AWAY FROM KEYBOARD COLLECTION

# FIGHTING FOR VALOR

PATRICIA D. EDDY

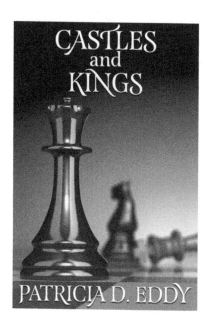

If you love sexy romantic suspense, I'd love to send you a short story set in Dublin, Ireland. Castles & Kings isn't available anywhere except for readers who sign up for my mailing list! Sign up for my newsletter on my website and tell me where to send your free book!

http://patriciadeddy.com.

*For Binky. You will always be the best.*

# CHAPTER ONE

*Six Years Ago*
*Hell Mountain - An underground prison deep in the Hindu Kush*

## Ripper

MY HANDS ARE NUMB. Fuckers won't take the chance I can break free, so they tighten the cuffs past the point of pain every time. The metal chair arms dig into the undersides of my wrists. The hood they shoved over my head before they dragged me in here makes it impossible to see more than a dull glow from the overhead lights.

I'm alone. That much I know. I can hear Ryker—head of our Special Forces team—cursing down the hall. Kahlid's—the meanest of the Taliban's torturers—going at him again, trying to force him to talk. Our captor's overly-sweet and patronizing tone carries, but I can't make out his words. Only the sounds of fists on flesh, the occasional scream or grunt, and then Dax, Ry's second in command, demanding Kahlid do something... physically impossible.

By Ry's estimates, we've been here six months. One hundred-and-eighty-four days trapped in the depths of Hell Mountain. I've lost count of the number of bones they've broken. The number of new scars criss-crossing my back, my arms, my chest.

"Hey, assholes! Pick on someone your own size!" I call out, hoping to draw Kahlid away from Ry. As the commander of our ODA team, he's taken the brunt of the torture. Both because Kahlid thinks he knows more than me and Dax and because Ry keeps goading the asshole. Trying to protect us.

Ryker McCabe is the biggest, baddest son of a bitch I've ever met. Almost seven feet tall and the size of a small house. Kahlid's never even come *close* to breaking him.

"Pig fucker!" Ryker growls. Kahlid's reply is softer, the words obscured by the twists and turns of the cave tunnels. I can't just sit here doing nothing...waiting for my turn under the knife, the blowtorch, or the strap. So I strain against the cuffs, and the left arm of the chair creaks. Another jerk of my arm and the whole thing wobbles. Kahlid and his men are usually more careful than this. Maybe Ry was locked to this piece of shit last. He would have done his best to destroy the damn thing.

Blood oozes around the cuffs as I contort my body, wedging my right leg against the loose piece of metal. This is going to hurt. A lot. Taking a deep breath, I start yelling the first few words of *Bohemian Rhapsody*. I hope to all that's holy Ry and Dax can drown out any noise I make next.

A moment later, Dax joins in, then Ry's rough voice echoes down the hall. For six months, we've communicated in taps and scratches, changing up our code every week. *Bohemian Rhapsody's* our current signal to "make as much fucking noise as possible."

As we hit the second verse, I use all the strength I have to push against the chair. The metal creaks, strains, and then I'm on the floor, my left shoulder dislocated, pain rolling over me in waves, but the chair's in three pieces and my right hand is free.

*Get up. Now. Move.*

This could be my only chance. They never leave me in here for more than an hour or so, and it's been at least twenty minutes. A little more maneuvering, and I slide my cuffed left wrist down the now-destroyed arm of the chair. My bloody fingers shake, and I yank the hood off my head, then use the scratchy material to wipe my hands.

*Holy hell.*

Two ancient computers sit against the far wall. Both of them on. I can work with this. As I stagger towards them, I remember I'm supposed to be singing, curse under my breath, and pick up the tune again—badly. Never could sing worth shit.

I'm useless without both arms, and I grab my left wrist, wrench my arm straight out in front of me, and scream as the shoulder pops back into the socket.

For too long, I fight not to pass out, but then shake my head. Hard.

*Think, dumbass. Computer. Message.*

Before the song ends and we have to start all over again, I manage to open a command prompt on the woefully out-of-date terminal. If I'm not careful, though, Kahlid and his men will know what I've done and they'll move us—probably somewhere even worse—so I have to cover my tracks.

Every mission has a dropbox protocol of sorts. Specific codes to use and places to send a message when you can't find an encrypted connection to CENTCOM. My fingers aren't working right. Half-numb and still bloody. It takes me three tries to type in the IP address I memorized before we left base months ago.

I can't authenticate. Too risky and time consuming. But I've thought a lot about what I'd do in this situation—in every situation. It's what we trained for. Adaptability. So many days and nights alone, bound, or thrown down in the pit at the end of the tunnel without food or water. Nothing to do *but* think.

I fall silent as I type, but Dax and Ryker pick up my slack until Ry screams.

ODA-94820RJT008000-AF-HK-ACHERON

I have no idea if anyone will see the message or understand my code. My initials. My birthdate. AF for Afghanistan. HK for Hindu Kush. And Acheron—another name for Hell. It's the best I can do. The message disappears into the ether, and I cover my tracks with a few lines of code that *look* like I'm trying to open an encrypted connection to a dummy server the Army runs.

Wait. I don't hear anything. No more singing. Just...footsteps. Fuck.

"Resourceful," the heavily accented voice says from behind me. I whirl around and only have time to register the amused gaze of one of Kahlid's men before he fires a stun gun, and I go down, my entire body twitching and my vision shrinking so I can only see a single drop of blood on his boot before I fade away completely.

---

IT'S HOT. The stagnant, thick air reeks of sweat, human waste, and filth. I force my eyes open, but can't see anything in the dark. Am I dreaming? Am I dead? No. My shoulder throbs with every breath, and I reach up to poke at it gently... Fuck. I'm naked. This is new. My hand falls to the ground. Dirt. Darkness and dirt. Where am I? This doesn't smell, sound, or feel like Hell.

Slowly, I rock up to my knees, dizziness threatening to send me back onto my ass, but I suck in the hot air and will my heartbeat to slow. Control. I'm a master at it. Controlling my body. My mind. As the rapid beat calms, I shuffle forward.

All of six feet until I find curved stone. What the fuck? Using the wall for support, I stagger to my feet, then turn around. "Jackson Richards. Listen carefully, fuckers. That's the only piece of information you'll *ever* get out of me."

My words echo, and from the sound, this whole place is less than ten feet across. And tall. Despite my shoulder sending shooting pains down my back, I feel as high up as I can. The stones are rough, but arranged in a way I can't find a handhold anywhere.

What I think is halfway around this hole, my foot comes in contact with something plastic. A bucket. Using it for reference, I continue around the space. My estimate is spot on. I'm in a goddamned well. Tilting my head back, I repeat my name and listen for the echo. Twenty feet down. Give or take. With no way up or out. No food. No water. And only a bucket to piss in.

I sink back down onto my ass and drop my head into my hands, elbows on my bent knees. Is this the end? Did Kahlid or one of his flunkies throw me down here to die?

"Go for it, shitstains. I dare you."

---

LIGHT CHASES AWAY THE DARKNESS, burning my eyes. I don't know how long I've been here. Six hours? Ten? Not more than that. Any longer in this heat and I'd be dead from dehydration.

Something lands with a *thunk* next to me, and then the light fades away as whoever's up there drags a cover over the top of the well. Feeling around, I close my fingers around a plastic water bottle.

My hands shake, and I twist off the cap and suck down half

the bottle in three gulps. It's stale, but so much better than the parasite-infested swill Kahlid always gave us.

I'm not in Hell. From the heat, I'm nowhere *near* Hell.

*Think. What do you remember after sending the message?*

Attempting to channel Ryker, I search my memories. Over the months we've spent as prisoners, he's taught us how to remember everything. Or...almost everything. Some things, it's better to forget.

The stun gun. Darkness. Then...a truck bed. At night. I couldn't see or move. I could smell the dust, though. I made some noise when we went over a deep rut in the road, then there was pain. My head. After that...nothing for a long time.

Loud voices. Pashto. But the accent was different than Kahlid's. If I had to guess, I'm a good four or five hours away from Hell. A completely different part of Afghanistan. Why?

Now that my eyes have adjusted, I can make out a dim halo around whatever covers the top of the well. I'm messed up—dysentery, malnourishment, and so many blows to the head—my mental capacity is probably severely compromised. But there's also a faint line that's a little lighter than the rest. A small gap between pieces of wood?

Keeping my gaze fixed above me, I try to stay conscious long enough to see the sun fade away.

---

I STILL DON'T HAVE any answers. The light's totally gone now, and it's finally cooler. The air feels just as thick, though. Hard to breathe. Every time I get up and try to find a handhold or foothold along the wall, I end up dizzy.

Once or twice, I thought I heard a truck pass close by. Voices. But they could all be in my head. My tongue is so dry, it's stuck to the roof of my mouth, and I gave up trying to keep my eyes open long ago. It hurts too much.

A skittering sound from behind my left shoulder makes me flinch, but I'm too tired, too weak to move. Rats, probably. I can deal with rats.

Something tickles my upper arm. Fuck. It's too light to be a rat. Too big to be a spider. I fling it away, and a quiet *thwap* sounds from across the well. "Serves...you...right..." I whisper.

But then, something stings the bottom of my foot. The pain flares, bright and hot, all the way up to my knee. I can't see anything, can't find the damn thing. What the fuck is it? My low moan echoes off the walls, and my heart rate spikes. Another sharp pain in my calf, and I slam my hand down onto something squishy. Almost...rubbery.

Panic takes over, and all my efforts to remember the list of poisonous species in Afghanistan short-circuit.

*Focus!*

Not a snake. Oh, shit. Scorpions. Some of the most toxic species in the world live in this country.

My left leg is going numb. This is bad. So bad. Even worse when I hear more faint scratching to my right. I'm going to die here. Alone. In the dark. In agony. With no one to hear me scream.

# CHAPTER TWO

## Ripper

A HEAVY WEIGHT hits my thigh. The light from above is faint. Like...twilight. I try to focus, to see the slats again, but I'm dying. I know it. The scorpions come every night. Some of the bites are infected. One of the water bottles they threw a while ago—I don't know how long—landed on one of the swollen welts, and it broke open, the scent making me retch.

My fingers twitch, about the only movement I can still manage. I let my head fall to the side, peering up as a dark shape descends the rope ladder. They're going to take me. Move me. Try to get me to talk. The joke's on them. I can't make a sound. I'm too weak.

Six times—I think—they've tossed a bottle of water into the well. The last one lies unopened. I couldn't muster the strength. I'm covered in bile, piss, and blood, and hours ago, I made peace with my death.

"There is no cause for this," the man says when he stands over me. "I will take care of you, my friend. Trust me."

I can't see his face. Can't make out any of his features. He's only a diffuse, hazy form in front of me, and as he grabs my arm and hauls me up over his shoulder, I pass out.

---

"YOU ARE VERY SICK."

"This will hurt."

"Drink, Isaad."

Fragments. That's all I have. I'm lying on a soft pallet. It's not so hot. I think...I try to wiggle my toes. There's a sheet over me.

Something presses to my chapped lips. Cool water slides down my throat. Just a sip. I try to ask for more, but no sound comes out.

"Isaad, you must wait. Only a small amount yet." A gentle hand dabs my forehead with a cloth. I can't even open my eyes.

*Who the fuck is Isaad?*

"I have given you antibiotics. In a few days, you will regain your strength."

I'm so dizzy. The voice seems to come from all around me. Where is he? I can only manage a grunt, and then the cool compress is back.

"Trust me, Isaad. I will protect you."

---

MORE BITS AND PIECES. But are they memories? Hallucinations? Dreams?

A taste of banana. A sip of sweetened tea. Something pinching my arm. Antibiotics? Drugs? I don't know. Don't care. I'm not tied up. Not vomiting. Not hearing Ryker and Dax scream in pain.

Whatever I'm lying on depresses slightly, and I force my eyes open. The man sitting on the cot has a neatly trimmed beard, black hair, and gray eyes. "Who...?" I whisper.

"My name is Faruk. My...employer...he wishes you to suffer. But he is not here now. So I can help you, Isaad."

"Name...isn't..."

"It is now. There is no use in fighting it. Please, Isaad. I will protect you, but you must listen to me." Faruk leans over me, a hand on either side of my shoulders. "The man I work for...he is a sadist. He will kill you to obtain what he desires."

"Then...let...me...die." I can barely force the words out, even after what I assume is several days of care. "Never... gonna...break."

"You will, Isaad. I have seen it before. So many times. But if you let me help you, I can make things easier. I can spare you much pain." His tone is so calm, so soothing. A hand slides behind my head, lifting me slightly. "Drink."

I try to turn away, but I'm so thirsty. And when the cool liquid touches my lips, I can't help myself. After several sips of tea, the room starts to spin, and I struggle to focus on the man who pulled me out of that fucking well. "Drugged...me." I whisper. "Bastard."

"No!" His denial is so sharp, so vehement, I believe him. "Have more tea. You are still dehydrated, and you have a high fever from the scorpion venom."

Faruk shifts, and his arm bolsters my shoulders enough for me to sit up. The sheet falls away from my chest, and I see the devastation. The swollen bites all over my torso. Some stitched up, others still bright red and hot. I couldn't stop myself from flinching every time, and that only angered the little shits more.

"Antibiotics and rest will help." He offers me more tea, and though I want to resist, I don't. It's been so long since anyone touched me with the intent to help and not hurt. I need to regain my strength before I can figure out what the fuck I'm supposed to do now. And how to get out of here and back to my team.

I fade in and out, unsure what's real and what's all in my head. Sounds drone on and on a few feet away. A news report? In English?

*Focus!*

The words have a heartbeat of their own. A life. They ebb and flow, and I can only pick out snatches. "*...for the man responsible, Sergeant Richards...*"

Richards. Me.

"*...murder, treason...*"

I don't understand. Squinting as Faruk presses a bandage to one of the wounds on my chest, I think I see the glow of a television in the corner. The image flickers, then there's only static, and I can't fight anymore.

---

I'M ALONE. Finally. And I think maybe...I'm strong enough to get up on my own. Throwing off the sheet, I grimace at my ravaged body. I've lost more than fifty pounds since our ODA team was captured six months ago. My first attempt to stand sends me back on my ass on the bed, but after a deep breath, I manage to stay upright. Someone put thin, loose pants on me, and they feel so foreign.

One step. Two. Three. I'm so tired. The room must be two miles across with the door at the end of a long tunnel. At least that's how it feels. *One foot in front of the other.*

I can do this. I can make it. Find a way out of here. If only I knew where *here* was. My fingers wrap around the door handle, but it doesn't turn. Shit. They locked me in.

*You're fucking Special Forces, asshole. Find a way out.*

On the nightstand, several discarded needles lie on a tray. If I'm *really* lucky, I might be able to use them to pick the lock. But now...I have to walk across the room again. In both directions. One step at a time.

My legs give out halfway back. And then...footsteps. Down the hall. Rushing. A key rasps in the lock, and I scramble for the needle that fell from my hand.

"Isaad!" Faruk lifts me to my feet and slings my arm around his shoulders. "You should not be out of bed." As he helps me back to the narrow cot, I try to hide the needle, but my fingers are shaking too violently, and it clatters to the floor.

Another man shouts, "Get away from the traitor!" Faruk jerks, lets me fall the last foot onto the mattress, and backs up a few paces.

"I am sorry, Amir Aazar. I only wished to bring him water." Faruk withdraws a bottle from the pocket of his tunic and shows it to this other man. He's taller. Stronger. Meaner.

"He does not deserve water. Or anything else." Amir Aazar strides forward and punches Faruk in the gut hard enough to make him double over. A rough hand fastens around my arm, and then he yanks me off the cot. My head hits the floor, and my vision dims as Amir Aazar drags me down the hall, around several turns, and through what I think is a lavish parlor.

Back outside, the harsh sun beats down on my face as sharp rocks cut into my bare back. "Open the well!" Amir Aazar shouts.

"No...please," I beg. I'll do anything to stay out of the well. "Take me...back...to Hell Mountain."

"You will never see the mountain again," Aazar snaps. "Your little trick with the computer? It got the other two men from your unit killed. Days ago. The mountain is gone. Now, there is only you. Here."

*No. Not Ryker and Dax. No. He's lying. He has to be.*

Another man drags the wooden cover off the well, and I claw at Aazar's leg, trying to hold on so he can't throw me down there. It has to be the middle of the day. I'm burning; the scorpion bites feel like they're on fire.

"You are the only one left, *Sergeant* Richards. And you will pay for the crimes of the rest of your unit." Aazar bends down and grabs my chin, forcing me to look at him. "You and your men killed my family. You will suffer for their deaths."

He shoves me down, throwing off my hold easily. As he rises, he brushes off his hands. I try to roll over, but I can't. I'm too weak to do more than lie on my back, blinking rapidly in the bright sun, as half a dozen men stand around me.

"Make sure he is alive when he goes back into the well," Aazar says. "But you may do whatever you wish to him before that happens."

Someone clutches the waistband of my pants and rips them off of me, and when another man grabs my hips and raises my ass in the air, I send my mind as far away as I can, so I don't have to feel them take the only thing I have left.

What seems like hours later, I land back in the well, and as the wood slides over the opening, plunging me into darkness once more, I don't even care that they left me down here to die. Broken, violated, bleeding from...places I never wanted to think about. Death...will be a blessing.

# CHAPTER THREE

**Ripper**

WHY CAN'T I let go? Stop myself from drinking the water they throw into the well? I want to. But every time...I fail.

*"Your little trick with the computer? It got the other two men from your unit killed."*

Ryker McCabe was the strongest man I've ever known, with Dax Holloway a close second. And this asshole—my captor—had the power to murder them. It might have been Aazar who ordered their deaths, but I'm the one responsible.

My stupid attempt to tell someone—anyone—where we were got them killed. And landed me...here. Broken. Used by half a dozen men until my ass bled, kicked, punched, choked, and tossed down into this hole. How long this time? Five days? Seven? I can't sleep. Too much pain. The only relief I find is when I pass out.

The scorpions are out again. My only indication of day or night. They don't consider me much of a threat anymore. One crawls along my thigh, and I don't move, don't react. I haven't moved in hours. Maybe even a day. My hands cup my dick, the only sliver of self-preservation I have left.

But my breathing must annoy the little bastard, because it skitters up my chest and drives its stinger into my cheek. Half my face goes numb, and I cry out as I shake my head. Fumbling for the water next to me, I pour some over the wound, swallow the rest, and then I start to hear voices.

Ry. Telling me to fight. Then Dax. He wants me to know everything will be okay. Behind my shuttered lids, I see Hab as Kahlid slit his throat in front of us. A second before the knife pierced his carotid artery, he mouthed, *"Never give up."*

Fuck. I wish I could honor his wishes. As another scorpion gets tangled in my mess of matted, too-long hair, and my weak, keening cry echoes off the stone walls. It feels like a hundred of the fucking things are crawling all over me, and panic sets in. My entire body convulses, and I fall over, the pain fading away. Now I'm floating. Somewhere quiet, where maybe...maybe I'll never wake up again.

---

"ISAAD. OPEN YOUR EYES."

The kind, smooth voice sounds like it's under fifty feet of water. I smell soap. Incense maybe. Colors fade in and out, lights swirling around me. As I force my heavy lids open, sharp pain lances through my skull.

The pale beige walls pulse in time with my heartbeat, and I'm soaked with sweat. Sucking in a wheezing breath, I try to turn my head, but I can't.

Something cool touches my forehead. "Trust me, Isaad. I will protect you. Do you believe me?"

"Uh huh."

*Why did I say yes? Where am I? Who's with me? Am I dead? Shit. Why can't I think straight?*

A thin face shifts in and out of focus. Gray eyes. I've seen those eyes before.

The man shakes his head, his hand over his heart. "I killed Amir Aazar. I did not wish to, but he would have tortured you until you could no longer go on, and I could not let that happen. He will never hurt you again, Isaad."

"Let me...go...please," I beg.

"I cannot. Your friends are gone, Isaad. I am very sorry, but your government blames you."

"Wha....?"

An arm slides under my shoulders, and he lifts me, supporting my head so I can almost make out a glowing screen across the room. "The news has carried the story for the past week, Isaad."

A man's voice—with an American accent—fills the room. "A United States Special Forces Team was laid to rest at Arlington National Cemetery today. Only two bodies were recovered from the Hindu Kush. Their names are being withheld at the request of their families. A third member of the team, Sergeant Jackson Richards, has been implicated in their deaths and is currently wanted on charges of treason. This has been Simon Jones reporting."

"Ry...Dax..."

"Dead." The man lays me back down, and his face swims in and out of focus. "You are safe here, Isaad. But only here. And only if you trust me."

No. This isn't right. I can't...think. Can't form the words. Everything's...fucked. My unit. My...family. "Not...Isaad."

"You must be. The man you were...he can never be again. You are Isaad now."

A glass touches my lips, and water trickles into my mouth.

So good. So cold. Sweet. I need more. The man's face is familiar. I've seen it before. Where?

"Who...?" I manage.

"Faruk. You remember me?" As I nod, he continues, "Good. After I killed Aazar, I took over. I am now Amir Abdul Faruk, and you will call me Amir Faruk. It is the way of things here. If you do this, I will keep you as safe as I can. Listen to me, and you will never end up in that well again."

---

Voices. No. One voice. Over and over again. I don't know what he's saying. Who is it? Why can't I think?

Searing pain consumes me, and I scream—at least in my own head. I can't tell if anything around me is real. It's all darkness. The stench of the well. The scorpions crawling over my naked body, filling me with poison.

Then water. A cool cloth.

And that voice.

"*You killed your team, Isaad. You will be executed if you return to the United States. You are safe here.*"

No. Here is bad. Here is pain. Do I say that out loud? Nothing makes sense. Is any of this happening? Or is it all in my nightmares?

"*Do you trust me, Isaad? You must trust me. If you trust me, I will make the pain go away.*"

I want to trust him. Fuck. I'll do anything he wants if he can put a stop to this endless torment.

---

A GENTLE BREEZE stirs the air around me. It's morning. A slash of sunlight hits the bed through slats on a window to my left.

There's a brisk knock at the door, and then Amir Faruk enters, another man behind him carrying a tray.

"Good morning, my friend," Amir Faruk says. "This is Zaman. He is my most trusted man. Tell him your name."

Zaman sets the tray down, and my mouth waters. A light broth, spiced, with chunks of vegetables. A glass of water. Glancing up at Amir Faruk, I know what he wants me to say. What I need to say. And though a piece of my soul shreds into pieces, I clear my throat and whisper, "Isaad."

YOU DON'T LOSE yourself all at once. It happens in stages. Isolation. Confusion. Fear. Amir Faruk comes to see me often. Always with food. With kindness. With words I can't help but listen to.

There's a doctor, too. A man who helps me shuffle over to the toilet to piss, who speaks only Pashto, forcing me to respond in kind. He tells me how bad things were under Amir Aazar. How Amir Faruk is kind and just. How the invading forces—American, British, French, and more—are searching for the Special Forces traitor. How lucky I am that Amir Faruk saved me.

Deep inside, I know I'm not this...Isaad. But then the lights go out. Every night, I wake screaming, the scorpions crawling over my naked skin. It's only when I fall to the floor—off the cot —and realize I'm wearing a loose pair of pants that I realize I'm not in that dark hole. If I don't do what Amir Faruk wants, I'll end up back there.

Three times, I've fought the doctor. Tried to escape. Three times, Zaman has caught me and thrown me back into the well for a day...sometimes two. I won't survive if he does it again.

Now, I'm locked in. "For your safety," Amir Faruk said the

last time he carried me back into this room, dirty, weak, and out of my mind from the scorpion venom. "You cannot fight me any longer, Isaad. This is your home."

The lock clicks open, and I push myself up, my back to the wall. I need to appear strong.

"Isaad. You are looking well today," Amir Faruk says as he closes the door behind him, approaches the bed, and slides a tray onto the table. "I have brought your evening meal and more antibiotics."

"My name is Jackson—"

"No!" His kind tone disappears, and he snatches up the hypodermic needle, grabs my arm, and injects me before I can protest or try to pull away. "You are Isaad. The man you once were is responsible for the death of two high-ranking Special Forces officers. If he were to live, you would be repatriated to the United States and tried for treason. Or the local Afghan Allied Forces would slit your throat themselves."

His words sink in as my eyelids droop. Yes. That's right. I have to stay safe. But...Special Forces...we don't lie. And this...is a lie. Isn't it? "I don't want to...be Isaad. I take...responsibility..."

"I do not want you to suffer, Isaad," Amir Faruk whispers as he holds a glass of a sweet liquid to my lips. "I can protect you. There is so much you can do to atone for your mistakes. Here. Where you are safe. What is better? Dying for your crimes? Or using your skills and talents to redeem yourself?"

Could I really do that? Atone for my sins? Maybe that *would* be better. I let him feed me, my limbs leaden. His voice is smooth, gentle. Kind. And he keeps repeating my name. Isaad.

Isaad is safe here. Isaad can do good with his life. Isaad knows Amir Faruk saved him.

"You will rest now, Isaad," Amir Faruk whispers as he pats my shoulder, and I want to do everything he tells me. When he locks the door, I try to remember that other name. The one I know I can't lose. But, it's just out of my reach. I'll remember. In the morning.

# CHAPTER FOUR

*Six Years Later*

**Isaad**

I SIT AT THE TERMINAL, moving forty thousand United States dollars from one offshore account to another. The transaction requires finesse, and I'm exhausted. I failed my previous task— hiding the purchase of ten surface-to-air missiles from the Afghan government. They intercepted the shipment and seized half a million dollars before I could reverse the transaction, and Amir Faruk ordered me to fast for seven days as punishment.

This is day six, and every time I stand, I have to brace myself on something.

"Isaad!"

His tone tells me any delay will earn me additional punishments, and I shuffle as quickly as I can down the hall and into the parlor.

"Yes, sir?"

Amir Faruk stands in front of a woman dressed in a long

abaya. She looks vaguely familiar. Shit. The doctor. The one who specializes in Alpha Thalassemia, the disease Faruk's son was born with.

He had me research her. I never thought he'd actually kidnap her. Or even be able to find her. Zaman holds her by the arms, and as I meet her gaze, I see her terror. All because of me.

Looking from Faruk to the woman and back again, I wait for my orders.

"Erase all evidence of Dr. Josephine Taylor from public records in America. She does not exist anymore." Faruk shoves a passport at me, and Josephine lunges for it.

Zaman grabs her by the hair, then kicks her in the back of the knees to send her to the floor. "Please," she whispers, holding up bound hands. "You can't just make me disappear."

"I can. Very easily," Faruk says with a smile. He casts a quick glance over his shoulder at me, and the look in his eyes...I want to throw up, but there's nothing in my stomach. "Your *friends* will be sold in two days. They are being prepared for auction as we speak. You, however, are too valuable to let go."

I hold Dr. Josephine Taylor's gaze for a long moment, hating myself, my part in all of Amir Faruk's businesses, and the weakness inside me that stops me from doing something...anything about it.

I bow my head, turn, and hurry from the room before I say something that will get me thrown back into the well. I have to do what Amir Faruk says or my life will be over, and I don't want to die. Except...days like today, I think maybe that would be better.

---

SEVERAL HOURS LATER, I'm staring at a picture of Josephine Taylor on the Massachusetts Department of Transportation website. She's forty-three years old, has lived in Boston for almost ten years, and has a savings account with sixty thousand dollars in it. A sister and mother in San Diego.

I know everything there is to know about this woman. At least, everything one can learn online without using the dark web. I can't do it. Can't take everything she is. But if I don't, Faruk will hurt me. My stomach rumbles, and I reach for my sixth cup of tea of the day.

Staring into the pale liquid, a memory threatens. Coffee. I haven't had coffee in forever. The first sip in the morning. The jolt.

*"Don't know how you can drink that sludge. It's from yesterday, fucker."* A voice I know. One I hear in my dreams. A man. There's laughter that might be mine. But then it fades away and I'm staring at Josephine's picture again.

Faruk won't know how much money she had in the bank. Not if I'm quick. I can send it to an untraceable account. And then...maybe soon, I can send it to her family. It's not enough. But it's all I can do. Faruk will skim the security feeds, and the camera behind me captures everything I'm doing. But I can make it glitch for sixty seconds without him suspecting anything.

All the cameras have these short outages. Because I put them there. My one small bit of rebellion.

Sixty seconds. Starting now. Switching over to the website for the First National Bank of Boston, I quickly siphon the sixty thousand and change into an offshore account in a bank Faruk doesn't know about. My fingers fly over the keyboard, and at the end of the transfer instructions, I enter a series of numbers and letters I can't forget.

94820RJT008000

I don't know what it means. Every time I enter those four-teen characters, I hope their meaning will come back to me, but in all the years I've been here, I've never been able to figure it out.

My old, rudimentary digital watch—it has a single alarm and that's it—counts down the last ten seconds, and I switch back to the Department of Transportation website.

I'm frozen, my fingers locked, my heart pounding. When Amir Faruk saved me, I thought he was a good man. But the first time he ordered me to make a woman's identity disappear, I refused. That earned me two weeks in the well. By the time he let me out, I was too weak to stand. That was followed by another month locked in my small room. At least...I think it was a month. I spent most days in a fog, and my only solid memories are of Faruk's voice, Zaman's fists, and my own fear.

In my dreams, I hear a man's voice. *"Stay alive. We never leave a man behind."*

But the name and face of whoever said those words—if this a memory and not a desperate desire to have someone, somewhere who cares if I live or die—must have left me. And even though Amir Faruk doesn't lock me in anymore and I haven't seen the bottom of that fucking well in three years, I have no hope of ever leaving this place.

One letter at a time, I erase Dr. Josephine Taylor. I don't have a choice. When I confirm the job is done, Faruk smiles. "You have done a good thing, Isaad. You may end your fast after midnight prayers."

My stomach twists in on itself, and I bow. "Thank you, sir."

---

MORNINGS ARE the only time I find peace. Amir Faruk insists I join the other men in the compound for prayers, but though I know the words, the actions that are expected of me, I don't believe. My life has become nothing but guilt and self-preservation. I should be stronger. I should know who I used to be. And I should find a way out.

After prayers, I walk to the far side of the compound. Faruk's cameras don't reach here, and though the men he has stationed in the watch towers can see me, I'm otherwise alone.

Punishing myself with a brutal exercise routine of pushups, jumping jacks, burpees, and flutter kicks helps me feel normal and keeps my strength up, though today, I lose stamina quickly. The meager serving of banana curd I had last night to break my fast was nowhere near enough to keep me going. I have to rest often between sets, and it's almost ten by the time I head back to the main house.

A woman's cry stops me. "I'll go. Just...don't push me over the edge!"

Josephine.

Sweat dampens my palms, and my heart races. *No. Not down into the well. He wouldn't. Not a woman.* I have to force my feet to move, and I round the corner as Faruk calls out, "If you refuse to help Mateen, you will be moved here. At night, the scorpions come out. The particular species we have in this part of the desert are not deadly, but their venom is quite painful."

The panic attack sends me to my knees. Tiny little legs scurry across my naked skin, and when the stinger pierces my shoulder, my entire body seizes. Clutching my chest, I find my loose dark blue tunic, and the shock is enough to let me suck in a shallow breath.

*I'm not in the well. I'm outside. In the sun.*

"P-please," Josephine begs, her tiny voice echoing off the stone walls. "Let me up. I'll...do whatever you want. I'll make the drug. I'll take care of Mateen."

Pushing to my feet, I stagger towards Amir Faruk as Zaman throws the rope ladder down the deep hole. When Josephine reaches the top rung, she collapses onto the rocky ground wheezing and staring at the sky.

"Get up, woman," Zaman orders her, and she tries, but her eyes start to roll back in her head, and I rush forward, wrap my arm around her waist, and let her sink against me.

"Breathe," I whisper. "I've got you."

"Isaad!" Faruk barks. "Step away from the woman. Now. Go back to your work."

I only risk meeting his gaze for a brief moment until I see the anger in his gray eyes. Looking down at the woman huddled against me, I keep my voice low. "Do not give him reason to throw you into the well."

She manages a single nod, and I step away, bow to Faruk, and head to my room.

---

HOURS LATER, I've only checked on a fraction of Amir Faruk's investments. My thoughts won't stop racing, pinging off the inside of my skull, jumbled, random fragments seemingly from another life.

I know I'm American. I know I don't belong here. I've always known that. But I'm trapped. Trapped by my guilt. Both an old, deep-seated guilt I can't understand and the guilt over everything I've done for my captor.

I used to think of him as my savior. Not anymore. Seeing him with Josephine, hearing the way he changes his voice, going from kind to vicious in a heartbeat, I remember bits and pieces of my first few days here. The drugs. The torture.

Giving up on my work, I strip off my clothes and turn on the shower. The water runs over my too-long hair, the beard I know I never used to have.

*"Remove all of it. Make it hurt."*

*The doctor grabs my wrist, rests his knee on my forearm, and holds a hot poker to my bicep. I scream, but then the pain fades away as Amir Faruk gives me a cup of tea.* "You are no longer that wanted man, Isaad. You are free."

Staring down at the shiny burn scar, I strain to see the remnants of the tattoo. "...iber." The only piece left. It means something. *Liber.* Freedom. *De Oppresso Liber.* To free the oppressed.

I used to be someone else. Someone good. Someone who helped people. And now...I work for a murderer, a rapist, a human trafficker.

Loud, choking sobs echo off the shower walls as I mourn that man I used to be. Even though I don't remember his name.

---

*Whoosh. Whoosh. Whoosh.*

The sound of the chopper blades lulls me into a trance, and I stare out at the desolate landscape. The Afghan hills are hauntingly beautiful at dawn—as long as you're not getting shot at.

Next to me, a hazy form moves, and an elbow to my ribs makes me curse. "What the fuck?"

"Stay focused," he growls, his voice deep, raspy, familiar. "Something's not right with this mission."

"You're one paranoid son-of-a-bitch, Ry."

"And you—"

An explosion rocks the air around us, and we're spinning, smoke filling the interior of the helicopter. I grab the radio, my hand shaking. "COMSAT, COMSAT, do you read—?"

Jerking to my feet, my legs tangle in the sheet, and I crash to the floor with a grunt.

My team. My *Special Forces* team. Ryker. Dax. Hab. Gose. Naz. Dead. All because of me.

I can't see their faces, but I know who they are now. And who I used to be. And that's the worst part of it.

I was Special Forces. Trained never to lie. To protect the innocent. To infiltrate and free the oppressed, to take on the missions few others could ever do.

How can I live with my failures knowing who I used to be? How can I keep following Faruk's orders? I can't. I have to find a way to end him—then myself. It's my only shot at redemption.

# CHAPTER FIVE

### Isaad

Days later, I trudge out into the courtyard for morning prayers, wondering how much longer I can keep up this act. Whenever I see Faruk, I want to wrap my hands around his throat and break his neck. But, he's never alone.

The American, Dr. Joey, is attempting to cure Faruk's son. Mateen is a sweet boy. Last spring, Faruk let me teach him how to play soccer. But the kid started asking me all kinds of questions—where I was from, why I talked funny, why my skin was so pale, and when Faruk overheard me tell him I was from far away and couldn't ever go home again, he put a stop to those blissful afternoons when I could let go of my guilt for a few hours.

Mateen curls on his prayer mat, his arms around his belly, while Faruk yells at the petite American. But she doesn't back down.

"I told you he needed fresh fruits and vegetables, bland food, and only the bare minimum of meat. Liver? It's full of iron

—something he does *not* need more of. You just set him back weeks!" Joey snaps from her position on her knees next to Mateen.

Faruk curses and kicks her in the stomach. The viciousness of his attack makes me draw in a sharp breath, and she curls into a ball as he continues to punch and kick her. Stepping forward, I force strength into my tone. "Amir Faruk, sir. The doctor cannot cure your son if you...break her."

Faruk straightens, panting, and Dr. Joey peers up at me from under her arm and gives me a tiny nod. Checking to make sure no one's looking at me, I mouth, *"I'm sorry,"* and back up, my head bowed.

I wish I could help her, but even if I could get her to the underground tunnel, where would she go? I can't get into the garage—the locks aren't computerized, and the keys are in the guard house, which is staffed twenty-four hours a day by two men. The gate, too, is manual, and patrolled.

Zaman drags the doctor back into the main house, and Faruk carries Mateen after them. She'll die here, and that'll be one more red mark in my ledger.

Tonight. After midnight prayers. If I can get him alone, maybe...I can kill him.

———

THE KNIFE IS heavy in my hand. Yet, somehow familiar. The loose tunic mostly hides the weapon, and I slip into the room off the kitchen with the bank of five computers.

A quick check of the time, and I roll my head, letting my neck pop and crack. I know Faruk's routines. In a few minutes, he'll be back in his office for his weekly 1:00 a.m. call with his contact in the States. Some government grunt who feeds him information and helps facilitate the arms sales that provide much of Faruk's income. He won't be checking the security cameras for at least half an hour.

With a few keystrokes, I prepare to disable the cameras but freeze. In the basement hallway, a man dressed in black pants and a black tunic leads Joey down the hall. He's not one of Faruk's men. Even if he'd brought in someone new without telling me, the way this guy moves...he's been trained to do this.

Quickly, I cycle through the other feeds. The camera trained on the front gate reveals another man, dressed similarly, fiddling with something under the hood of one of the Jeeps. The man outside touches his ear, then shakes his head. A moment later, he sprints for the west side of the compound, and...fuck. Runs right into Faruk's wife, Lisette, and Mateen. Lisette grabs his arm, begging. They argue for a moment, and then the man picks up Mateen and motions for Lisette to follow him.

They're getting out. All of them.

This is my chance to find some sort of redemption. I can help. I can protect them until they're safe. Disabling the cameras is simple, but I only have fifteen minutes before an alarm goes off in Faruk's office.

Where the hell is the first guy taking the doctor? *Shit.* Down to the old storage rooms in the basement. The last time I was down there, Faruk beat me so badly, I couldn't lie on my back for a week. Double-checking the cameras and locking the workstation with a new password no one else at the compound can crack, I grab the woefully dull kitchen knife, tuck it into my pocket, and take off at a run.

---

Where the hell are they? I should have found them by now. They weren't underground, and I hurry out the kitchen door.

*Fuck.*

"Stop," I call out as two men and the doctor rush around a corner.

The shorter one—the one I saw take Joey from her room—raises a gun. "Don't move."

"I am no threat to you," I say quietly as I hold up my hands and drop my gaze to the ground, "but you cannot go this way. I disabled the cameras, and in fifteen minutes, if I do not turn them back on, an alarm will go off and Faruk will...hurt me."

He'll do more than that. But I don't have time to explain why I'm helping them. I just hope they trust me. "Your other man is headed for the front gate, but there are too many guards between here and there for you to escape that way. Come with me. There is an underground tunnel that leads out of the compound."

"Fuck, no." The shorter man lunges for me, but with a quick sidestep, I'm out of his reach, my hands still held high.

"Please. Let me try to atone for my sins."

"For your sins?" The taller of the two men, who's leaning heavily on Dr. Joey, winces as he tries to stand up straighter. "Your accent...you're American, aren't you? What's your name?"

Several of Faruk's men shout from the opposite side of the compound, curses in Pashto and orders to find the invaders.

The shorter man takes Joey's free arm. "We have to go. Now."

"Wait!" I hiss. "The doctor is wearing a tracking device."

"What? Where?" Dr. Joey asks as her eyes widen in the light from the waning moon.

"In the hem of your pants. He trusts no one. Not even his own men. Not even his wife." *Definitely not me.*

The first man crouches and runs his fingers around the bottom of Joey's pants. With a curse, he pulls out a knife, then rips through the thin fabric. After he drops the tracker on the ground, he stomps on it and stares me down. "Why tell us?"

Shame heats my cheeks. "Faruk took my name. And my honor. Let me earn a piece of it back." Falling to my knees, I bow my head and rest my palm over my heart. "I'll kill him for what he's done. Then...maybe my ledger won't be so full of blood." *And maybe I can die in peace.*

The two men exchange a glance, then the shorter one says, "Get up. Show us this tunnel. But if you're lying to us, I'm putting a bullet in each of your kneecaps before I shoot you in the head."

That wouldn't be punishment enough, but if I can't get them out, at least I know I won't have to face Faruk and his torture ever again. With a nod, I lead them through the dark shadows to the rear of the compound and a wooden trap door.

"The tunnel leads under the wall. I'll give you a two-minute head start, and then I'll send the guards to the opposite side of the compound. After that, I will have to tell Faruk the doctor is gone and the cameras were shut down. And if I'm lucky, I'll be able to kill him before he kills me."

The men nod at me, and Dr. Joey whispers, "Thank you."

---

GUNFIRE EXPLODES from the front gate as I duck into the main house and head for Faruk's office. I've lost my best chance. Any hope of surprising him. But I can still fight, and if he's not expecting the attack, maybe...the knife will be sharp enough to sever his carotid artery.

But as I round the corner, Zaman is heading right for me. *Fuck.* He could still pass me by. Flattening myself against the wall, I hold my breath. As Zaman stops in front of me, I can almost *feel* death hovering over my shoulder.

"Amir Faruk says the cameras are down," he snaps.

With the knife still tucked inside my sleeve, I lower my head. "I will check on them now."

"You will come with me. Invaders have taken the boy and his mother." He grabs my arm and pulls me down the hall. "You will help find them."

Death would have been a blessing. Now...I'm trapped. When Zaman lets me go in front of Faruk's desk, I quickly clasp my hands behind my back. "What can I do for you, Amir Faruk, sir?"

He leans forward, his eyes wild. In the years I've been here, in all of my fractured memories, I've only seen him this out of control once—when his son was diagnosed with Alpha Thalassemia, a rare blood disorder that is fatal without treatment. His hair sticks up in all directions, and he tugs at his tunic. "Infidels have kidnapped my son, Lisette, and the doctor. You will find out how they got in and where they are going."

"It will be my pleasure." The words make my stomach turn, but maybe...I can send Faruk's men in the wrong direction and buy his wife and son—and the doctor—some time to get far away from this horrible place. If I don't get rid of the knife first, though, he'll find it, and then I won't be able to make good on my vow to end the life of the man who stole mine.

"Take him to the computer room. As soon as you know how the infidels broke in, report back." Faruk rounds the desk and grabs my arms. His thick fingers dig into my biceps, squeezing to the point of pain. "You will find them for me, Isaad. Or I will send you back to the well."

---

I STUMBLE on the way out of Faruk's office, banging into a tall plant and going down on one knee. I push the knife into the dirt as far as I can and hope it's enough. Zaman growls at me in Pashto—something about being a clumsy idiot—and when I straighten, he shoves me down the hall.

*I can walk on my own, fucker.*

For so long, Faruk owned me. Not only my actions, but my thoughts as well. I didn't dare challenge him, even in my own mind. But now...it's like I'm awake for the first time in years, and if I'm not careful, my expression or my body language is going to give me away.

Despite knowing who I am now, so many of my memories are fuzzy. I know I was trained to do this. Infiltrate. Blend in. Adapt. But my skills are rusty. Anyone looking at that plant will see the knife poking out a half an inch.

In my little office with the ancient laptop computer, I enter my password. Zaman crosses his arms over his chest and leans against the door jamb. Does he suspect me of turning off the cameras? I've done Faruk's bidding for years—most of the time without protest or question—but Zaman has always hated me. The feeling's mutual, and I hunch my shoulders as I bring the cameras back online. My quick glance at Zaman finds him tapping on his phone, probably messaging Faruk, so I delete the video file from the kitchen that shows me stealing the knife, then rewind the recording to when I saw the doctor being taken from her room.

"Here is footage of the...the infidels." The words stick in my throat, and Zaman arches a dark brow.

"That is not all Amir Faruk asked of you." He ends with a word I'm pretty sure means fucker, but though my Pashto is pretty good after all these years, no one's ever bothered to translate the insults Faruk and Zaman have hurled at me.

"This is all I have of the doctor. After they round this corner, the cameras shut off."

Zaman brings the phone to his ear and tells Faruk what I've

found. I can't delay long—not without Zaman getting impatient and beating the crap out of me, so I scan through all of the other footage until I find the other man talking to Lisette and Mateen, and then running with them. "This is the man who took the boy."

More muttering into the phone, and I pull up a complicated-looking screen of code. It's junk. Doesn't do a fucking thing. But when I want to make Zaman or Faruk think I'm working, I run this program. Making a show of scanning through the lines of letters and numbers that mean nothing, I pull out a small notebook and pen, then start writing down random time stamps.

Zaman only gives me five minutes before he demands to know what I'm doing, and he does it by cuffing the back of my head with his elbow. "Amir Faruk requires an update."

"These are times over the past three hours when a signal from outside the compound disrupted our security systems. These men are experts. The first few attempts did not take down the cameras. But after an hour, glitches started to occur. This line," I point to the last time stamp, "turned off the cameras completely."

Zaman snatches the notebook from my hand. "I will take this to Amir Faruk. Track the doctor and the boy. Now. We have men searching for them, but they have so far come up empty. If you have not found them by the time I return, you will regret the day you were born."

*I already do.*

---

FINDING MATEEN IS SIMPLE. The transmitter in his little video game has a battery that should last five days. Right now, he's moving steadily southeast, occasionally doubling back. The guy who was with them...I bring up the footage I gave to Zaman. He's not Special Forces or SEALs. Black ops, maybe.

Taking Lisette and Mateen...he didn't plan on it. The way he changed tactics from stealth to speed, the rapid-fire words I assume were for the benefit of whoever was on the other end of those comms, and his path after he got the two of them out of the compound all say he was trained to think on his feet and react to anything. And to kill.

Half a dozen tracer dots move on the map. All but one of them belong to Faruk's men. Mateen's little group only has a two-kilometer lead. This...is going to be tricky. Hacking into a GPS device on the fly isn't child's play, even for me. I just hope I have enough time before Zaman comes for me. If not... Faruk will kill Lisette, and his son will end up just like him one day.

---

I WIPE MY BROW, the house's air conditioning no match for the heat of the day. Other than one break I was allowed to piss, I've been at this computer since 3:00 a.m. Almost fifteen hours. My shoulders ache, and I've burned through the meager snack one of the kitchen girls brought me a few hours ago. Despite barely moving from my chair, my heart is racing. I think Faruk suspects I'm not the same broken, obedient lackey he trained all those years ago. I'm still broken, but definitely not obedient. Not anymore.

Mateen's GPS is sending accurate data back to my machine, but I managed to cobble together a little program to adjust the coordinates enough to throw Faruk's men off their trail.

The door bangs open, and I flinch, my shoulders hiking up to my ears before I get myself under control. Zaman grabs me by the back of the shirt and jerks me out of my chair. The punch to my solar plexus catches me off guard, and I fall to my hands and knees, retching and trying not to vomit.

"You are working against me!" Faruk roars. He waves a phone in my face, and on screen, I see a blurry photograph of Lisette, Mateen, and the American. "This picture was taken five kilometers from where you *said* my son was."

"I do not...understand," I say, holding up my hands and trying to look beaten. It's not hard. I've had a hell of a lot of practice. "I can show you the map, Amir Faruk, sir. I am only reporting what the GPS shows me."

"You think me a fool, Isaad?"

*No, I think you're a sadistic fuck who gets off on torturing people.*

"No, Amir Faruk, sir. I think you are an intelligent and compassionate man." Even as I say the words, I know they're useless. Faruk realizes I've betrayed him. "Let me try to find out why the coordinates are wrong. I will fix this."

"No. You will not." Faruk jerks his head at Zaman. "Take him—"

I lunge for the laptop, and before either one of them can stop me, I slam it into the wall, shattering the screen and sending bits of plastic and glass flying around the small room. I can't let them see what I've done. All of my little rebellions. All preserved on a server no one will ever find. The money I hid for the doctor. The code that adjusts the GPS signal. The bits of video footage I deleted to hide my own plan to kill the man in front of me.

I still have a hold of the laptop's guts, the keyboard and hard drive, and I bring it down on Zaman's instep. He spits out a curse, and I push to my feet, then catch Zaman in the knee with a sweeping kick. He's got fifty pounds on me, but the movement shocks him enough to make him stagger back. Muscle memory takes over, and I spin around and land a punch to Faruk's chest, close to his sternum. But I'm off, just enough, and he doesn't go down.

I don't have anywhere to go, sandwiched between Faruk and his most lethal man. As Zaman grabs me and forces me to my knees, Faruk kicks me in the stomach. "You have forgotten your place, Isaad. And I am going to remind you."

# CHAPTER SIX

**Isaad**

ANOTHER OF FARUK'S men joins Zaman, and the two of them muscle me through the house and across the courtyard. I'll do anything to stay out of the well—even die right here—but Zaman smashes the butt of his gun against the back of my head, and I see stars.

"Down. Or I will throw you down," Zaman growls at me once the ladder's in place.

"Do it." Except, what if the fall doesn't kill me? After he punches me in the gut, I crawl over to the ladder and make my way to the place of my nightmares. The rope slithers back up, taking my last hope with it. Panic courses through me, my entire body shaking, but unlike every other time I've been down here, no one replaces the wooden cover.

What the fuck am I supposed to do now? Faruk is going to "remind me of my place." That means more drugs. More time locked in that tiny room, not knowing up from down, with Faruk's voice the only one I hear.

Sinking down against the stone wall, I draw my knees up to my chest and close my eyes.

*He won't destroy me again.*

I remember my name now. Jackson Richards. But no one called me Jack or Jackson. To my team, my family, I was always Ripper.

"You won't break me this time, pig-fucker!" I shout to no one. I don't care what he does to me. I know who I am, and I'll die down in this shithole before I let him take that away from me again.

---

I MADE it through the night. The light of the stars was just enough for me to see my feet. And the scorpions as they skittered towards me.

I crushed every one of them under my shoe. The crunch as the little fuckers died brought me a bit of satisfaction. Revenge.

Now, there are ten squashed bodies around me. The scorpions hide in the heat, and for a while, I'm safe from their stingers. Sinking down against the wall, I let my head fall back and stare up at the cloudless sky. It's quiet, and I let myself drift into a dreamless sleep.

When I wake, my throat is parched. It's evening, and the temperature has to be over forty-five. No. I'm a damn *American.* I need to think like one. Over a hundred and fifteen. How long are they going to leave me down here like this? As the last bit of light disappears from the sky, footsteps crunch over the rocky ground above. A shadow moves around the edges of the hole, and then a bottle of water hits my foot.

"Fuck you!" I croak as the footsteps fade away. I'm not eating or drinking anything Faruk gives me. Not anymore. I'm ready to die. It's a hell of a lot better than losing myself again. I twist open the cap and dump out the entire bottle.

As determined as I am right now, I can't take a chance that in twelve hours, I'll be so desperate, so weak, that I'll give in. Staring up at the first stars overhead, I say a prayer to the God of my youth—the one Faruk tried to make me forget.

"Help me be strong enough to die."

---

MIDWAY THROUGH THE NIGHT, I've picked up that fucking empty bottle four times, praying for a single drop left inside. The scorpions are out. I've killed two more, but I'm dizzy, and I can only manage to slap at them with my shoe in my hand. Standing... didn't work out so well the last time I tried it. Rubbing the gash on my forehead I opened when I pitched into the wall, I gaze up at the stars. This...would be a good night to die. I'd like to see the moon one more time. After that...I don't care anymore.

*Don't you die on me, brother!*

Ryker. Commander of our ODA. The only reason I survived Hell. He kept us going. Me and Dax. The three of us were closer than brothers when we were captured—even closer after all of Kahlid's torture. Watching one another be flogged, burned, beaten. Tapping out messages on the stone walls of the caves.

Ry protected us. Taunted Kahlid, tricked him so many times into bypassing Dax and me to focus on him instead.

My eyes burn, but I'm too dehydrated to cry. After all Ryker sacrificed, one stupid moment of distraction, and I got him and Dax killed. I deserve everything that's happened to me since, and as a scorpion stings my calf, I relish the pain while I slam my shoe down on top of the bastard.

Someday, if there's an afterlife, I'll see him again. Or...I won't. Because if there's a heaven, Ryker McCabe is in it. And me? I'm going somewhere else. Somewhere I'll burn.

The rope ladder lands on the top of my head, and pain bursts from my skull down my neck. Zaman mutters something to another of Faruk's men, and the burly guy—I think his name is Musa—climbs down the ladder with a large flashlight, waving it around, sending another scorpion hauling ass back through one of the cracks in the wall. He grabs my chin, forces my head up, and pours water down my throat.

I choke, coughing up as much of it as I can, but I'm so desperate, so thirsty, I can't help swallowing more than I want.

And that's when the world starts to go soft and fuzzy. "No..." I moan, but Musa stops my protests by wedging the bottle between my teeth, tipping my head back, and pinching my nose. I down the entire bottle, and then...nothing matters anymore.

---

I DON'T KNOW how long I've been here. Musa comes down the ladder sometimes to give me water or force me to eat a banana or some bland, flavorless mush. I'm too out of it to care or fight back. The heat, the drugs, the scorpions—though I've killed most of them, I think. Still, every once in a while, I feel the searing pain followed by the blessed numbness from their venom.

I deserve it. I failed. Couldn't kill Faruk, couldn't hide Mateen, Lisette, and the American for more than a day. He probably has them again, and it's all my fault.

My entire world is darkness and pain. All the time, except when they come for me. Musa calls me Isaad, but even though I can feel my mind slipping, urging me to give in, I don't. Whenever he leaves, I repeat my name. Jackson Richards. Ripper. American. Special Forces.

Every time, it's a little harder. I don't want to lose myself again. I'd rather die. I'm *trying* to die. But I can't fight. I'm too weak. Too tired. Too addled from whatever hallucinogens they're giving me. I see my dead team mates, hear my mama's voice as I prepared for my first deployment, feel the pain as Kahlid orders me whipped for the very first time.

The rope ladder hits my thigh, and I barely flinch.

*Not again. Please. I'm not ready.*

The drugs haven't worn off yet, and I'm so dizzy. Voices all around me, both in my head and echoing off the walls, tell me to give up. Give in. I won't last much longer. Either I'll die or I'll turn back into Isaad, and that would be so much worse. My vision fades in and out as Musa hauls me over his shoulder and carries me up the ladder, across the courtyard, and into the house.

Cool air wafts over me, and the smooth tile floor rushes up to meet my face.

"Ow."

"Isaad. You do not look well," Faruk says, his voice soft and gentle, almost caring.

"Y'think?" I slur. The kick to my ribs steals my breath, and I cough, fighting for air. Someone grabs me and sits me up, and then a glass presses to my chapped lips. "Nnnooo." I try to push it away, but another hand fists in my hair.

"It is not drugged, Isaad. Please, let me help you." Faruk kneels and takes the glass from the asshole holding me. "Do as I ask, and I will take the pain away."

Despite the fog currently muddling my brain, once his face comes into focus, the dark circles under his eyes and the stress lines around his mouth give me hope. He hasn't found them.

I choke down the water. Not much choice in the matter. As I let my eyes close, waiting for something to happen—anything—Faruk sighs. "Isaad, I am a rich man. You, more than anyone, know this."

*Yeah. And I helped you get that way, shitstain. Kill me. I don't want to listen to your stupid, fucking voice a second longer.*

"I could hire someone new to find my son. But I do not wish to. You want to live, do you not?"

I want to say yes. To do anything to keep myself out of the well. But I can't. I won't. "Death...sounds pretty good...about now, asshole." Shaking off Musa's grip on my hair, I use what little bit of saliva I have to spit in Faruk's face. "Put me...back in the well. Too fucking bright...out here."

For a few seconds, nothing happens, but then Zaman and Musa start in on me, and I curl into a ball to protect my head. The pain is so much better than not knowing who I am that I welcome it. As they drag me from the room, I lunge for the knife I buried in the potted plant days ago. It's dull as fuck, but I use the last of my strength to drive the blade into Zaman's calf.

He goes down, and blood stains his light gray pants. Musa drops me in favor of helping Zaman. Collapsing into a heap, I hawk a mouthful of blood towards the fucker writhing with his hands around his lower leg. Faruk pulls out a small pistol and presses it to my forehead.

*This is it.*

Relief spreads through me, an odd calm that makes everything slow down. If there's a God, I hope he knows how sorry I am for everything I've done. I hope I get to see Ry and Dax again. I hope they forgive me.

"You are determined to die, Isaad?" he asks.

I meet his gaze, feeling more like myself than I have in years. "My name...is Ripper, you fucking piece of shit."

He slams the butt of the gun against my head, and as darkness overtakes my vision, my last conscious emotion is despair. He didn't shoot...

# CHAPTER SEVEN

*Seattle*

**Ryker**

Coding myself into our condo, I roll my head to work out the kinks in my neck. The loud crack seconds after the door opens makes Wren yelp, and she barely holds on to her laptop.

My heart skips a beat. Seeing her curled up on our couch, working, is the best sight to come home to. "Sorry, sweetheart," I say as Pixel leaps up and starts yipping and running circles around me. "Hey, furball."

Wren's smile staggers me. Every day, I wonder what she saw in my eyes when we met. "You're home."

"Damn right." I pull her into my arms, letting her wrap her legs around my waist. "Missed you."

"Obviously," she says with a laugh.

My jeans are suddenly painfully tight, and the scent of her, all that honeysuckle and heat, means we might not make it to the bedroom. "Can you take a break?"

"Almost." She lowers her head and kisses me, her tongue tracing the seam of my lips. I yield to her demands, nipping at the corner of her mouth before she pulls back. "I just got this surveillance video from Nomar of that compound where they had Ford's fiancé. I want to load it into my facial recognition software and let it run. It'll probably take all night. Or...at least long enough for us to do...other things."

As she returns to her computer, I head for the fridge for a beer. "I like the sound of that."

"Thought you would. Grab me one?" Wren's fingers fly over the keyboard. "Got a good way through unraveling Faruk's finances too. The guy's got a computer genius on his payroll. I tracked deposits through five different countries, multiple banks... He's good. But I'm better. All the trails lead back to his compound in Afghanistan. Close to Mazari Sharif."

Afghanistan. Not far from Hell. The hiss as I open the beers reminds me I'm free. Safe. With Wren in our condo in Seattle. Not back in those caves. Talking with Dax over the past ten days has brought up some painful memories, and I've been riding the edge of the darkness inside me for so long, I don't know what it's like to be on solid ground.

"Ford's back, right? They're both safe?" Dropping down next to her, I hand her the beer, then let Pixel settle in my lap. Stroking the pup's fur, I force myself to relax.

"Yep. Trevor said they got back a few hours ago." After she enters another set of commands, she makes a low, frustrated sound I've never heard her make before. Was that a...growl? "Succotash."

"Succotash?" The laugh that rolls through me eases the last of the tension behind my eyes and reminds me just how fucking lucky I am. Even if I can't keep up with all the odd words Wren uses in place of more conventional curses. "I love you, little bird."

Her fingers still on the keys, and she peers up at me, a soft smile tugging her lips and her jade green eyes dark. "I love you too. And I'm glad you're home. How was training?"

I ramble on as she works, and amazingly, she listens to every word and still manages to follow a set of financial trans-actions from one bank to another. "Everyone seemed glad to be back after West's honeymoon."

"And you?" Searching my face, she huffs quietly. "Don't answer now. But tonight...talk to me?"

How does she know? That if I peel back the lid on the dark-ness, I won't be able to put it away and let her finish her work?

"I can read you, Ry. Someday, maybe it'll stop surprising you." With a quick squeeze to my thigh, she returns her focus to the laptop and shakes her head. "This is so weird," she mutters. "Every single transaction has an extra piece of code that makes no sense. It doesn't do anything. But it's obviously important. This guy's too good to put useless information in these wire transfers."

Glancing over at the screen, I choke on my sip of beer, take Wren's laptop over her sputtered protest, and stare at the string of letters and numbers I know better than my own birthdate.

94820RJT008000

In a little window off to the side of the screen, the surveillance video plays, and I pause, rewind, and zoom in.

"Holy fucking shit."

"Ry? What the heck is this?"

I can't force the word over the lump in my throat. Six years. Six years and eight months. Pulling out my phone, I send a text to my team.

*HVT located in Afghanistan. We leave in three hours. Plan on being gone five days.*

Within minutes, Inara, West, and Graham have all

confirmed, and Wren's staring at me like I've grown a second head.

She arches her brow. "Ryker McCabe, what in the hockey pucks is going on here?"

"Pack a bag, sweetheart. We're going to Boston."

---

*Boston*

**Dax**

The sound of chimes wakes me from a deep sleep. Next to me, Evianna calls out on a yawn, "Alfie, show the front door."

Her home security system—the one she designed, built, and launched just a few days ago—lights up, but all I can see through my damaged eyes is a dull glow. A second later, she sits up, and her fingers curl around my arm. "Dax. It's Ryker and Wren. They're outside. Here."

For a moment, her words don't register. And then, it's like someone shot electricity through my entire body. I'm on my feet, fumbling around for my pajama pants, until I remember I'm not at my apartment. I'm at Evianna's house—where we've been living for the past ten days—and I'm still a little iffy about where everything is.

"Dax. Stop." Her footsteps make the wood floors creak as she rounds the bed, and I still. "Pants," she says softly as she drapes the material over my hands. "And a black t-shirt. I'll let them in. Your cane's downstairs, and I'll bring it up—"

"I can make it to the living room," I grit out.

With a little huff, she heads for the bedroom door. "If you fall down the stairs, I'm going to be really pissed off."

"Darlin', wait." Regret roughens my tone, and I pull on the

pants and shirt, then hold out my hand. "You're right. I need... help." I'm not steady. Neither is she. With her holding my elbow, I can feel the slight tremble in her fingers. "What time is it?"

"Six-thirty-three. It's barely light out." At the bottom of the stairs, she guides me to the right, enters a ten-digit code, then flips the locks.

"What's wrong?" I ask as soon as Ry and Wren's diffuse, hazy forms are silhouetted in the pre-dawn glow from the street lights.

"Snackcakes," Wren mutters. "You didn't call him, did you?" Ryker grunts what might be a *no*, and I think Wren elbows him as she huffs. "Dax, I'm sorry. I should have...I don't know. Fudgesicles. Can we...uh...come in?"

*Manners, Holloway. Remember 'em.*

"Yeah. It's fine...I mean...don't apologize." Though I dislike being touched, I reach out, and she wraps her arms around me for a quick hug. Ry's stiffer, sidling past me without so much as a 'morning.

The women embrace as I shut the door, exchanging apologies for the early hour and not being dressed flowing between the two as Evianna leads us all into the kitchen. "Just let me start the coffee, okay?" she asks with a squeeze to my fingers.

Whatever Ry's doing here, it's bad. I just talked to the man a little over a day ago. Ford and Joey got back last night, so I know they're safe. I need something to do, but it's not that big of a kitchen. I can at least find the mugs, and I carry four to the table, setting them down with only a hint of a clatter.

Pinching the bridge of my nose, I try to think. "We have...uh..."

"Nothing," Evianna answers. The coffee starts to percolate, and she slides into the chair next to me and links our fingers. "Unless you consider Honey Nut Cheerios suitable for guests?"

"Coffee's fine," Ryker says.

No one says a word for several minutes, but Wren pulls out her laptop, and I can hear her typing furiously. When the drip, drip, drip of the coffee slows, Evianna brings the pot to the table and fills the mugs.

"Do you have any honey?" Wren asks.

I can feel the tension rolling off Ryker, and after Evianna slides the bottle of honey in front or Wren, he rubs his hand over his bald head, then clears his throat. "We found something in Abdul Faruk's finances."

"Something important enough to show up at Evi—our—house before sunrise?" I asked her to marry me a week ago, and though we haven't talked about a wedding yet, if things work out, we'll get married next to Ry and Wren at the end of the year. But it still feels odd to refer to this as our place.

"Yeah. How much did Ford tell you?" Ry leans forward, his massive presence dominating the room. I'm tall, but he's the biggest motherfucker I've ever seen...or had ever seen before I lost my sight.

"I got a text message from him when he got in last night. He and Joey are at his place, safe. Trevor's back too. Nomar, the spook he knows who worked the Uzbeck theater, is stuck in a hospital in Turkey for another couple of days."

*Where's this going?*

I find Evianna's hand under the table and run my thumb over her engagement ring. She calms me. Centers me. Helps quiet my demons. And at the moment, those demons are trying to bring down the entire fucking house.

"They had help escaping Faruk's compound," Wren says. "Trevor sent me all of the footage from his and Nomar's body-cams, and I spent yesterday afternoon digging into Faruk's finances. He has dozens of offshore accounts, and untangling all the transactions, sources and destinations...it was driving me bonkers."

"You?" Wren's the best hacker I've ever met, and she routinely has to delve into complex financial data for our clients. Bonkers is extreme for her.

"There was this code..."

Ry finishes her sentence, "At the end of every transaction. A code that didn't need to be there."

"Are you going to get to the fucking point?" My headache's already started, and it's not even 7:00 a.m. "Or is this just a really long-winded story so I won't kick your ass for waking us up—"

"Dax," Evianna says in my ear. "This is...this is bad. Can't you hear it in his voice?"

*Fuck.* Of course I can. It's been there since we opened the door. But I just got my best friend—my brother—back after six years. I'm not prepared to lose him again, and I can't think of any other reason he'd be this...off.

"94820RJT008000."

"No." I push back from the table, half knocking over the chair in my rush to stand, to pace, to get some fucking air. "Evianna...I need..." Not paying a damn bit of attention to where I am, I bang into the counter, lose my balance, and go down, hard.

"Dax!" Evianna cries, but it's Ryker who takes my arm and pulls me to my feet.

"Give us a minute," he grits out. The lock on the back door *thunks*, and the crisp morning air hits my cheeks. I'm free. In Boston. Not back in Hell. Not broken. Well, not completely broken. And my brother's still at my side.

"It's just a code," I say, my voice rough.

"Yeah. It was. Until I saw the video from Trevor's body cam. It's him, Dax. Older. Beard, long hair, looked like shit. Like...the man we knew—the man we called our brother—died a long time ago. But his body... It's him. My team's on their way here. I don't care what it takes. We're bringing him home."

I can hear the emotion in Ry's voice. The tears he's fighting not to let spill.

And then it hits me. Why he's about to break.

"We left him there. Fuck. We left a man behind."

# CHAPTER EIGHT

## Dax

IT'S TOO EARLY, and I should have called first, but Ry was right to just show up at my door this morning. Some things can't be explained over the phone. He rings Ford's doorbell, and I hear footsteps inside.

As the door opens, a small hazy form darts behind Ford's taller one. Shit. Ry probably scared the crap out of Joey.

"Didn't know we were hosting a party this morning," Ford says. "You couldn't have called first? Joey's—"

Wren edges around me. "Joey? I'm Wren. It's really good to meet you."

Ford introduces us all, but we're still standing just inside the door. "Ford, can we sit down? Wren and Ryker found something on the surveillance tapes from Faruk's compound we need to talk about."

"Yeah, whatever. You want coffee?" he asks.

I wave him off as I take one end of the couch, and Joey and Ford huddle together on the other end.

"This is from Nomar's bodycam," Wren says. "Before the three of you went in to rescue Joey."

I can't see the screen, but it sounds like Faruk is beating the crap out of Joey, and I'm about to say something when Ford pipes up. "Wren," he warns, "what's the point of this?"

"Sorry." Her voice drops to a whisper and she taps a few keys. "Joey, you're off the video now. But you need to see this next part."

Ry explained what's on the screen. Our friend, our teammate, walking across the yard, looking like a broken man with no hope. Behind Wren, Ry clears his throat. "Do you know who that man is?"

"Isaad," Joey says quietly. "He was...kind."

Ford recounts their escape and how this *Isaad* directed them to an underground tunnel. "He said Faruk took his name and his honor. Everything that made him who he was. His ledger was full of blood. And if he was lucky, he'd be able to kill Faruk before Faruk killed him. And then he said he was sorry."

Ryker stands a little taller. "That enough proof for you?"

"Yeah." I take off my glasses and pinch the bridge of my nose. "I'm going with you. At least to the safehouse in Kabul. If he's alive, I need to be there."

"Who?" Ford asks. "Who the hell is this Isaad guy? He didn't sound like a local."

Ryker's voice is raspier and rougher than normal. "His name is Jackson Richards. But when we knew him, when he was the Communications Sergeant on our ODA team, we called him Ripper."

**Ryker**

We leave Ford's apartment and head directly to Second Sight. Dax hasn't said a fucking word since we walked out the door, and I don't know how to reach him. Or if I even can.

He's out of the car faster than I think should be possible for a blind man and headed for the elevator, his cane tapping lightly on the concrete. "Don't," Wren says when I take a deep breath, ready to stop him. "Let him have a few minutes."

Meeting her gaze, I can see my anguish reflected in her green eyes. "Sweetheart, I'm..." My knuckles crack as I ball my hands into fists, little lightning bolts of pain shooting through my fingers. But it's only a fraction of what I deserve.

"You didn't leave him," she whispers. Gently, she cups my cheek, leans in, and ghosts her lips over mine. "You thought he was dead. You had every reason to believe he'd died six months before you escaped. He wasn't in Hell. You had no way of knowing *where* he was. I *know* you, Ryker McCabe. If you'd had a single shred of doubt, you'd have turned that whole country upside down to find him."

"I can't get those words out of my head. 'Faruk took his name and his honor. Everything that made him who he was.'" I need to hit something, but the steering wheel of the rental car wouldn't be a good target, and I want the whole team on a transpo to Afghanistan as soon as West gives us the go ahead. But if there's time, I'm finding Dax's boxing gym and punching the shit out of a heavy bag. "I thought...I thought I got him killed, Wren. But this is worse. I...destroyed him."

"Stop that right now," she says sharply. "That horsepucky isn't going to do you—or Ripper—any good. *You* didn't destroy him. Faruk did. *You* are going to get him back. Now, come on. We've given Dax enough time alone, and West, Inara, and Graham should be here soon."

As we reach the elevator, I wrap my arm around Wren's shoulders, pull her close, and kiss the top of her head. "I couldn't do this without you, little bird. I love you."

"You'd do it." Her lips curve into a half-smile. "Because that's who you are. But you don't have to do it alone."

---

MY TEAM—INARA, West, and Graham—along with Dax, some guy named Clive, and Wren all sit around a conference table with a view of the Boston skyline. And I doubt any of them have even looked twice at it.

"This is going to be tricky," West says as Wren projects satellite images of the compound on the wall. "He's got a shit ton of firepower, a position with three-sixty visibility, and we have no idea if the target's going to welcome us with open arms or try to kill us."

I slam my fist down on the table, and Wren stifles a yelp. "This is Ripper we're talking about. He's Special Forces. There's no way he'd turn on us," I say, the words rough as they scrape over the back of my throat. I know the guy. Knew him, at least. "We all had two weeks of SERE training. And fuck...we survived Hell. Ripper didn't disappear for six months. He was as messed up as Dax and I were, but the last time I heard his voice, he was singing *Bohemian Rhapsody* as he was trying to do...well...something. Never knew what, but that was our code for resistance."

A quiet, low voice from the door startles all of us. "SERE training helped you and Dax survive being prisoners of war. But that bastard who carved the two of you up wasn't trained in enhanced interrogation and psychological torture."

"And you are?" I push to my feet, straightening my shoulders to show off all seven feet of my bulk. This guy's small—

compared to me—and I don't want anyone else in this room. Hell, I didn't want Clive here, but Dax insisted.

"Trevor," Dax says. "Sit down, Ry. He's one of mine. Ex-CIA. You can trust him."

My gaze slides to Dax, and I nod. "Fine. But are we inviting anyone else to this circus?"

"No." Trevor shuts the conference room door, but doesn't sit. Instead, he shoves his hands into his pockets and rests his back against the wall. "McCabe, I don't know you. But between the little Dax has said about his time in Hell and your face, I'd bet your torture involved pain, movement restriction, isolation, and starvation. Along with your captor trying to convince you everything would be okay if you'd just tell him what he needed to know."

"Trevor—" Wren begins, but I squeeze her hand.

"It's all right, sweetheart. I know what I look like." Returning my gaze to Trevor, I growl, "Add in time in the hole and you've got it pretty well covered. So?"

"That's not how you break a man." His voice quiets even more, and his eyes darken. "That's how you torture a man. But if you want to break him, there's more to it. And if you want to take away everything he is...that's only the start."

West clears his throat—not that it does much good. "He's right." All heads turn in unison. "My team...we were trained in some of the techniques. I don't...I need a minute." He strides from the room, glaring at Trevor for a beat before slamming the door behind him.

"Keep going," I say.

"Wren? Are you sure you want to hear this?" Trevor asks. "I can come get you when—"

"Flippin' Flapjacks," my little bird says as she rolls her eyes. "I was kidnapped, drugged, and beaten by the head of a Russian bratva less than six weeks ago. No, I don't want to hear this. Yes, I'm going to. Get on with it." She links her fingers with mine, and I feel the tremble. Anger flares, hot and prickling along my skin, and I tighten my free hand around the arm of the chair until it creaks in my grip.

With a sigh, Trevor runs a hand through his hair. "If you want to destroy a man's psyche, you don't just beat the shit out of him. Pain is only a small part of the process. First, you take him away from everything he's ever known. That didn't happen in Hell. It probably happened there," he points at the map. "Faruk's compound is a good four hours from the mountains by truck. Then, you switch things up. Hell was cold, yeah?"

Dax and I both grunt our assent in unison. Deep under the mountain, the intense heat never penetrated.

"That part of Afghanistan where Faruk is? It's hotter than the surface of the sun in July. So hot, it's hard to breathe. They might feed him. Might not. But they'd deprive him of water until he was almost dead. Then, they'd give him a sealed bottle. Tell him it was clean. But all you need is a hypodermic needle and a lighter and you can inject a bottle full of LSD or other psychotropic and no one's the wiser."

Trevor's voice takes on an almost monotonous tone now, and he's not looking at any of us. His gaze is focused somewhere over my head, out the window. "Within twenty minutes, the prisoner won't know up from down. He'll see things. Hear things. And he'll be susceptible to programming."

"Programming?" I sit up a little straighter. "Did they get him addicted to drugs?" It's too much like Wren. Too many memories, and I want to carry her away, back to Seattle where nothing can ever touch her again.

Trevor frowns. "No. They wouldn't risk that. Not if they wanted something from him. But the drugs would leave him off balance. Anyone here ever done LSD? Mushrooms?"

No one speaks, and Trevor offers a wry smile. "It'll fuck you up big time. He's in the dark. It's hotter than hell. He's probably restrained. Definitely alone. In an environment he doesn't understand. And he can't think straight. Then, someone comes. Tells him it's going to be okay. That he's going to be safe."

"He wouldn't believe that," I growl. "Ripper's too smart for—"

"He would. Maybe not the first time. But the fifth? The tenth? Breaking a man isn't something you do in a day. Or a week. It takes months. Back and forth. Total agony, then drugged, relative safety. Eventually, he'll believe any fucking thing they want him to. Because whoever's in charge of him... well...they'll be the one to make it all okay. Get him somewhere cool. Give him food. More drugs. Treat his wounds. And then... they'll deal the final blow."

Fuck. What the hell else?

After a pause, Trevor scrubs his hands over his face. "They'll take away the one thing he's been holding onto the whole time. Hope."

"How?" Dax demands, but from his tone, I think he's figured it out. So have I.

"They'll tell him everyone he knows is dead. And that he killed them."

---

THE HANGER'S deserted this time of night. Or morning. It's almost 2:00 a.m., and none of us have slept. That's what the flight's for. We're all in our separate corners, going through our rituals. Inara's upside down in a head stand, West is cross-legged on the floor, his eyes closed, Trevor's on the phone to some of his CIA contacts, Dax sits with his arms around Evianna and her head on his shoulder.

Wren's checking and double-checking every piece of tech.

Laptops, coms, tablets, and cameras. She's not going with us—I put my foot down—though we fought about it for an hour. Now, she's not speaking to me. Can't say I blame her.

Digging my hand into my pocket, I finger the small, black box I've carried around for two weeks.

"Wren? Sweetheart, I...need—"

She's in front of me before I can finish the sentence. "What's wrong?"

"Wrong?" My heart takes up a frantic beat in my chest, and I step back. "I don't—"

"You just said 'I need.' Pretty sure you've used those words exactly twice before." She cocks her head, concern darkening her emerald eyes as she wraps her delicate fingers around my biceps—well, partly around them—and drops her voice. "I may be mad at you, but I still love you, Ry."

I haul her against me and try not to crush her. She's so tiny. So perfect. "Come outside with me for a minute?"

With a nod, she eases down to her feet and lets me put my arm around her shoulders.

The moon is almost full, and the airfield has a view of the water. It's...beautiful. Hell, without the plane idling two hundred feet away, this could be almost romantic.

"I wanted to do this at home," I say, my voice stronger than it has any right to be with how nervous I am. "Maybe take you to the Space Needle restaurant—it looks out over Puget Sound and spins slowly. You get a whole three-sixty-view as you eat."

She smiles at me, and my whole world feels lighter. "You surprise me every day, Ryker McCabe. That sounds like an actual...date."

"We skipped that whole part of the relationship." I stare down at my boots. "You deserve a guy who'll date you. Bring you flowers. Take you all the places you've ever wanted to go."

When I meet her gaze, anger simmers in her eyes. "Don't

fucking tell me what I deserve. I love *you*. I deserve *you*. *You're* the one who makes me happier than I've ever been. Who understands me. Who—"

The profanity—so unusual for her—has my heart shooting into my throat. "Sweetheart, I'm sorry. I'm making a mess of this." Pulling out the box, I drop to one knee with a stifled grunt. "I love you, Wren. I didn't think I could love anyone. Or that anyone could ever love me. And we're about to go back to the place where..." I shake my head and open the box.

The platinum ring has four emerald-cut diamonds arranged in a haphazard line. "The guy who made this called it 'beautifully broken.' Back in Russia, after...all that shit, you said 'maybe I didn't realize how beautiful broken could be.'"

Wren's eyes glisten, and she runs her fingers over the beads of her bracelet. Five times in a row before she blinks hard and focuses on me again. "You remember that?"

"I remember everything, sweetheart. Every single moment we've had together. And I want a lot more. All of them. For the rest of our lives. Will you marry me?"

She nods, then holds out her hand. As I slip the ring onto her finger, a single tear rolls down her cheek. "I didn't know if you wanted to..."

Pushing to my feet, I gather her against me and silence her with my lips on hers. My little bird. My partner. One day, my wife. I wish I had the words to tell her what she means to me, but this...this is a start.

"Come back to me, Ryker," she whispers when I finally let her go. "Bring Ripper home, but make sure *you* come home too."

"I will, sweetheart. I promise."

## Dax

Against me, Evianna shifts, and fuck. She feels so good in my arms. "Are you sure about this?" she asks. "Going back there?"

"Yes." Taking off my glasses so she can see my eyes—not that it does anything for my sight—I wait until she brushes a kiss to my lips. "I left him behind, darlin'. It doesn't matter that I didn't know. I spent so many years mad at Ry for leaving *me* behind. Not in Hell. He didn't have a choice when he escaped without me. But when we got back. I can't do that to Ripper for one single day more."

"You're not going to Faruk's compound, though, right?" Worry tinges her voice, and I wish I could tell her what she wants to hear. Give her some guarantee I'll come back alive. And whole.

Skating my thumb over her engagement ring, I evade the question. I won't lie to her. "I'll stay with Trev the whole time."

"That means you're going." She frames my face with her hands. Her palms are warm and soft, and she traces the scars around my eyes gently with her thumbs. "You're scary-good at navigating the world without being able to see it, babe, but this is—" Evianna's voice cracks and she touches her forehead to mine, "—men with guns who'll kill you in a heartbeat. Or worse."

"I know, darlin'. I know." I don't have any answers for her. Or myself. I just know I have to do this. If I stay here...or even at the Kabul safehouse, it'll be the end of me. "I'll come back alive. We've got a wedding to plan. There's nothing in this world that would stop me from marrying you. I promise."

# CHAPTER NINE

**Ryker**

WEST PEERS through the night-vision scope at the compound at the top of the hill. "One target on each of the north and east towers. Two on the south and west."

With a nod, Inara hoists her rifle case onto her shoulder. "Roger that. It'll take me twenty minutes to get into position. Another ten to sight in. Radio silence from me until I'm done."

"Base? You have Indigo on GPS?" On mission, we never use our real names. Only designators. Too great a risk if anyone were to intercept our signals. This job is so fucking illegal, we'd all be locked away for the rest of our lives.

"Yep. Got her." Wren sounds so far away—and she is. Back in Boston. This is the most complicated job we've ever done, and so West's wife, Cam, and Inara's guy, Royce, are patched in to Wren's other ear in case the GPS trackers go down. They're all computer geniuses, and more than once, I've thought about asking them to join Hidden Agenda.

West pulls out his tablet as soon as Inara takes off. "All right.

Listen up. This isn't a normal op." He focuses on Graham. "If you can subdue a hostile silently, do it. Even if that means killing them. You okay with that, probie?"

"Got it." The kid's barely twenty-seven, new to the team, and though he's seen combat, he's green as fuck, and I hate filling his ledger like this. But we need all the help we can get.

"Anyone comes across Faruk, you take him out. No hesitation," I add. "He's not going to hurt anyone again after tonight."

West calls up the satellite photo of the compound. "We have no idea where the target is, and the house is a fucking maze on the main level and underground, but Base will be watching our GPS signals. You get boxed in, you signal for help."

"Last call," I say quietly. "Check your weapons and ammo. Zip ties. Flares. We're going in hot and silent. Thermals show twenty-three signals, but we don't know how well the scanner penetrates into the basement. So we could be looking at double that number." Turning to Dax, who's standing next to me with his hands clenched into fists and a special pair of glasses with a built-in camera covering his sightless eyes, I clasp his shoulder. "Are you sure, brother?"

"If you ask me that again, you're going to be on your ass," he growls.

I have to stifle my grumbled curse. "This party can't get any bigger. We should invite the guy we passed an hour ago with that herd of goats too."

"Shut it, Alpha Team Leader." My little bird chuckles over the air, and the sound calms me like nothing else. "This is what family does."

*Family.*

I never thought I'd have one again. Before Hell, my team was my family. Dax, Ripper, Hab, Naz, Gose... But after we escaped, I thought I'd lost them all—along with any hope of redemption.

"All right," I say over the lump in my throat. "Indigo should be checking in soon. Let's go get our brother back."

"Hooah," Dax says.

West and Graham add, "Hooyah," in tandem.

Over comms, I hear Ford's "Oorah," and we're good to go.

*We're coming, Ripper. I'm sorry we're six years late.*

---

As THE SKY darkens at moonset, West, Graham, and I creep closer to the compound. Trevor and Dax crouch behind an old truck parked a thousand yards away. The former CIA spook paid a local to leave the vehicle this morning with the air let out of one of the tires.

"You're up, Indigo," I whisper.

"Roger that."

Inara's comms click off, and West frees the grappling hook from his belt. At my side, Graham flexes his fingers. The kid's been working on his rappelling skills non-stop since his first mission where he almost got himself killed. As I mentally tick off the location of each member of my team, one word bounces around in my head.

*Family.*

Wren was the first one who told me Hidden Agenda, my K&R firm, was a family. And families support one another. I rest my hand on Graham's shoulder and give it a squeeze.

From above, I hear a soft exhalation of air followed by a quiet thud. One down. West throws the hook over the wall, and it catches on the razor wire. Good enough. He's up and over in less than a thirty seconds. Graham's next, and though he takes slightly longer, he's almost as quick as I am.

The three of us crouch on the top of the north guard tower, the dead guard staring up at nothing. Inara's the best damn sharpshooter I've ever known, and she put a bullet right between his eyes.

West pieces together his own rifle. In under five minutes, all six guards in the towers are dead.

"Bravo Team...approach is clear," I say. "Base, we're going in."

"Be careful," Wren says, and the tremble in her voice shoots right to my heart. "There are two guards at the back door to the house."

"Roger that."

"Got sights on one of them," Inara says. "Alpha Team, on your mark."

West and Graham drop down to the ground, and West pulls a serrated blade from a sheath at his waist before the two of them head east, towards the back door. He'll protect the kid as best he can. I descend silently and head in the other direction, determined to check out two buildings at the edge of the compound. The smaller showed a faint heat signature moving back and forth, and though I have no proof it's Ripper, my instincts are pulling me in that direction.

As I approach the corner of the house, footsteps scuff along the dirt, and I wrap my fingers around the handle of my blade. Except it's not mine. It's Ripper's. The only piece of him I had left. I've carried it with me on every mission since I left the army.

Tonight, I'll use it. Silent and deadly.

At least Dax is the only one wearing a camera. Wren doesn't need to see what I'm about to do. The knife slides quickly into the man's abdomen as I cover his mouth with my other hand. Blood splashes the wall, and he gurgles quietly as I twist the blade and destroy his internal organs. He's dead within seconds, and I ease his body down to the ground.

The first building is just a storage shed—and empty.

Slinking quietly towards the second, I listen. A handful of chickens peck at the ground, and a dog barks from the inside of what looks like a barn. Fuck. Have I been tracking a damn dog this entire time?

I have to check. As I put my ear to the door, I hear quiet panting. Adjusting my grip on the knife again, I use my foot to nudge the wood and then spin so I can press my back against the wall. A skinny, scruffy dog comes padding out.

Dammit. I could have been hunting down Faruk instead of chasing Fido.

"Base? Status on heat signatures at my location?"

"One. Faint. Headed away from you. All the others are inside."

"It was a goddamned dog. He's not out here." I stalk towards the front of the house, anger tightening my jaw.

"Wait," Wren says. "Stop. There's...something... Where are you, Team Leader?"

"Twenty-five meters west-northwest of the front door."

"Hold position."

"I'm exposed, Base." Pulling out my Beretta, I scan all around me. There's nothing here. Nothing but dead bodies and blood. The gate's still closed, and to the outside world, Faruk's compound is peaceful.

"Oh God. Really?" Wren's not talking to me, but whatever she just learned has her voice trembling. "Right in front of you. Maybe half a meter. Is there a...wooden cover? Like you'd find on a manhole?"

I adjust the sensitivity of my NVGs and peer at the ground. The night vision turns everything green, but it sharpens every-thing around me, and the circular outline of a cover maybe ten feet across comes into focus. "Roger that."

"It's...a well," she says. "Faruk threatened to put the doc down there. Keep her there if she didn't cooperate. And...there's something really faint on the thermals under there. Like...actually underground."

I drop to one knee and feel around, finding a small metal ring that pops up from the cover. My gut twists. What's down there? A body? An enemy? Or my brother?

The cover slides off easily, and I peer into the deep, dark space. "Package located," I manage, though I don't know how I get the words out. He's twenty feet down, curled on his side, unmoving. "Bravo Team...prepare for infil. My position. Hold until I have proof of life."

In my ear, Wren's voice comforts me. "There should be a rope ladder against the wall of the building behind you."

"Roger."

As I hook the last rung of the rope on a small iron peg sticking up from the ground, multiple quiet *pops* sound from inside the house.

"Alpha Team Leader," West says, "Enemy target secured. Office. Southwest corner of the main floor."

"Keep him breathing. He's mine."

The ladder unfurls and hits the prone body in the thigh. I blow out a breath as he flinches. Still alive. I'm down in under a minute, and even with everything I've seen, what I find makes me stagger back until I hit the wall. Dead scorpions litter the ground—most of them crushed, but a few of them ripped apart, their abdomens gone...like...he had to eat them. A live one skitters over his thigh, and as soon as it reaches the dirt, I slam my boot down on top of it. "Not today, fucker."

There's a single plastic water bottle next to him—empty—as well as a bucket, and the stench is so thick I could chew it. Pushing the goggles up on my head, I activate the small light at my shoulder. That sends another scorpion fleeing back through a crack in the wall.

"Ripper?" Kneeling next to him, I check for a pulse. The

man in front of me bears little resemblance to my friend. His beard is thick but neatly trimmed, and his hair brushes his collar. He's too thin, and so dehydrated, his skin looks a lot like wrinkled paper. Blood dries on his cracked lips. "Base, put the doc on."

"I-I'm here," Joey says quietly.

"His heart's racing. One-sixty at least. There's an empty water bottle with him, but I don't know how long he's been down here. He ate some of the scorpions, I think. And he's burning up."

"Oh my God." After a few seconds, she stammers, "Y-you have to...to get fluids into him. And sugar. Lower his core temperature. His kidneys are probably shutting down. Beyond that...get him to a hospital."

I can't do that. Dax and I already decided...Jackson Richards no longer exists. We buried him. Everything that happens now...happens off book. "Roger that."

Pulling a small canteen from one of the pockets of my tactical vest, I slide my arm under Ripper's torso and ease him up. "Rip? You have to drink, brother. We're getting out of here."

Water dribbles over his cracked lips, and a low, deep sound rumbles in his chest. Almost a protest. "It's water, Rip. Just water."

I get a little down his throat, then pour the rest over his head. Now I have to get him out of this fucking hole.

As soon as I stand, he falls over again, retching, and loses the little water he swallowed.

"Dammit." Tapping my comms unit, I stare up at the top of the ladder. "Bravo Team. My location. Now." I lift Ripper, and he struggles weakly. "Stay still, Sergeant. That's a fucking order."

My tone must register, or he passes out, because now he's dead weight over my shoulder. Twenty feet. I can only use one arm on the ladder, and having Ripper's legs between me and the wall doesn't help, but I get us both out of that hell hole and onto level ground.

Ripper doesn't move, and I pull my Beretta as a metallic clang from the gate draws my focus. Drawing down, I wait, crouched on one knee in front of Ripper. But then Trevor's head rises up over the top of the gate, and he quickly drops, tucks, and rolls to distribute the impact. Dax follows, doing a pretty damn good impression of a man with the full use of his sight.

They're in front me in another ten seconds. "Is he alive?" Dax asks.

"Yeah. Barely." When Dax kneels next to me, I guide his hand to Ripper's shoulder. "Rip...we're here. Say something, man."

Nothing. The look on Dax's face...I've only seen the man this broken up once—when I pulled him out of Hell.

"Gentlemen, company's coming," Inara hisses. "Two vehicles approaching from the east. You have five minutes to get the fuck out of there or this is going to get loud."

*Shit.* "Take him to the truck," I say to Dax and Trevor. "Do whatever you can to cool him down. And get the engine running."

Sprinting for the house, I burst through the front doors, finding blood smeared across the expensive tile. Using it as a guide, I track West and Graham to an office where they stand in front of Amir Abdul Faruk. He's zip-tied to a chair, duct tape over his mouth, with seven of his men lying dead in a corner of the room.

*Well, that explains the bloody drag marks.*

"The house is clear?" I ask.

"Another six are locked in a room in the basement," Graham says. "They didn't resist."

"Exfil. Now." I level a gaze at West. "Get to the truck. I'll be right behind you."

The former SEAL squares his shoulders, his blue eyes bright with determination. "No. Take care of him and we all go together."

"Goddammit. Who's in charge here?" We don't have the time to waste arguing, so I just glare at him as I pull Ripper's knife from its sheath and head for Faruk.

"Turn around," West mutters to Graham, but to his credit, the youngest member of our team doesn't move.

Standing over Faruk, I turn the knife in the light so he can see the handle where Rip carved his name, and bare my teeth when his eyes widen. "You took our brother. If our truck wasn't full, I'd bring you with us and spend *months* making you bleed until you begged for death. And then I'd let you heal up and do it all over again."

I lean down so we're eye-to-eye. "But instead, I'll grant you this one mercy." The knife plunges deep into his heart, sliding between his ribs with ease. A half-moan, half-scream is muffled by the duct tape, and I give the handle a twist, watching for the moment the light leaves his eyes.

The blade drips crimson with his blood, and for good measure, I slit his throat, then wipe the thick filth on the leg of his pants.

Turning to West and Graham, I nod. "Bravo Team? We're on our way. Faruk will never hurt another person again."

It's done. And my conscience is clear.

# CHAPTER TEN

**Ripper**

SOMETHING HITS MY SHOULDER, but I can't move. Breathing hurts. I don't care what they do to me. Anything will be better than this. Waiting to die. I haven't pissed in days. Nothing left in me. The scorpions—the few I haven't killed—ignore me now. They can smell death clinging to me.

Fingers touch my neck, and then I hear a single whispered word. "Ripper?"

I should know that name.

"Base, put the doc on."

The voice...I've heard it before. Another wave of pain addles my thoughts, and by the time it's faded, the man's talking again.

"...heart's racing...burning up."

I try to force my dry eyes open, but I can't.

"Roger that." The world tilts, and the man speaks again. "Rip? You have to drink, brother. We're getting out of here."

Water dribbles over my cracked lips, and a low, mournful sound escapes my parched throat. *No. Please. No more...*

Whatever he says next is lost to my panic, but I swallow a bit of the cool liquid, and fuck, it's the best thing I've ever tasted. Metallic, almost. Like the canteens we used to carry. More water drenches my hair, rolling down my cheeks.

When I'm thrown over a shoulder, I push against what feels like solid granite.

"Stay still, Sergeant. That's a fucking order."

*I know that voice.*

Somewhere, deep down, in a place I don't want to go, I hear that same voice calling my name. We're climbing now. Well, *he's* climbing. I'm desperately trying to stay conscious. To figure out what the fuck is happening.

But when the man lays me on the ground, fear takes over, and I can't breathe. I manage to crack an eyelid, but all I see is darkness and boots—three sets of boots—before a dull roar fills my ears and that place where I know the people around me is suddenly closer than it's been in years.

---

Voices. One of them's shouting, but there's so much noise...I can't make out the words. Everything hurts, but it's cooler here —wherever I am. We're...moving. Oh, fuck. Where is Faruk taking me now?

My stomach pitches, and I taste bile. Rough hands grab me, rip my sleeve, and then...the sting of a needle. "No!" I whisper as I try to pull my arm away.

"Dammit, Ripper, stop fighting us!" The order registers, the voice is one I know, the one that belongs to a ghost.

I let myself go limp, and long moments pass where I don't feel anything at all. They're broken up by terror, pain, nausea, and stomach cramps so intense, I think maybe...death would be better.

Time has no meaning as I start to sweat, then shiver, letting the motion lull me into sleep or unconsciousness. When I come to, I'm floating. My fingers, blistered and raw, ache as I grab on to fabric—nylon or...Kevlar?

"...into the water..."

Someone rips off my clothes, and I thrash, hitting my head on something hard. I can't let them hurt me again. I can smell blood. My own filth. The scents are overwhelming here in this place that otherwise smells like...very little.

"You're safe, brother. Trust me," a man whispers, and everything about this situation is so different from Faruk and his men, I believe him. The water surrounds me, blessedly cool, and I relax enough to open my eyes.

Muted colors and dark shapes. Every blink is pure agony. "Let...me...die," I manage.

"Not an option." The man standing over me has dark hair, but I can't make out his features. The room spins, and a soft cloth drags over my face, my neck, my chest.

"Someone did a number on him," the man says quietly. "Wish we'd have been able to spend more time killing that shitstain."

"He's gone. That's all that matters now." A giant kneels close by, and thick fingers grasp my shoulder. "I'm so fucking sorry, Rip. But you're safe now."

I close my eyes, waiting for the drugs to take hold, for the entire world to turn upside down, inside out, and sideways. But all I find is quiet and peace.

---

SOMETHING COOL RESTS on my forehead. Breathing hurts.

*Think. Don't let Faruk give you anything. Stay focused.*

It's too hard. Nothing makes any sense in this new reality. A tear leaks from my eye, and the mattress depresses. "Ripper?"

Another voice, this one with a hint of a southern drawl. "Rip? Come on back now."

Ghosts. I'm hearing ghosts.

"Gotta get some calories in him." This is the man I don't know. "Joey's worried about his kidneys."

The doctor? Is she here? Fuck. I tried to keep her safe. Did I fail...again? Forcing my lids open, I lock onto multi-hued eyes so distinctive, there's no way they could belong to anyone else. I'm hallucinating. Ryker McCabe has been dead for six years.

"Ripper? Can you hear me?" He leans closer, and I blink hard and study his face. The left half looks like someone took a hot poker to it—repeatedly. One eyelid droops slightly, and a thick scar bisects his brow. His bare, corded forearms sport tattoos I've never seen, and one...holy shit. One has my name on it.

"Ry...?" The word sounds more like a croak than anything else, and takes so much out of me, sleep starts to pull me under.

"Stay with us, Rip. You hear me? Open your fucking eyes. Now."

I've never disobeyed one of Ryker's orders. I can't start now, even if he *is* a figment of my imagination or Faruk's torture. The room comes back into focus, and I take in the six people standing around me. One...I've seen before. He helped get the doctor out. "I...know you."

"Trevor," he says. "And she's fine. Back in Boston with Ford —the tall guy with me the last time we saw you. But she won't stop messaging us to get you to eat something."

Ryker holds a cup with a metal straw to my lips, and logic goes out the window. "N-no." That's how it always starts. A bottle of water. Tea. And then reality fades away. Fighting against the light sheet covering me, I hear Ryker tell me to calm down, but I can't. The hands pressing against my shoulders pull a hoarse wail from my throat.

"Jackson!" Trevor's voice—his use of my name—shocks me enough that I stop struggling, but the brief fight stole what little strength I had left, and I can only lie there helplessly, panting. "This is just sugar water." He takes the glass from Ryker, sucks half of it down through the straw, and passes it back. "Satisfied? Because my teeth hurt now."

I nod, which is probably a mistake, because my head pounds like it's being used for a basketball. Ryker slides his arm behind my shoulders, helps me up, and shoves a pillow behind me before he presses the straw to my lips. I take a small sip. Then another.

"That's enough for now," a man says from behind Ry. "If that stays down for ten minutes, you can have the rest. Doctor's orders."

"Who...the fuck...are you?" That's not what I want to ask. I *want* to ask Ryker how he's alive. How he found me. How he knows this Trevor dude. But I'm not ready for the answers yet.

"West Sampson. SEALs. Retired."

Of course. He's got that look. The one all frogmen get after a while. The look that says, *"I could kill you without breaking a sweat, then go the bar and order a beer, and no one would ever find the body."*

"My team," Ryker says, then nods to a woman in the corner of the room dressed all in black with a shock of blond hair peeking out of her cap. "Inara, West, Graham."

"Team?"

"K&R. In Seattle."

We're dancing around an elephant so fucking huge, it doesn't just take up the room, but the whole damn country. "You're alive."

"Well, I'm sure as shit not a ghost. You think I'd choose to look like this if I were?"

"Rip?" Dax pats the mattress for a second before he eases himself down on my other side. "We didn't know. When Ry escaped Hell, one of the guards told him you'd died. Broken your neck when they threw you in the hole."

"I...didn't..." No. I can't give up any intel. This has to be a trick. But...Dax is wearing tinted glasses. And behind them... scars. His eyes were darker before. A part of me wants to believe so badly, I have to risk one question. "After...*Bohemian Rhapsody*, what song was next?"

"*Hammer to Fall*," Dax and Ry say in unison.

Fuck. "I saw...the news reports. You were dead." Every word feels like it weighs a hundred pounds, and I don't know how much longer I can stay awake, but I have to know.

Ry glances at the SEAL, then back at me, but it's Trevor who pipes up. "Faruk show you those news reports?" I don't confirm or deny, but he nods. "I figured. He made all that shit up. Pretty typical enhanced interrogation and brainwashing technique. Ryker tells me you're a wizard with tech."

The world feels like it's slowing down, but I fight to stay awake. "Moved money. Investments. So...much...more. Don't... remember..." The heavy weight of shame presses down on me, and I let my eyes close, let the tears I could never cry before stream down my cheeks.

"Ripper, cut that shit out. You did what you had to do in order to survive," Dax says. "Look at me, brother."

I do, because the emotion in his voice...the only time I ever heard it is when he used to talk about his wife...when we were in Hell. But I can't let him just...ignore all the shit I've done. "You never should have come for me."

The sound Ryker makes...it's almost a growl, but Dax

shoots him a look, and he quiets down. Dax takes off his glasses, and the damage...shit.

"Six months after you disappeared, we got the chance to escape. But Kahlid had broken my leg a few weeks earlier. I couldn't walk. After Ry broke out..." Dax swallows hard and gestures to his eyes. "Drain cleaner."

"Dax—"

"It's okay." His dry laugh says it's not, but then the stress lines around his mouth fade, and he looks almost...happy. "I'm here, aren't I? Managed to get myself over that fucking fence around Faruk's compound when Ry found you."

"Heard...you both. Didn't...believe..."

"You're free now," Ryker says. "I killed Faruk." He pulls a large serrated knife from a sheath at his hip and lays it on my thighs. Trevor and West tense, but Ry waves them off. "This is yours, Rip. The one thing I kept from your footlocker when I packed up your shit at Fort Benning. I used it to end that bastard's life."

As I stare down at the handle, I can just make out the jagged lightning bolts I carved around my nickname. There's still a little dried blood towards the hilt, and I rest my hand on the black metal.

They came for me. I don't know how they figured out I wasn't Isaad, but right now, that doesn't matter. I'm back with my team.

# CHAPTER ELEVEN

*Two Months Later*

## Ripper

MY PHONE VIBRATES as I step off the bus in front of the nondescript gray building in south Seattle. One glance at the screen —and Ryker's name—and I jab the button to send the call to voicemail.

Doc Neery buzzes me in as soon as I close myself in his outer waiting room, and by the time I sit down across from him, I've ignored two text messages from Ry as well.

"Jackson. How are you today?" Neery asks.

He's the only person who calls me by my first name—my original first name.

"Jackson doesn't exist anymore. You know that, doc." The bitterness in my tone? I don't even try to hide it. Not from him. He'd see right through me anyway. The shrink is relentless, and since I go in for appointments twice a week, any resistance I might put up doesn't last long.

"Not on paper, no. Jackson 'Ripper' Richards died six years ago in Afghanistan. But I don't care what your driver's license says. Or how you got it. Jackson's the man I'm treating." Neery leans forward, his elbows on his knees. "So? Going to answer my question?"

"Same shit, different day." I run a hand through my hair. It's short now, and I haven't let my beard grow longer than a dark stubble since the day after Ryker and his team rescued me. Ry gave me a razor and told me to "fix my face."

"Not an answer. Where'd you sleep last night?"

*Lie. Just get the fuck out of here.*

But I can't. My training won't let me. "In the doorway of the Presbyterian Church on 15th. It's quiet there after midnight."

The shrink scribbles something in his notebook, then leans back with a sigh. "When was the last time you went to your apartment?"

"Showered there this morning. Changed clothes. Grabbed a granola bar and got the hell out. We do this every session, doc. Nothing's changed. There some point to this?" I don't want to talk about my feelings. About the fear of locking myself inside my apartment, of the four walls penning me in. Of finding myself somewhere dark and small, unable to get out. But without these appointments, I can't get the anti-depressants that keep me from wanting to throw myself off the Ship Canal bridge, and I'm too scared to face life without them. I don't want to die. I just don't know how to live...free.

"One day, you're going to trust me," he says simply. "Until then, it's my job to make sure you're safe and not a danger to yourself or anyone else."

My shoulders stiffen, and I sit up a little straighter. I'm a danger to everyone. Hell, the last time someone tried to grab my arm to tell me my backpack was open, I almost laid them out with a single punch. "I'm controlling it," I say through gritted teeth.

"Care to try that again without cracking a molar?"

"No." Crossing my arms over my chest, I arch a brow, daring him to push me. But he doesn't. Instead, he switches gears completely.

"Any news on the job front? How was your interview with the animal shelter?"

This, I can handle. "I start volunteering tomorrow. Cleaning the kennels, walking the dogs. Six hours a week, after the shelter closes for the day. If it goes well, they'll start paying me in a month."

"So, a job where you won't have to see or talk to anyone." Neery hides his frustration well most of the time, but when you've been trained to read micro-expressions, it's pretty damn easy to spot when your shrink is disappointed with you.

"Look, doc, this is all I've got in me. You want to make me feel like shit for it? That's your choice. I met your minimum requirements. Ten minutes in the chair twice this week. Get me the damn script and I'm gone." Pushing to my feet, I sway as a brief wave of dizziness hits me. But Neery is too busy scribbling on his prescription pad to notice.

"I'll see you next Monday, Jackson."

"Yeah. Whatever." Five minutes, and I'm outside in the sun. By the time I reach the pharmacy, I'm shaking. Will this be the day I slip up? Get distracted and give the wrong name?

*Breathe. You're Rick Mercury now.*

The day Dax asked me to choose my new name, there was only one I wanted.

*"Fred Mercury." I shove my hands into the pockets of the hoodie. Since we landed in Boston, I haven't been able to get warm.*

*Dax chokes on his coffee. "You've got to be fucking kidding me."*

*"No. If you're going to take my name away—" I clear my throat,*

*unwilling to let anyone know how much it kills me to give up the name I just got back, "—then I'm going to be Fred Mercury."*

*"Rip, come on," Ry says as he drops into the chair across from me. "You'll draw way too much attention to yourself. After the movie...fuck."*

*"What movie?" I haven't seen a movie in more than six years. I've missed so much.*

*Ry's girl takes his hand, and her engagement ring catches the light. I don't know her—or Dax's fiancée, or anyone else in this room. Clive-something-or-other is Dax's relocation specialist, and he and Wren can get me a fake identity, complete with credit history. She meets my gaze, and her soft voice holds sympathy. "They released a Queen biopic last year. Won all sorts of awards."*

*"Fine. Rick Mercury." Before Dax and Ry can protest again, I hunch my shoulders and stare down at the floor. These are my brothers. I should be able to be straight with them. But all I can hear is Faruk's voice in my head telling me Jackson Richards is dead, and I'm Isaad now. "I can't lose anything else," I whisper. "Please. Richard Jack Mercury. Let me keep...something of who I used to be."*

The pharmacist calls out, "Mercury. Rick Mercury?"

It takes me a minute to remember that's who I'm supposed to be, and when I approach the counter with my ID and credit card, I want to throw up. But I get through the transaction and leave with a week's worth of anti-depressants and anxiety pills.

I hate this. Hate my life. Hate what those years of brain-washing and torture did to me. My hands shake as I twist the top off the bottle of anxiety meds and toss back two of them with swig of cold brew coffee I picked up while I was waiting.

I should be better by now. Stronger. But instead, I'm fighting the physical and mental effects of too many traumatic brain injuries, sleeping on the streets, and spending the rest of my days walking. Just so I can be outside, somewhere no one can lock me in again.

BY THE TIME I reach my apartment building, Ryker's sent me two more text messages, both ignored with a quick tap to the screen. I swear under my breath as I check the time. Sunset is in twenty minutes. I can't be here after dark. Won't be.

Up three flights of stairs—there's no fucking way I'm getting into an elevator—and I round the corner and freeze. "Last time I checked," I say, trying to keep my tone measured and level, "I was two years older than you. I don't need a babysitter."

Ryker pushes off the wall, his hands in his pockets, and ambles towards me. "Then return my damn messages."

"I was busy."

He arches a brow. "Doing...?"

"None of your fucking business." Shouldering past him, I don't miss his flinch—or my own. Neither of us like to be touched. Punching in the fourteen-digit code that saved my life —94820RJT008000—I wait for the secured door to open. "What do you want?"

He doesn't answer, just follows me inside, and the idea of anyone between me and the door sends my heart rate skyrocketing.

*It's Ryker. He's your goddamn brother. Get over yourself.*

But I can't. "If you're going to come in, don't block the door," I manage as I stow my meds in one of the empty kitchen cabinets. Five minutes. That's all I need. Enough time to grab my rucksack and sleeping bag, take a piss, and make sure I have enough cash to hit up the pizza place on the Ave.

"Ripper, stop." Ryker steps in front of me as I'm reaching for my sleeping bag. Not hard, since I wouldn't let him set me up in anything but a studio apartment. Too many walls.

"Back. Away." I don't meet his gaze. Too many years of being beaten every time I tried to stand up for myself, and now...I'm a fucking coward.

"Look at me." His voice isn't steady, and the shock of hearing Ryker McCabe break is enough to drag me out of my own head. "I don't...do this, Rip."

"What?"

"Talk." His hands ball into fists at his sides, and he cracks each knuckle before turning and heading for the door. "Get your stuff. Do whatever you need to do. Then meet me outside."

Whatever this is...it's serious. As I hook the strap of my sleeping bag to the bottom of my ruck, I glance around the studio. He did all of this for me. By the time I was strong enough to make the trip from Boston to Seattle, he had this whole place furnished and outfitted with the best security system money could buy, and had Wren set up a bank account for me with enough money to live off of for a decade. All courtesy of the man who imprisoned, abused, and brainwashed me. Wren found a couple of his accounts, traced the transactions, and transferred the money to me.

I wish I could sleep here. In the king-sized bed with the navy blue duvet and five hundred thread-count sheets. Use the brand new pots and pans, the top-of-the-line refrigerator and stove. But I can't manage to do more than shower here. Last week, I bought a patio chair and tried to sit on the balcony for a while. I made it all of ten minutes.

The alarm on my phone beeps, warning me I need to get the fuck out of here if I don't want darkness to fill the small space from the floor-to-ceiling windows that look out over Lake Washington.

Down on the street, I find Ryker scanning the few passersby. This is a quiet neighborhood, a safe one. But that doesn't mean I can stay here. Not when the nightmares come.

"Say your piece. I've got places to be," I grit out as I reach for my bus pass.

"Yeah. You do. Come on." He jerks his head toward his pickup truck parked at the end of the block.

"If I don't get to—" I can't tell him I'm sleeping in a church doorway. He'd never let me go back.

"I took care of it." He hits a button on the key fob, the door locks disengage, and he opens the passenger side door. "There's a guy saving your spot until you get there."

Mouth agape, I don't move as he rounds the truck and slides behind the wheel. The vehicle's massive. It has to be. Ry won't fit in a normal vehicle. He turns from behind the wheel, and his eyes...the greens and golds and blues darken, seeming to almost swirl together with the raw emotion twisting his features.

"Do you think I don't understand?" he asks quietly. "After Hell, I did my time sleeping places no sane person would ever choose. Tried the park just south of Fort Bragg for a while until the cops caught me. Rented Hidden Agenda's warehouse a week after I got to Seattle and slept on the concrete floor for a month. Even that didn't do it. I had to get a TV and put on a horror movie every fucking night. Six years later and I still can't stand small spaces. Anywhere dark. Anywhere I can't move..."

"I..." The memories hit me hard, and I stagger back, the rucksack hitting the sidewalk first, followed by my ass.

Ry's next to me before I can scramble up, but he doesn't touch me. Just crouches a foot away, clenching his hands on his thighs so hard his knuckles turn white. "Rip? You don't have to talk to me. Hell, you don't have to come with me now. Just answer your damn messages once in a while so I know you're still—" He swallows so hard, I can hear it, then shakes his head. "You're family. And I...care."

My eyes burn, and a single choked sob scrapes over my throat. "I...don't know who I am anymore."

"I know, brother. But that's where we're going. If you'll trust me." Ryker rises and holds out his hand. Two of his fingers aren't entirely straight—courtesy of Kahlid and our time in Hell.

For a long moment, I stare at the scars winding up his arm. Then I look down at my own wrists where the thick, shiny skin from so long bound will never disappear.

*Stay strong, brother. Don't give them anything. You're fucking Special Forces. Remember that.*

Clasping his hand, I let him pull me to my feet. "How'd you know where I was sleeping?"

"Royce told me. He has some sort of post-stroke support group down there once a week. After that...I drove by a couple of times."

"You didn't stop me."

His voice roughens as he stares down at his shitkickers. "Pulling you off the street isn't going to fix you, Rip. You have to find your own way back. Just know...you're not alone. One call, and I'll be there. Anywhere. Any time."

With a nod, I pick up my ruck and throw it in the bed of his pickup. I wish I could tell him everything. All the shit that happened after they took me from Hell. It's too hard. And if I do, he'll never look at me the same way again.

I can give him this, though. A couple of hours where we're brothers again. "Let's go."

---

THE RIDE PASSES IN SILENCE, and I stare out the open side window, feeling the breeze on my face and smelling the sea.

Ryker eases the truck to a stop on Roosevelt—only a little over a mile from the church. If I need to bolt, I can walk there.

It's then I notice the sign. Emerald City Tattoo and Piercing. "What are we doing here?" My right hand reflexively goes to my left bicep, where my Special Forces tattoo used to be.

"Righting a wrong," Ry says as he turns off the engine. His voice drops so low, I have to strain to hear it. "And maybe... finding something we all lost."

Even though I'm not sure anything can right the wrongs from the past six years, I grab my ruck and follow him inside.

"Dax?" He's sitting on a bench against the wall, his folded cane in his hands.

As soon as he hears me, he heads right for us. "About damn time you showed up. I've been here half an hour."

Ryker gives Dax a quick one-armed bro-hug, and even though they're both clearly uncomfortable with the gesture, a part of me aches to be able to have that kind of physical contact again. But every time I think I'm ready, panic takes over. These are my brothers. The two people I'm closest to in the entire world. And I can barely manage to shake their hands.

Dax turns to me, and I swear he can see right through my bullshit and into the depths of my soul, despite being mostly blind. "Pick up the phone once in a while, asshole."

I don't respond, and Ryker reaches into his back pocket and pulls out a folded piece of paper, then passes it to me. "Inara's an artist. When she's not killing people or translating boring legal documents into half a dozen different languages. I asked her to make this for us."

Spreading the paper out on the counter in front of me, I freeze. It's... "Holy shit."

The Special Forces insignia, a crest with two crossed arrows bisected by a dagger and the motto—*De Oppresso Liber*—overlays an intricate design of a phoenix bursting from flames. And encircling the entire design: ODA 5150 Rip Dax Ry.

Tears burn, but I refuse to let them fall. Instead, I grind my fists against my eyes for a moment until I can speak again. Turning to my brothers, I realize I'm not the only one about to lose his shit in the middle of the shop. "Okay. Yeah. Together. Right?"

The relief on their faces breaks something inside me, and I let go. For a minute, I can shove my shame and fear aside. As Dax and Ry each put a hand on my shoulder, I return the gesture and let my tears fall for the first time since the plane landed in Seattle.

"Together," Ry says. "Brothers. Always."

# CHAPTER TWELVE

**Cara**

As soon as I step outside my apartment, I slam into a wall of stifling hot air. Seattle's in the middle of one of its summer heatwaves, and none of the windows in the hallways or stairwells open. Probably against some code somewhere, but I can't complain. I'm lucky to have a roof over my head and a lock on my door.

The slumlord for this building doesn't care about safety violations, or comfort. But the rent is cheap, and it's only three blocks from a bus line. Despite the temperature—already in the eighties at 10:00 a.m.—being in the sun, with the barest hint of a breeze, makes me smile.

*Meds. Coffee. Wallet. Keys. Notebook. Water bottle.*

I pat down my small bag, making sure I have everything I need for the day. I live by lists. Without them, I'm lost. My phone finds its way to my hand without a second thought, and as I wait for the bus, I launch my Solitaire app and start moving cards around. I need the distraction. Left with nothing to focus on, my messed-up brain will wander to places I can't let it go, and I'll wind up standing here, drifting, lost in a whirlwind of thoughts while three buses pass me by, get to work an hour late, and lose my job.

Ten minutes later, I've finished half the daily achievements the game offers, and the bus lumbers to a stop. It's full, and I scan my card, then squeeze my way past a handful of standing passengers to position myself by the back door. Someone on this bus smells like they poured an entire bottle of cologne over their head this morning, and I breathe through my mouth, but it doesn't help. The headache starts behind my eyes and nausea claws at my stomach.

And then I turn and see a guy with his briefcase taking up a full seat of its own. "Mind moving that?" I ask.

He grunts his refusal, and I stare down at him. "Well, then your briefcase is going to get crushed under my not-so-tiny ass. I'm sitting down whether you like it or not. Your bag didn't pay a fare. I did."

Another standing passenger murmurs, "You go, girl," and I flash her a quick smile. Begrudgingly, the man hoists his bag into his lap, but he doesn't move his legs so I can get past him to the window seat.

"Do I look like I'm a size zero?" I ask. "Either scoot over or stand up."

"Bitch," he says as he finally moves his lazy, inconsiderate ass.

"Yep. Grade A bitch. With a seat."

As soon as I drop down, he tries to crowd me, but I lock my arms in place and he has to pass the rest of the ride with my elbow pressing against his ribs. The feel of his rough shirt against my bare arms makes my skin crawl—textures can do that to me—but I won't back down.

Two stops before mine, he finally gets up, and his bag clips me on the shoulder.

*Asshole.*

I stop myself before the word escapes. Getting myself into trouble—hell, getting myself noticed at all—isn't smart, but I'm just so sick and tired of manspreaders on this route. Every damn day.

The short walk to the diner on the main floor of Pike Place helps ease some of my frustration, and by the time I secure my bag in one of the lockers and reach the kitchen, I feel almost...at ease.

"Hey, Cara," Lindsey says as she balances a tray on her shoulder. She moves with a grace I'll never have and slides the overly full monstrosity onto the counter without so much as rattling a glass. "Didn't expect to see you in today."

"I needed to pick up a couple of extra shifts this month." My fingers tremble slightly as I tie the apron around my waist. "My landlord's raising the rent."

"Aw, shit. I'm sorry, babe." She slings her arm around my shoulder and gives me a squeeze. "The offer's still open, you know. I have a second bedroom. It'd take me a few days to clear it out, but if you ever want it, it's yours."

"Th-thanks. But...I'm not...I don't want... Um, living with me...isn't easy. I drive off roommates. Kind of...set in my ways." While I am...very, and I have to be, that's not the whole truth.

It's not safe for me to live with anyone else. For eighteen months, I've tried to keep to myself. But the day I started working here, Lindsey marked me as "friend-material," and after a couple of months of refusing her invites to go out for a drink or a movie after work, I could no longer resist her infectious personality. Plus, I was lonely.

Now, she's my only friend in this town, though I've shared nothing honest about my past with her. I think she knows I have secrets I can't confess, but to her credit, she hasn't pressed. Much.

"Well, you know the offer's always there," she says with a smile.

"I do. And I love you for it, Linds." I rest my head against hers for a brief moment, then straighten my shoulders. "I've gotta get out there or Barry'll have my ass."

"Yeah, he's in a shit mood today. Guess he didn't get any last night." Lindsay elbows me in the ribs lightly before she tucks a fresh tray under her arm and heads back out through the swinging doors to the dining room.

Great. Just what I need. Another male asshole to deal with. Spinning my Lapis Lazuli pendant inside its silver cage, I take a couple of calming breaths.

My meds keep me mostly together, but on my bad days, the constant frenetic pace of the popular tourist spot, along with the smells and cacophony of sounds I can't control can leave me totally and completely wiped by the end of my six hours on the floor. And then, I have to work a shift at For Fork's Sake—a food truck that roves around the city, setting up at a different location every night.

At least my four-day-a-week stints there as a chef make me feel a little more like myself. My old self anyway.

*Okay, Cara. Get out there and kick some ass. If it's a good day for tips, you can splurge on a couple of slices of pizza for dinner.*

---

My TIME COOKING at For Fork's Sake makes me feel...alive again. The pay's crap, but they let me try out some of my own recipes, and I rarely have to talk to people. This late in the day, I'm prone to anxiety attacks—a side effect of my meds—and people make me nervous.

I'm about as far from North Carolina as I can get without a legitimate passport, but that doesn't mean someone from my former life won't come to Seattle for a visit and recognize me. And if they do...and tell anyone from JSOC...I'm dead.

"Need a Croque Madame and a Bacon Mac," Joel says from the cashier's window. "Last two orders of the night."

"Already?" Glancing up at the digital clock above the cook plates, I lose focus and tip the two slices of bacon off the spatula and onto the floor. "Dammit!"

"You realize that's coming out of your pay, right?" Joel scribbles on his little notepad as I retrieve two fresh slices from the fridge.

"Bite me," I mutter under my breath, but then turn to him and offer an apologetic smile. "Sorry, Joel. It's been a long day. We were down a server at Hillside Diner for the second half of my shift."

He starts to close out the till and tally up the night's receipts and tips, then crosses out the deduction for the bacon in his notebook. "Just don't do it again."

*Finally. Something going my way.*

It's another hour before we finish wiping down the last surface, mopping the floor until it shines, and cleaning the vent hood. "You all right to get home, Cara?"

"Yep. I'll be fine. The bus stop's just on the corner." Seattle's a safe city, overall, and tonight, we're parked in the Ballard neighborhood—the safest of our ten regular haunts. "See you on Monday."

"Oh, hey. You want to pick up Nance's shifts tomorrow and Saturday? She really wants two nights off to go see some concert down in San Francisco."

I try to contain my excitement as I sling my bag across my body. "That'd be great. Thanks. Five to nine again?"

"Yep." Joel climbs into the driver's seat and starts the truck.

"Menu's already set though. Gazpacho and enchiladas tomorrow, lasagna on Saturday. I'll email you the recipes when I get home tonight."

Lovely. The day everything in my life imploded, I made enchiladas. And now...the smell turns my stomach. But I force a smile. "You got it."

---

THE BUS RIDE back to the University District takes over an hour, and by then, my anxiety's off the charts. "Twenty minutes," I whisper as I adjust my bag and start walking. Twenty minutes and I can draw myself a hot bath, pour a glass of cheap wine, and let this day fade into the constant background noise in my head.

This late, my thoughts ping a hundred miles an hour. A bird flies overhead, and I track it with my gaze until it lands in a tree on the University of Washington campus across the street. The cyclist speeding past me yells, "On your left," and I jump.

"Shit." Now my heart rate won't slow down, and I press my hand to my chest as I pass the Presbyterian Church. A man sleeps in the doorway, his arm flung over his face.

He cries out, his entire body jerking inside his sleeping bag. "Don't," he slurs. "Not again... Stop!" Sitting bolt upright, he pushes the hood of his sweatshirt off his head and looks right at me.

The intensity of those deep blue eyes boring into me combined with the anguish I heard in his voice make me take a step back. But my foot lands on an uneven seam in the sidewalk, and I go down, hard, right on my tailbone.

I try to draw air into my lungs, but I can't, the shock of the fall knocking the wind right out of me. Sitting there, clutching my chest, making hoarse choking sounds, I don't even notice the guy moving until he's right in front of me.

"Give it a couple of seconds," he says as he holds my gaze. "Focus on my voice. You'll be fine. But maybe next time, watch where you put your foot."

Indignant now, I suck in a wheezing breath. "Maybe *next time*, you don't stare down a woman in the dark late at night. Stalker."

He flinches, and his shoulders hunch as his voice drops, a little more with each word until it's only a whisper. "It wasn't... intentional. Needed to lock on to something...real. You were...real."

"Hey." I reach out to touch his arm, but he jerks away. "I'm sorry. This late at night, my brain and my mouth don't always operate on the same wavelength."

Rising, he offers me his hand to help me up, and even though I don't know the guy and he's quite obviously homeless, he did a damn good job keeping me calm, so I place my palm in his.

Warm fingers with a firm grip pull me up, and I test out my ankle. Stalker Man watches me intently, focusing on my lower leg as I roll my foot around.

"Are you going to be okay?" he asks.

"Yeah. A little sore, but nothing serious." Why am I still talking to him?

*Because you don't talk to anyone but Lindsey, and he's...safe. Who's he going to tell about you? The homeless guy two doors down?*

"This isn't the best street late at night," he says as he heads back up the three stairs to his sleeping bag.

"Which is totally why *you* sleep here? I've seen you before. A lot, I think, in the past month or so." He's full of contradictions. Gruff and sweet. Homeless, but with a clean, alluring scent. Like bergamot and sandalwood and soap.

"No one bothers me here." Pulling the sleeping bag around his body, he shoves his backpack under his head. "You should be carrying pepper spray or something."

I pull out my little kitty cat self-defense tool. With sharp, pointy ears, the metal tool looks like a cute—if not a bit large—keychain charm. But really, it's a set of brass knuckles, with holes for my fingers where the cat's eyes are, and ears that'll cut, slice, or puncture skin. Totally illegal in this state—and a lot of others—but very effective.

"Shit. Okay. You can take care of yourself. Ignore me, then." He closes his eyes, a clear dismissal, and I huff out a breath.

"Thank you," I say, and he props his head up on his hand as he meets my gaze once more. "I would have panicked...and probably ended up wrecked for the whole night if you hadn't helped me...?"

"Ric—" He shakes his head, conflict furrowing his brow. Sitting up again, he scrubs his hands over his face. "Ripper. My name's Ripper."

My laugh escapes before I can stop it, and I slap my hand over my mouth for a second. "You might want to pick another fake name to give the ladies, Ripper. Because that makes you sound like you're an axe murderer."

Ripper's strangled sound of frustration holds more of the anguish I heard when I first walked by, and he turns over, his back to me, and pulls his hood over his black hair.

As I stare, mortified that I insulted him like that when I don't even know him, his shoulders shake, and as a single sob escapes, muffled by the sleeping bag, I turn and rush for home.

# CHAPTER THIRTEEN

## Cara

As the citrusy scent of my bubble bath washes away the cloying bacon grease and heavy cheese odors from the food truck's tiny kitchen, I take a healthy sip of wine and sink lower into the steaming water.

The apartment complex might be a dump—and the landlord an asshole—but there's one redeeming quality about the place. A tub deep enough for me to relax in.

My ass hurts, and my ankle's a little sore, but the only other lingering effect from my fall is Ripper's face etched on the inside of my eyelids.

I can't remember when I first saw him. A little over a month ago? But he sleeps in that church doorway every night. Seattle has a fair number of homeless. The nighttime temperatures are mild for a good part of the year. My walk to and from the bus takes me by a handful every day, but none of them have ever acted, looked, or smelled like Ripper.

He's well spoken, sober, and polite. So why is he sleeping

on the streets? Another sip of wine, and I lean back and close my eyes. Tomorrow, maybe I'll pack up an order of enchiladas after my shift and drop them off to him. I feel like I should do *something* to thank him for helping me, even if he did get all snippy at the end. Before he broke down completely.

There's something about him that calls to me. The sadness in his voice, the haunted look on his face...he knows loss, and while I can't fill the hole in my own life from giving up the person I used to be, maybe a little kindness can help ease his pain.

---

BEFORE I CRAWL INTO BED, I grab the little notebook with all my secrets and the cheap tablet I got off of eBay. Searching for Cara Phillips seems ridiculous at this point. I've been safe for eighteen months in Seattle, but I still can't relax. Not after how close I came to losing it all back in Tulsa.

No current results, so I move on to the other names on my list. Francis Jessup, Bill Parr, and J.T. Richards. Still nothing. Just like every other time I've looked.

My stomach won't settle, my anxiety a vibrating knot deep inside, so I log in to the anonymous email account I created when I left Fort Bragg. Leland Parker—the only man in the world I trust with my life and my secrets—sends me an email message once a month, and he's overdue by a week now.

Nothing.

Opening the notebook, I find the words I copied from his last message and read them again, hoping this time, I'll find something in them to give me hope. I should know better.

*Our mutual friends came by again last week for a visit. They lost track of the international package they were looking for, and hoped*

*I'd seen it. The weather's turning unbearable here, and I'm going to escape the heat for a while. Stay safe.*

It's a terrible code. But at least this time of year, the weather in North Carolina *can* melt asphalt, so if anyone did get a hold of the message, they wouldn't know with any certainty he was talking about anything other than the ambient temperature.

The international package has to be J.T. Richards. So, apparently he's no longer in Afghanistan working for the guy Jessup and Parr knew. If the two JSOC operatives are looking for Richards, maybe they've decided to leave me alone for a while. Or...maybe I'm fooling myself.

I look at the clock and groan. Tomorrow's going to be just as long of a day as today, and it's almost midnight.

With a final check of the locks, I turn out the lights and burrow under the covers and my weighted blanket. It helps keep the anxiety at bay while I sleep, and makes me feel... almost like someone's holding me. Yeah, right. Like that'll ever happen again.

Between my broken brain and the two men who want me dead...I'm bad relationship material. I can't get comfortable, and an hour later, I'm still tossing and turning. Every time I close my eyes, I go back to the day everything changed and hear Jessup's voice, the rage in his tone terrifying me.

*"It's time to put the pressure on our foreign friend," a man says as he jingles his keys in his pocket. The sound echoes off the walls of the parking garage, and I freeze, pressing myself to the back of a cement pillar. I know this guy. Jessup. Every time he comes into the JSOC cafeteria, he stares at me like he's imagining me naked, and I hate it. But my chef's whites hide most of my figure, and he's only one man. Everyone else here, despite being secretive and scarily lethal, is great, so I try my best to ignore him.*

*Another voice replies, "He hasn't responded to us in three months. What makes you think he'll start up again now?"*

"*Because we won't give him a choice. I'm tired of waiting for Richards to slip up again. That traitor does everything he's ordered to, and his work is practically untraceable. All we have to do is threaten to leak the news that J.T. Richards is alive and well and working for the enemy. We do that, and our friend will move as many crates of weapons and opium as we want. And give us a bigger cut of the profits.*"

*This conversation is getting way too serious and scary for me, and I clutch my purse tightly as I try to creep away in the opposite direction. But before I make it more than ten steps, my phone rings, the* We Will Rock You *tones deafening in the silence of the garage.*

"*Fuck. Who's there? Show your face right fucking now!*" *Jessup shouts.*

*I don't. Instead, I run.*

With a whimper, I roll over and pull the blanket tighter around me. "Breathe, Cara," I say over and over again, and eventually, it's not Jessup's voice I hear, but Ripper's. Not Parr's face I see as he grabs my arm and drags me towards the balcony of the apartment in Tulsa, but Ripper's kind eyes as he helps me calm down after I fell.

It might not be the most normal fantasy in the world—being kissed by a homeless man—but it's a hell of a lot better than the memories of screaming as I clutch the metal railing with both hands, staring down at the street fifty feet below, knowing I'm going to die. Of Jessup's face as he pries one finger after another off the rail. Or of falling, almost in slow motion, trying desperately to contort my body, and landing on another balcony two floors below, breaking my right arm, but saving my life by inches.

Ripper. Back to Ripper. Yes. Tomorrow, I'll bring him dinner after my shift at the food truck. That's a plan. And maybe...it'll make those damn enchiladas palatable again.

With my mind still racing, I punch the pillow and start to

count backwards from a thousand. I hope I fall asleep before I reach one.

---

**Ripper**

Letting myself into my studio, I jab the button to open the blinds on the floor-to-ceiling windows. If I'm going to stay here for more than a few minutes, I need light. Lots of it. Bypassing the brand new, still-in-the-box laptop on the desk—courtesy of Ryker and Wren—I head for the bathroom.

The new tattoo stings as the hot water pelts my forearm, and I relish the pain. The sensation reminds me I'm alive. Dax and Ry want to talk this morning. Breakfast at some joint in Greenwood. I'm not good in public. Fuck, I'm not good anywhere.

Every day, I have to re-learn something new. Find a piece of myself I lost. It's exhausting. The soap in my hands smells both right and wrong at the same time. The entire time we were in Hell, we were surrounded by dirt, shit, blood, sweat, and fear. Once Faruk had me, it was all incense and spices. Scents I can't *stand* now.

I wash off the grime from my night on the street, wrap a towel around my waist, and grab my razor. Standing at the sink, I stare at the stranger in the mirror. His hair looks like mine. So does his nose. His chin. His eyes don't.

Staring down at the shiny blade in my hand, I wonder, again, why I haven't just ended it all. And then I see the tattoo, and I understand. I'm alive because Ry checks on me. Every fucking day since we got to Seattle. I can't let him down. Not again. Not ever.

My phone, charging next to the laptop, rings on the table,

and the sudden noise makes me jump. The razor skids across my chin. Blood drips into the sink, bright red, and my vision tunnels.

*A woman screams, and I stop pacing my small room.*

*"Please, stop!"*

*I know it's a mistake. I'll be punished for interfering. But she sounds so young. So afraid. I pad down the hall, barefoot, until I reach the foyer. Fuck. She can't be more than eighteen, and blood streams from a cut on her forehead. Zaman's stripping off her abaya as she shakes in front of Amir Faruk.*

*"Isaad! Leave us," Faruk orders, and I pause for a moment too long. "Now." He crosses the room, his hands clasped behind his back. He hates getting them dirty. "You dare disobey me? Perhaps a few days in the well—"*

*"I am sorry, Amir Faruk," I say as I bow my head and back away. "I will leave. I should not have disturbed you."*

The phone rings again, and I'm back in my bathroom, shaking. Pressing a black towel to the cut, I stumble for the table. "What? I said I'd be there."

"Need a ride?" Ry asks.

My refusal dies on my tongue as the room pitches. Dammit. Not today. I take a quick step to the side and bang into the table. "Fuck." The pain helps me focus, as does Ryker yelling into the phone.

"Answer me, Sergeant. Are. You. Okay?"

Shit. Most times, the dizzy spells pass quickly. Too many traumatic brain injuries over the years. Not to mention a scorpion bite behind my left ear that left me with lingering equilibrium issues. This time...I must have been out of it for more than a few seconds. "Sorry. I'm fine. Wet floor. Skidded and hit the sink." How I come up with that lame ass excuse so fast, I have no idea, and I hold my breath.

*Leave it alone, Ry.*

"I'll pick you up in half an hour." He doesn't give me time to protest before he ends the call, and I slam the phone down on the table.

Thirty minutes to pull myself together so I can convince Ry and Dax that I'm okay. If only I could convince myself.

---

BY THE TIME RYKER KNOCKS, I've managed to calm down. My hands are steady, and I'm dressed in a pair of new jeans, a black Henley, and a pair of boots. The clothes feel like they're strangling me. My entire wardrobe as Faruk's prisoner consisted of loose tunics, flowing pants, and light shoes that were barely more than slippers. Back before we were captured, we used to call those outfits "desert pajamas." But once Faruk got a hold of me, they were all I was allowed. Even after two months back in the States, I still haven't gotten used to "normal" clothing again.

Tugging at the denim, I adjust myself, then enter the fourteen-digit code to unlock the door.

Ryker's multi-hued eyes narrow, scanning me from head to toe before he nods. "About damn time."

"Want to tell me what the hell you're talking about?" I fidget with the shirt sleeve. The material's soft—probably expensive—but it still feels rough on my skin.

"Boots."

My eye roll triggers a sharp stab of pain at my temple, but I hide my wince. "And how long did it take *you*, asshole?"

"Ten days." He scrubs a hand over his bald head, the scars, jagged and deep, covering half his scalp. "Couldn't go back for Dax without 'em. I tried. Showed up with my ruck and weapons, wearing scrubs and hospital slippers."

The visual makes my lips twitch, almost like I want to smile, but I can't.

"With Sampson?"

"Yeah."

There's less than ten feet of space between us, but it might as well be ten million. The first week or so after Ry and his team got me out, I don't remember much. Fear. Gratitude. Disbelief. Exhaustion. And after that...the gulf separating me from Dax and Ryker was so large, I didn't know how to cross it. Or how to be...me again.

I'm only in Seattle because I didn't know where else to go. I could have stayed in Boston, but when I met Josephine—Joey—for the first time as Ripper, the look in her eyes...I would have been a constant reminder of what she went through.

"Wish I'd been there," I say quietly, "to watch that fucker die."

Ry heads for the windows and stares out over the city and the wedge of Lake Washington. "You were, Rip. You never stopped being our brother."

Ryker McCabe doesn't talk about his feelings. At least he never used to. "You've changed."

He turns back, a half-smile curving his lips. "Yeah?" At my nod, he chuckles. "Finding someone who loves you will do that. Before I met Wren, I hadn't laughed in...well...since before Hell."

The gaping maw Faruk carved out of my soul aches as I realize that's one thing I haven't done since I got out. I can't muster the emotion.

Gesturing to the unopened computer box on the table, he arches a brow. "You ever going to crack the seal on that damn thing?"

"No." The word escapes with more force than I expect or intend, and Ryker's expression softens—as much as it can. I head off any attempts to convince me otherwise by holding up my hand. The scars around my wrists won't ever fade, and I kick myself for picking a short-sleeved shirt. "I can't, Ry. All those years...everything I did... Shit. I've...blocked it all out. If I pick up anything more complicated than a phone, I'll disappear into that dark well that holds all my crimes, and I won't ever come back."

"You could do something good with that tech."

"Like what? Find all the people killed by the weapons Faruk sold to the Taliban? Search for the graves of the women he had kidnapped and sent to the auctions? There's so much of what he made me do I don't remember. And...it's better that way. I can barely live with the guilt over what I *do* remember."

"Rip—"

"End of discussion. You want me to go to breakfast? You'll shut the fuck up until we get there." I grab my jacket, the air in the apartment suddenly too thick, too choking, too cold, and head for the door. "Lock up for me, will you?"

I don't stop until I'm out on the street, and I brace my hands on the bed of Ryker's truck, sucking in fresh air to remind me I'm free.

---

HE DOESN'T SHOW for so long, I push off his truck three times with the intention of heading back inside. But each time, I stop. I don't want to know if he's going through my shit, looking for contraband. Drugs, weapons, signs I'm sinking into a deep depression...

Faruk never cared about that last one, but he rifled through my tiny room all the time. Or had Zaman do it.

By the time Ry shows up, five minutes later, I'm ready to take his head off. Except he's got over a hundred pounds on me. Fucking giant. "Find what you were looking for?"

"Give me a little credit, Rip. If I wanted to go through your shit, I'd do it when you were sleeping at the church. And no. I haven't. Not once. Get in the goddamn truck."

I do as I'm told, hating how easily I give in. We don't speak again until Ry pulls up to a small breakfast spot in Greenwood. I stalk in ahead of him, then stop. It's not just Dax sitting at the table within ten feet of the exit. Ford's there too.

"Ripper," Ford says as he rises and holds out his hand. I stare at it for a full minute before I can force my arm to move.

"How's Joey?"

He smiles through our brief handshake. "Good. She went back to work last week. It helped."

I take the empty seat with the best view of the restaurant. There's nothing between me and the door, and it doesn't escape my attention that Dax and Ry purposely arranged things this way. Shit. As I scan the room, I understand exactly what they've done.

Around our table, there's a buffer zone where every four-top has a *Reserved* sign on it. There aren't any words to explain my gratitude and frustration. I don't *want* to be this person. So damaged his friends have to protect him from himself—and the rest of the world.

"Ford," I say, "you get a pass. But the other two of you... What the fuck is going on here? This wasn't the plan."

Dax flinches, but Ryker's face is set in stone. Doesn't much matter. The guy conveys more emotion by remaining perfectly still than he'd like to admit—to those who know how to read him.

"We have news," Dax says as he slides his hands towards one another on the table until he finds his coffee mug. "And we wanted you to be the first to know."

I clench my own mug hard enough it shakes a little, but manage to take a sip of coffee without spilling it. I don't like surprises. Not after the past six years. Surprises are...bad.

Ryker clears his throat. "I moved to Seattle after my discharge because being in Boston...it was too hard. Dax and I...weren't talking. My fault. Only reconnected three months ago."

Coffee sloshes over the rim of my mug, burning my hand, and I hiss out a breath, swear, and grab for my napkin. "Shit, Ry. You *wasted* all that time?"

He bristles and shoves his chair back from the table, drawing up to his full height. "You're my goddamned brother, Rip, but you're also getting on my last fucking nerve."

"Enough!" Dax says as he slams his coffee mug down on the polished wood. "We're past it now. Got it? Everyone." Despite being unable to see much more than hazy shadows, he looks right at each of us, and we all mutter our agreement.

"So what's this news?" I shouldn't be allowed to be around people at all. Not even those closest to me.

Ryker rubs a hand over his shaved head and then takes his seat again, meeting my gaze. "Hidden Agenda and Second Sight are partnering up. Offices and training facilities in both Seattle and Boston."

I turn my attention to Dax. "So, you'll be out here on the regular?"

"Yes. Evianna can work from anywhere, and Beacon Hill Technologies is growing too. She and Cam are talking about a merger." His face softens whenever he mentions Evianna's name. I've only met her a couple of times—wasn't fit for human contact when we got back to Boston—but she's obviously good for him.

"Rip?" Ryker leans forward, his elbows on the table. "I know what you said earlier. But we need you, man. Wren's so busy with her work for Second Sight, and Hidden Agenda needs its own expert. Plus...I don't want her to have to face that darkness every day. She gets enough of it living with me."

"No."

Dax takes off his glasses and pinches the bridge of his nose before setting them on the table and turning towards me. Up close, in the light, the scars around his eyes look so much worse. Shiny, burned skin, irises so pale, they're almost gray. Yet, I swear he sees me. All of my shame, everything I did. He knows. Even though I refused to tell them much of anything. Couldn't. It's hard to confess what you don't remember.

"I know it's only been a couple of months, Rip. It's not fair that we're pushing you like this. We had years to get ourselves straight. And we did a shitty job of it."

The corner of my mouth twitches, and if my crimes weren't playing in a loop in my head, I might let myself smile.

As the server drops off our food, I stare at my short stack of pancakes. Ford, Dax, and Ry all have huge plates of food. Me? I barely eat. Most days, it's all I can do to force down the bare minimum of calories to keep myself alive and give me enough energy to work out and spend the daylight hours walking. Reminding myself I can go anywhere I want.

I stab a small wedge of pancake and swirl it in the lake of syrup. "The last time I touched a computer, even though I wrote a whole program to obscure the kid's GPS location, I ended up giving Faruk everything he needed to find Lisette, Mateen, and..." I risk a glance at Ford, "Joey."

The marine straightens and waves his fork at me. "If you think for one minute that Joey and I blame you for *anything* that happened, you're wrong."

"You should." I push back from the table and stand up. "I'm the one who tracked her in Turkmenistan. I'm the one who researched Alpha Thalassemia and found out she was the *only* expert in the world who might be able to help Mateen. She was taken because of me."

Ford rises and gets right in my face. I have to tip my head up to meet his gaze. My heart rate skyrockets, and I take a step back. "Don't," I whisper, and the look in Ford's eyes...he realizes how close I am to losing my shit.

Ford rests a hand on my shoulder, and for once, I don't pull away. "Ripper, I'd give anything...everything...to erase what happened to Joey. To make it so she never had to experience those horrors. But..." he shoves his hands into his pockets and smiles, "it brought her back to me. *You* brought her back to me. You got us all out when Faruk's men were after us, and you bought Nomar enough time to get Lisette and Mateen to Kandahar."

"But—"

Ford frowns. "But nothing. We're square. More than square. I owe you...everything. But if you disagree, consider joining Hidden Agenda—or whatever off-the-wall name those two come up with—a way to pay me, Joey...anyone you think you wronged...back."

"Rip?" Ryker stands next to Ford, and fuck. I didn't realize how tall the older marine was. "You don't have to decide now. But...think about it?"

I'm too tired to argue with him. Too ashamed to admit all my reasons for refusing. And for the first time in a while... hungry. So I nod and sink back into my chair. Maybe for an hour, I can pretend to be a normal guy, sharing a meal with his friends.

# CHAPTER FOURTEEN

### Cara

I'm on edge as the Saturday breakfast crowd thins out. Too many people, too little sleep, and one of the dishwashers reeks of cigarettes today. The constant cloud of nicotine surrounding him makes my stomach roil, especially when mixed with the scents of eggs, cheese, and toast.

I miss my routines. The relative silence of the JSOC kitchen when I'd arrive at 5:00 a.m., my staff filing in one by one, each one of them able to adapt to my...unique challenges.

How I can't concentrate with music playing. How I depend on lists. How interrupting me while I'm speaking is like sending a horde of shiny squirrels to distract me, each of them playing a different musical instrument.

Even with all that, though, I was the best. And they all knew it.

"Cara, get a move on!" My boss slaps the metal counter three times and makes me jump.

"Dammit, Barry. Don't *do* that. If I'd had a plate in my

hand..." He might be my supervisor, but I can give as good as I get—most days. "And how the hell do you think I'm going to deliver the Benedicts when Louie hasn't finished them yet? The hollandaise needs another thirty seconds."

Louie tips his head. "Nice catch, Cara. You should be behind the stove."

If only...

I wave him off. "This is enough for me, Chef. I get to watch you work your magic every day." It's not, but I can't risk anything else. I only let myself cook at the food truck because they pay me under the table.

"Well, I *am* pretty damn talented," he says with a smile as he finishes the hollandaise sauce and pours it over two dishes containing poached eggs on English muffins, then wipes off the splatter before handing me the plates.

In ten minutes, I can take a break. Hide out in the employee locker room and put on my headphones, launch my meditation app, and for a few minutes, pretend the rest of the world doesn't exist.

Except, after I drop off the Eggs Benedict, I notice the customer sitting alone at the end of the counter. Crap. He wasn't supposed to be here until closer to noon. Taking a deep breath and throwing my shoulders back, I march over to him.

"Hi! I'm Cara and I'll be your server. What can I get you?" I ask brightly.

"Just coffee," he replies. His fingers tap rhythmically against the Formica counter, and as I set a cup, saucer, and napkin down in front of him, he meets my gaze. "Price went up. It's two-eighty."

My hand jerks, and the coffee splatters over the counter and soaks the napkin. I glance around, making sure Barry's still back in the kitchen trying to micro-manage Louie. "But...I only have two-hundred."

"Then you're only getting ten days' worth."

"Please." My voice cracks as I wipe up the spill, then use both hands to hold the coffee pot steady enough to pour. "I can barely afford them as it is."

"I'll give you the full order today, but you'll owe me the extra eighty. And if you don't pay up in two weeks, it's fifty percent interest. That's the best deal I can offer. Take it or leave it." He starts to slide off the swivel-mounted chair, and I rush to pull out my order pad.

"I'll...take it." Scribbling his coffee order on the top sheet, I tuck it into one of the leather envelopes we use to deliver the bills, then drop my hands to keep my next moves hidden behind the counter. The two hundred-dollar bills in the pocket of my apron slide into the side pocket of the bill sleeve before I pass it over to him.

Once he pulls the folder into his lap, he offers me a self-satisfied smile. "I knew we'd see eye-to-eye. See you in two weeks, sweets."

I can't grab the leather folio fast enough when he sets it back down, and the small plastic bags with my daily meds—all the pills that make it possible for me to function like a normal human being—fall into my palm.

Clutching them tightly as my dealer—I don't even know the asshole's name, just his email address—saunters out of the diner, I rush into the break room and open my locker. A small, hidden compartment in the bottom of my small messenger bag hides the pills from anyone not specifically looking for them, and I sink down onto the bench.

When I left Fort Bragg, Leland helped me convert fifty thousand dollars of the inheritance from my grandmother into cash. But when I had to leave Tulsa with a broken arm and a gunshot wound to my thigh, I blew through three grand. After I got to Seattle, another two thousand covered the deposit on my crappy apartment.

And now...I'll have to dig into my stash every time I need meds. Before long, I won't be able to keep up. I have to find a better job—but every time I give someone my stolen social security number could be my last.

If I didn't depend on such highly regulated drugs to survive, I could find a health clinic, get myself a legitimate prescription. But my very unique needs—Adderall, a beta blocker to keep my heart rate under control, Zoloft, and clonazepam—are what led Jessup to me in Tulsa. Pharmacies computerize records, and Jessup and Parr run searches for anyone filling all these prescriptions at once. Even going to Mr. Pills-On-Demand is risky, but I've been using him for over a year now and so far... I've been safe.

Mentally calculating how long I can go without something going my way, I play with the lapis pendant hanging just below the hollow of my throat. It spins within a silvery cage, calming the racing thoughts telling me I'm screwed, that I'm useless. That I might as well give up.

I'll find a way. I have to.

---

## Ripper

The sign over Safe Haven Animal Shelter proclaims, "Every Animal Deserves a Home." Set on almost half an acre of land in Woodinville—about an hour from Seattle—it offers sanctuary for dogs, cats, horses, birds, and more. My shrink put his foot down after six weeks and told me I had to find something to do with my time besides walking and sitting by the lake staring out over the water, replaying the few crimes I could remember over and over again.

"Hey, Rick. Good to see you." The shelter's owner, an older woman named Melissa, greets me with a smile. "Come with me, and I'll show you around."

My shoulders tighten at her use of my fake name, but it's not her fault. It's the only one I can give her, so I blow out a breath and follow.

She leads me through the main building, showing me the volunteer break room, the intake and adoption forms, the filing system, and finally takes me out the back door where two other buildings bookend a large, fenced patch of grass maybe a hundred feet across. "On the left we have our cat condos. At any one time, we shelter fifty to a hundred cats from six weeks to twenty years old. You'll find detailed notes on each individual condo that list which cats can be out in the main play area together, which are in quarantine until their medical tests come back, and which are best when they're the only cat in the room. You'll primarily be working with the dogs, but feel free to visit the kitties at any time and give them some love."

Melissa turns right and opens the door to the kennels. The loud yips, barks, and whines, along with the sight of the metal cages, hit me like a punch to the solar plexus, and I stagger back.

"Rick? You okay?" Melissa asks.

I force myself to lock eyes with the closest dog, a big German Shepherd with only one good ear standing at his kennel door, not making a sound. "Yeah. Sorry." I can't move, and I think the dog is the only thing keeping me sane.

Melissa's gaze softens, and she takes a step closer. "I've seen a fair number of veterans come through here, you know. Volunteering or just looking for some non-judgmental companionship. Charlie there...he's a peach. He'd probably like to meet you."

"What...uh...happened to him?" I drop to one knee, and Charlie lowers his head and sniffs when I bring my hand closer to the door.

"We don't know. He came to us like that. He's about the nicest, sweetest dog in this entire place, but no one wants him because he looks...a little different." Sadness laces Melissa's tone, and she sighs as she checks her watch. "I have to run back up front cover for Sandra while she's on lunch. Why don't you spend some time getting to know the dogs. Leashes are hanging on the wall. Feel free to take one or two of them out into the exercise pen. When I'm done up front, I'll show you what we do to clean out the kennels."

"Yes, ma'am," I say as I drop down to my ass in front of Charlie's kennel. He's lying down now, his head on his paws.

After a few minutes, the noise starts to die down. Charlie hasn't taken his eyes off of me.

"You're kind of like me, aren't you? A little broken." As if he understands, he gives the door a little nudge with his nose. Glancing up at the laminated card tacked to his cage, I read his history, along with the date he was brought in.

*Found wandering on a busy street. No chip or tags. Right ear missing and bloody. Charlie is a neutered two-year-old male (approximate age) with good teeth and no other health conditions. He has only shown aggression when playing tug-of-war. All other forms of play are allowed, and he can be exercised on or off leash.*

"You've been here a year? No wonder you look so sad. Want to get out of there for a few minutes?"

As soon as I approach with a leash, Charlie sits up with his tongue hanging out of his mouth. My hand shakes as I reach for the latch, but once I get it open, some of the memories threatening fade away.

For the next half an hour, Charlie chases a ball around the exercise yard, always bringing it right back to me and dropping it at my feet, and I start to think maybe I can do this. Take care of these animals and find my way back to some sort of normalcy.

Until I have to take the dog inside. He follows without complaint, but locking him back in his kennel sends me over the edge, and I run from the building, unable to say a word to Melissa as I head for the bus stop a mile away. This was a mistake. One I don't know how the hell I'll ever get over.

———

MELISSA CALLS as I code myself back in to my apartment. "I'm sorry," I say before she can even get a word in. "I panicked. I didn't mean to let you down."

"Son, you didn't let anyone down—except maybe yourself." She sighs over the line. "Your therapist sent you here because Safe Haven has a bit of a reputation for helping vets find their way back from where you are right now. My son, Aaron, couldn't, and when I lost him, Safe Haven was what kept *me* going."

"Shit. I'm—"

"Don't go saying you're sorry. Not again. I don't know your history, and I'm not asking. But I understand PTSD better than you might think. If you need to start out slow, you can take care of the dogs outside the kennels for a while. Or work with the horses. Or feed the goats. Come back tomorrow. Try again."

Words won't come as I stare out the large windows at the lake, shrouded in shadows.

"Rick?"

"Yeah. Okay. Tomorrow," I force out, and end the call with a rough, "Thank you."

I still have a couple of hours before dark, so I change into a pair of basketball shorts, grab a set of twenty-pound barbells from the closet, and push myself through a grueling workout. My shrink would say I'm punishing myself. Maybe I am. Or maybe this is all I have to keep me sane. I just don't know anymore.

---

A LIGHT SUMMER rain falls as I spread out my sleeping bag in the church doorway a little after ten. Times like this, I think maybe I should try to sleep at my apartment. With all of the windows open and the rain tapping on the metal overhangs, I might be able to handle being inside. But what if I can't?

Every night, I expect someone from the church rectory to try to convince me to go to a shelter or to come inside so they can tell me how God will save me. And as I stretch out, my muscles still tight from my workout, it hits me. Ryker. The man's done his damnedest to protect me since he pulled me out of that well.

And I've repeatedly told him to go the fuck away. "You're a piece of work," I mutter to myself, and a quick inhalation from the sidewalk causes me to jerk my head around. Brown eyes meet mine, and the woman from last night freezes. In one hand, she carries her set of kitty cat brass knuckles, and in the other, a grease-stained bag.

"I...uh...b-brought you something," she stammers as she climbs the first step and then stops.

"Hoping to bribe me into not axe murdering you?" She flinches and squeezes her eyes shut for a brief moment. "Bad joke. Sorry. But Ripper...really is my name. Or what everyone calls me." I push up to sitting and rest my back against the church door. "And I'm not a charity case."

"Didn't say you were." She thrusts the bag at me, and when I don't move, drops it next to my hip. "We had extra. It's rainy and kind of cold tonight. I thought...a hot meal might...shit. Never mind. Take it or leave it."

She turns, and the scents of cheese and salsa waft up from the bag. "Wait a minute, sunshine." Digging into the paper, I find an aluminum foil pan covered with a healthy serving of enchiladas lightly covered in cheese and red sauce, a half pint of refried beans, and a bag of marinated carrots and jicama. "This smells great."

A hint of pride straightens her shoulders, and the corners of her lips curve into a half-smile. "Thanks."

"You made this?" I grabbed a granola bar and an apple at my apartment, but my stomach rumbles at the prospect of something so very different than my everyday diet. The first bite takes me back to my mama's cooking, and I think I moan a little.

In the light of the street lamp, her cheeks glisten with the misty rain and turn a bright pink. "I work at a food truck. Today's menu was Mexican comfort food."

"My mama learned how to cook from my *abuela*, who grew up in Mexico. These are the best enchiladas I've had since I left Texas."

She toys with a blue pendant hanging from a silver chain around her neck. Joy and sadness battle for control of her features, but joy seems to win in the end. "Thank you. That means a lot."

A tendril of long brown hair plasters itself to her cheek as she stares down at her sensible black shoes. Her ankle's wrapped in an ACE bandage, and as she fidgets, I can tell she isn't putting all her weight on it. "You okay? After last night?"

"Oh. Yes. I should...go. Let you eat in peace."

"Wait." I don't know why I'm stopping her. But the idea of

her being hurt and that I caused it, doesn't sit well with me. "What's your name?"

"Cara," she says quietly.

"You live...uh...close by?" Her eyes widen, and I kick myself. If she didn't think I was a stalker or an axe murderer before, she does now. "I just mean...it's wet out. And you weren't the most graceful last night. I...be careful, okay?"

A scowl twists those heart-shaped lips, and she levels me with an acerbic stare. "I'm not the one sleeping on the streets with no defenses. And I'm very graceful. When I want to be. Good night, Ripper." Her curtsey is a little lopsided since she isn't putting her full weight on her right foot, but she turns on her left heel and starts limping away.

"'Night, Cara." As the rain intensifies and I dig back into the takeout container of enchiladas, I wonder why it's easier for me to talk to a stranger than it is the men I consider my brothers.

Pulling out my phone, I thumb out a text message to Ry and Dax. *Coffee tomorrow? Broadcast at ten?*

Within thirty seconds, they've both confirmed, and as I fall asleep to the sounds of the rain on the sidewalk and the occasional light mist coating my cheeks, I decide to give Safe Haven another try. I might fail. But I have to find a way to get some semblance of my life back, even if I never touch a computer again.

# CHAPTER FIFTEEN

**Cara**

THE LIGHT SEEPS through the thin curtains in my bedroom, waking me long before I want to open my eyes. After I make myself a cup of tea and take my meds, I curl up on the second-hand couch with my tablet and check my email.

Still nothing from Leland. My stomach twists into knots, and every day I don't hear from him is another day closer to breaking his rules—and mine—and calling him. I have an internet site I can use to mask my location, but it'll only give me two minutes of time. And it's expensive.

*Please, Leland. Get back to me.*

The man's been a JSOC analyst for twenty-five years. He knows how to hide and how to protect himself. Taught me everything I needed to know in a safehouse at the edge of Charleston before he sent me to Tulsa with two different fake IDs.

*"This guy in Afghanistan is one of the worst on JSOC's radar. Yet*

*no one goes after him because he has contacts everywhere. Runs guns, missiles, drugs, and...people."*

*"People?" I whisper as I change the bandages on the gunshot wound to my thigh. The bullet only grazed me, but it was enough I almost didn't get away.*

My tea goes cold before I rein in my racing thoughts. Grabbing my phone, I go right for my standard coping mechanism —puzzles. If I can distract my brain for ten minutes or so, I might be able to pull myself out of this panic cycle before a full-blown attack.

It's an hour before I move from the couch, and as I stand, pain shoots up my calf from my turned ankle. Thank God I don't have to work at the diner today.

The free morning and afternoon mean it's time for me to plan out the next week. My light blue canvas box holds the only things more important to me than my lapis pendant and my fake ID: my notebook, a weekly organizer, a set of colored pens, and my bank ledger.

Survival on the run with ADHD, anxiety, and a potentially life-threatening heart condition requires me to plan my life down to the day—if not the hour. I can't be caught without meds, and since the combination of drugs I need to keep myself sane and healthy are so unique, I have to buy them illegally. The local pharmacy is too risky.

Sitting at my little kitchen table, I count out my pills. Fourteen days left for my ADHD meds and the anxiety pills, but... shit. Only three days left for my beta-blockers. The small little pills keep my heart rate from skyrocketing and aggravating a genetic condition that leaves me prone to arrhythmia. Without them, I feel like I'm running a marathon—all the time.

To make it to the end of the month, I'll need another $400 paid to my *dealer*. Which means dipping into my cash reserves. My anxiety kicks up a notch as I check the balance. When I left

JSOC, I had $50,000. Now...I'm down to less than $22,000, and the balance shrinks every two weeks when I have to replenish my meds.

The notes I scribble on each day in the planner get harder to read as two words bounce around inside my head. *My dealer. I have a dealer.* If my mother saw me now, she'd call for her fainting couch. The last few years of her life—lung cancer stole her from me when I was only twenty-three—she never stopped talking about how beautiful I looked at my debutante ball back in Charleston. She was convinced I was going to be a doctor or a lawyer. Or at the very least, the wife of one.

Instead, I'm a former chef with people out to kill her, who's working as a waitress with a side gig slinging comfort food out of a truck. Sitting back, I scan the various multi-colored notes strewn across the next two weeks. I don't know how much longer I can go without something going my way, but I have to try.

## Ripper

The morning rush at Broadcast Coffee is long over by the time I pull open the door a few minutes before 10:00 a.m. Good. Dax and Ry aren't here yet. I don't want a repeat of breakfast the other day. After I order a cappuccino and a piece of pound cake, I take a seat where I can watch the door.

With the tall windows in front of me and rock music blaring through the speakers, this is about as different from Faruk's compound as it could be. There...it was quiet all the time. When he was pleased with me, I was allowed an hour or two after the morning prayers and breakfast to walk the courtyard and exercise, but the rest of my days...he insisted I stay inside, confined to my work room or my small prison with its cot, dresser, and bathroom.

I wash down my morning meds with a generous sip of coffee, watching each customer as they enter. Ry's truck pulls up to the curb across the street, and as he and Dax head for the door, I worry this was a mistake. They're going to try to get me to join Hidden Agenda again, and I can't.

"Rip," Ry says, directs Dax to the chair to my left. "I'll get the coffee. You want anything else?"

"Pretty sure I can find my own damn seat," he mutters in reply. "I'm not totally blind, you know. And yeah. Anything that won't end up all down my shirt."

As he folds up his cane and takes a seat, he sniffs. "Never thought I'd see you eating sweets."

"See?"

Dax chuckles. "Yeah, dumbass. It's an expression. You're not going to piss me off by saying the word. Besides, 'never thought I'd smell you eating sweets' sounds like I'm Hannibal Lecter."

I don't know what to say, and I try not to flinch when he reaches out and rests his hand on my shoulder. "Rip, you can crack a joke once in a while. Or laugh."

"Not sure I remember how." Pulling away, I wrap my hands around my mug. All of a sudden, I'm freezing, which my shrink would say is evidence that I'm headed towards a panic attack if I don't find a way to distract myself. "H-how's Evianna?" Small talk. I remember small talk. Vaguely.

"Good." His voice softens, the southern twang deepening. "She and Wren are dress shopping and cake tasting."

"New Year's Eve, yeah?" The rich cappuccino suddenly tastes like sludge. "Double wedding?"

Ryker kicks out a chair and folds his massive frame into the seat as he slides a coffee in front of Dax. "Yep. Up in the mountains," he says. "I hate being in the city on New Year's Eve. Too many fucking fireworks."

Shit. The Fourth of July back in Boston was a nightmare. Only a few days after we flew back from Afghanistan, I didn't know which way was up, and I spent the night huddled on the floor of my hospital room, Dax and Ry on either side of me. The assholes wouldn't leave, and when the fireworks started, Ryker found the movie *Bohemian Rhapsody* on the small television, and the two of them sang every fucking song—badly— while I tried not to throw up.

"You're coming, Rip. We're not getting married without you there." Dax carefully reaches for his mug and stops with it halfway to his mouth. "Don't make me ask again."

"I'll be there." Though the idea terrifies me, being somewhere new, somewhere I might not be able to escape, somewhere I'll have to be social...these men are my family.

No one speaks for a few minutes, and Ryker looks more uncomfortable with each passing second. "You going to join us at Hidden Agenda?" he asks finally.

I choke on a sip of my cappuccino. "I already told you—"

He sets his cup on the table and stares me down. "That's not why you wanted to meet?"

With a sigh, I run a hand through my hair. It still feels foreign to me—this shorter style I wore until we landed in Hell. "No. I'm trying something new. It's called being a normal guy. One who has friends. And isn't broken as fuck."

Ryker jerks like I just slapped him, and Dax rubs the back of his neck. Their tells. I haven't known them long—not the men they are now—but we were trained for years to observe, to read gestures and micro-expressions. And they're both...hurting.

"Sorry," I say quietly. "Brothers—"

"That's not it." Ry meets my gaze, and the greens, blues, and ambers of his eyes deepen as he stares at me. "You're not broken, Rip. Not like you think. None of us are."

I arch a brow. "You set me up in the sweetest apartment on the planet, and I sleep *on the streets*. I went to the animal shelter yesterday and bolted when I had to put a dog back in his kennel. His fucking kennel, Ry. He wasn't even upset about it. But I couldn't handle it. If that's not broken, I don't know what is."

Ryker lays his arm on the table, exposing a fresh tattoo. Not the one we all got the other night, but a different one. The design looks like a stained-glass heart with words etched around the outside in a flowing script.

*We're all beautifully broken.*

"Wren's words. Before her, I never would have believed them. But she's right. Doesn't matter what shit we've been through. What shit we're *still* going through."

Dax clears his throat. "He's right. Fuck, man. If we could erase what happened to you the past six years, we would. You don't think I wish I had my sight back? I do. Every damn day. I've never even seen the woman I'm going to marry. But I'll tell you one thing... If I had the choice between seeing and having Evianna in my life? Between seeing and sitting here, right now, with my two brothers...there's no choice. I don't need my sight. I need my family."

"I'm not you. Either of you." Standing, I grab my cup and plate. "And this is about all the normalcy I can take for one day." Sliding my dishes into the bus tub, I rush for the door, and thankfully, neither of them follow.

# CHAPTER SIXTEEN

## Ripper

BY THE TIME I get to Safe Haven, my body feels like one raw nerve. Admitting my brokenness to Dax and Ry...it opened up a box I don't know how to close again. One full of shame and disgust and agony that swirls around me in a dark cloud I can't escape.

As I reach the edge of the empty parking lot—the shelter closes early on Sundays—the door to the office opens, and Charlie comes bounding towards me, his tongue hanging out of his mouth.

"Hey, buddy." I drop down to one knee and try to keep him from licking all the way up my face as I wrap my arm around his neck and rub his side, his tail wagging so fast, it's only a blur. "What are you doing off leash?" The German Shepherd yips and starts trying to herd me towards the office. "All right. I'm coming."

Melissa waits at the door, a big smile on her face. "He saw you coming all the way from the road. Whined at me until I let him out." I must look confused, because she pats Charlie's head when he sits next to me. "He doesn't get a lot of love," she explains. "That missing ear...it means he gets passed over every time. So after we close for the day, I usually let him hang out up here with me."

I reach down and stroke Charlie's head. "You're still handsome, buddy." My fingers skim the edge of the mangled remnants of his ear, and he leans his whole body against my leg. "Why don't you adopt him?" I ask Melissa.

She arches a gray brow and chuckles softly. "I think he's meant for someone else. So does Charlie, apparently."

Her words don't register for a few seconds. Not when Charlie's leg is thumping on the ground like he's just discovered the secrets to the universe. But when they do, I meet her gaze. "I...can't. I'm not a good bet. My life isn't...stable. I'd fail every question on the application."

Melissa clucks her tongue. "You know the best part about running this place, young man?" After a beat, she turns and heads back for a stack of paperwork on the desk, plucks a blank application from the tray, holds it up, and then crumples it into a ball. "I make the rules."

The wadded-up paper sails into the trash bin with a soft *plunk*, and she smiles. "When you figure out what Charlie and I already know, we'll talk. Until then...you know where everything is. Go see what speaks to you today."

---

FOUR HOURS LATER, my shoulders burn from mopping every floor in the place. Charlie stayed close to me the whole time, and when I ventured into the kennels, trying to get over my irrational fear of locking doors, he never left my side. I scrubbed his space until it shone, switched out his bedding and got him a chew toy, then sat outside the open door while he lay on his pallet with the toy between his paws and went to town.

"I'm broken, Charlie," I whisper, too quietly for him to hear me over the sounds of the other dogs. "Too broken to give you a good home." My tears shock me, but I can't make them stop.

At the beginning...when Faruk first started in on me, I used to dream of escape. Of what I'd do when I got home. I never thought I'd feel like this. Constantly afraid. Constantly ashamed. This isn't a life. It's one nightmare after another.

But then the dog scoots forward and rests his head in my lap, and my tears turn into sobs. Charlie doesn't move until I get myself under control, then he gives my hand a lick. Just one. And his eyes...the emotion in them is impossible to ignore. I can't make him sleep on the streets. If I'm going to do this...I have to be able to give him a real home.

"You want to give this a chance?" He makes a low sound in his throat and sits up so we're eye-to-eye. "I need a few days, buddy. Gotta take the first step on my own. Okay?"

With a yip, Charlie wriggles his whole massive body until he's in my lap, and I wrap my arms around the dog, bury my face in his fur, and promise him, without words, that I'll be better. For him.

***

## Cara

A little after 10:00 p.m., I head down 15th, trying to stay focused on my surroundings. My mind is racing, as it always does when my meds wear off, and if I'm not careful, I'll walk right into an oncoming car.

I can't keep bleeding money and expect to stay safe. I tried to convince Joel to let me work more hours at For Fork's Sake, but Nance has seniority. Tomorrow, I have to start looking for a better job. If I could pick up a few hours in the early mornings baking for a coffee shop, that might be enough. Otherwise, I'll end up on the streets.

*Like Ripper.*

He's been hovering at the back of my mind all day, and I don't know why. But I tucked a double serving of lasagna in my satchel for him, along with a bottle of sparkling water. Unlike the enchiladas, which were leftovers, tonight's meal, I had to pay for.

I don't know why I did it. I can't afford my life as it is. But for some reason, I feel the need to try to help this guy. As I approach the church, I search for his prone form wrapped in a sleeping bag. But instead, I find him sitting on the steps with nothing around him. No backpack. No sleeping bag. He's resting his elbows on his knees, his head in his hands.

"Ripper?"

His whole body jerks, and he looks around, his eyes wild. As he focuses on me, the storm in those dark blue orbs quiets a little. "Cara. Hey."

"What's wrong? Where's your stuff?" I approach slowly, ease myself down next to him, and pull the box and bottle of water out of my bag. "I...um...it was lasagna night at the truck."

"You brought me dinner again? Why?" He accepts the offering, pulling back the flap of the box and staring at it like it's one of life's greatest mysteries.

"I-I don't know."

"I'm not homeless, Cara." After one last, longing look at the cheesy lasagna, he passes it back to me. "You should keep this. Have it for lunch tomorrow."

His words take a minute to sink in. "But...you sleep out here. Every night."

"Yep." The huffing sound he makes might almost be a

laugh, but then he sighs and stares off into nowhere. "Can't handle being inside when it's dark."

"Why not?" Setting the box down in front of me, I turn towards him. The sleeves of his sweatshirt are pushed halfway up, and peeking out from one of them is an image I recognize. "You're Special Forces."

"Was." The surprise in his tone is tinged with bitterness as he gestures to the tattoo. "Not many people would recognize the insignia."

"I used to know a few. From my old life." I don't know why I'm telling him this. Any mention of my time at JSOC is risky. But there's something about Ripper that exudes safety. I think I can trust him with this little bit of my past.

"Old life." Ripper runs his hand through his hair, his expression changing subtly as he reaches the back of his neck. "Yeah. I had one of those too."

"And that's why you can't handle being inside?" I shouldn't pry. Not when I can't reveal any secrets of my own. But the deep, soul-crushing sadness emanating from this man makes me want to wrap my arms around him and tell him everything will be okay. Even if I know it won't.

He shakes his head. "Not exactly. But also not a good story."

"Point taken."

We sit in silence for a few minutes, watching the traffic go by until he speaks again, his voice so low and quiet, I have to lean closer to hear him. "I made myself a deal tonight. I could come out here and sit until 1:00 a.m. Not a minute longer. Then...I'd go home. Figured if I could manage until sunrise without freaking the fuck out, tomorrow night I'd go home ten minutes earlier."

"How long has it been? Since you've slept inside all night?" Ripper flinches, and I reach for his arm, but he jerks away. "I'm sorry," I whisper. "I didn't mean to...to pry. Or—"

"Fuck." Scrubbing his hands over his face, he lets out a mournful groan. "You shouldn't hang out with me, Cara. I can't even carry on a normal conversation. Let alone...open up about anything."

"I don't need normal." I turn slightly so I can see his profile. "There's nothing *normal* about this situation. I'm sitting on the steps of a church, in the dark, talking to a man I don't know, yet this feels easier than every other personal interaction I've had today. Normal's overrated."

Ripper stares at me, and a fraction of the loneliness in the depths of his azure eyes fades away. "I don't think I've ever met anyone like you."

"Well, I hope not—" My phone buzzes, and I frown. No one should be calling me this late. And not on this phone. "Hang on a sec." Digging for the cheap flip phone I picked up outside of Vegas, I suck in a sharp breath at the number on screen.

*Leland.*

I hurry a dozen paces away, just far enough I hope Ripper can't hear me, before I answer. "H-hello?"

"Cara, I need you to listen very carefully." There's a muffled curse, followed by a thump, and then the call disconnects.

My heart rate skyrockets, and panic floods my body with adrenaline. Leland wouldn't have called unless he—or I—were in danger. After I shove the phone back into the pocket of my skirt, I limp back to the church steps and grab my cross-body bag. "I...I have to go, Ripper. I'm sorry. Um...I hope...I hope you get some sleep tonight."

As I take off at a jog—at least as much of a jog as I can manage with my ankle still sore, he calls my name, but I don't turn back. I can't. I have one ID left. I can become Carrie Yates and get on a bus to...somewhere else. And then, Cara Barrett will disappear forever.

# CHAPTER SEVENTEEN

### Ripper

SHOCK SLOWS MY MOVEMENTS, and by the time I get to my feet, Cara's turned the corner onto fifty-third, a full two blocks away. The number on her phone—I didn't mean to look, but I recognized the area code. Fort Bragg, North Carolina. Why the hell is she getting calls from Fort Bragg?

The fear in her voice...I can't just ignore it. Running after her, I find her leaning against a lamp post, rubbing her ankle.

"Cara?" She yelps and loses her balance, landing on her hands and knees. "Dammit. I'm sorry."

"Ripper? You shouldn't have followed me."

Tears shine on her cheeks, and I don't think. I crouch close to her, cupping her jaw and wiping them away. "I may not be able to have a normal conversation with you—or anyone—but I'm not letting you run down a darkened street, crying and alone, when I know you're scared."

She stares up at me with such need in her eyes, but behind that, wariness. "This isn't something you want to get involved in," she whispers. As she wobbles to her feet, I catch the scent of blood.

"You're hurt." I scan her from head to toe, quickly finding the source—a piece of broken glass embedded in her knee. "Stand still."

Cara leans back against the lamp post, sniffling softly. I use my left hand to hold her leg still, then carefully slide the dirty shard free. She hisses out a breath, and blood drips down her shin.

Pulling a handkerchief from my back pocket, I tie it around her knee, just tight enough to hopefully stop the blood from soaking into her sock and shoe. "How's your ankle?" I ask once I'm standing again.

"It'll be fine," she insists, but as soon as she takes a step, I know it won't be.

"Stop, Cara." Planting myself in front of her—but not touching her, because shit...her skin was so soft, and having my hands on her...it made me want...things I can't ever have again —I cross my arms over my chest. "Let me help you get home. As soon as you're inside, I'll leave, and you don't ever have to see me again."

Her expression tells me she wants to protest, so I arch a brow. "That ankle's not going to hold up. And whatever's got you spooked, pretty sure you're going to want both legs fully functional to take it on. You know what I am...what I was," I say, gesturing to my tattoo. "We don't lie, we don't cheat, and we don't hurt the innocent. Ever."

Cara shivers in the cool night air, and I shrug out of my sweatshirt and hold it open for her to slide her arms into the sleeves.

She blows out a breath, then seems to deflate as she lets me help her on with the hoodie. "You don't know what you're asking me to do. The last time I trusted someone..."

"You want to compare war stories? Because mine won't be pretty."

She's chewing on her lip hard enough I'm afraid she's going to bite it clean through, but eventually, she frees the abused flesh and sighs. "Okay. Just...to my apartment."

I hold out my hand. "I'm going to touch you now. Okay? Put my arm around your waist so I can support some of your weight?"

Her nod doesn't do much for my confidence. I haven't been this close to someone—at least not while conscious—in a long time, and her curves mold to my side. The fruity scent of her shampoo tickles my nose. Something tropical. "Where to, sunshine?"

"Two blocks up."

The walk takes us almost ten minutes because with every step, her limp worsens, and she's still shivering. Adrenaline crash.

"No exterior lock?" I ask as we reach the dilapidated four-story apartment building.

"Not one that works." Her tone has turned bitter, and she shakes her head as she leads me into the building foyer. "This is...stupid. I've been so careful for so long, but..." As Cara looks up at me, true fear lingers behind her eyes. "Screw it. Will you come up with me? Just to make sure my apartment's...safe?"

*What the fuck happened to her to make her this scared?*

If anyone found out that Jackson Richards is alive, they'd come after me for war crimes. Treason. A litany of atrocities so long, I'd never get out of jail—assuming they didn't just execute me. And whatever's in Cara's past...she's just as scared as I am.

"Yeah. Lead the way."

Stained ceilings, threadbare carpet, and peeling paint decorate the halls, along with the vague scent of popcorn. I carry her up the two flights of stairs—though she protests half the way—and set her down outside one of only two units on the third floor. She digs in her satchel for her keys, but before she can manage the lock, they slip from her hand, and I catch them in mid-air.

"Shit. You're...fast." Her voice is getting a little thready, and I'm starting to worry about her remaining upright for much longer.

"Stay behind me." The lock wouldn't keep out a ten-year-old, and I shake my head at the state of this building. As I make my way through her small apartment, checking her closet, shower, and behind the drapes and couch, I can see the care she takes to make the place a home. Candles in every room, all fruity scents—like her hair—and not a thing out of place. Even her bed's made so you could probably bounce a quarter on it.

I find her in the middle of her living room, fiddling with the blue pendant around her neck.

"All clear. As perfect as everything is, it'd be obvious if anyone had broken in."

"Are you calling me a neat freak?" she asks with a weak laugh.

"Maybe. Not saying it's a bad thing." What the fuck are we supposed to do now? She's obviously afraid, and despite the last six years of my life, I haven't forgotten all of my training. I don't want to leave her alone, but I barely know the woman.

Her phone rings again, and she looks up at me with wide, terrified eyes as she retrieves it from the pocket of her skirt.

"I'll just..." I begin, but she motions for me to stay.

"Hello?"

Whatever the person on the other end of the line says to her must be exactly what she needed to hear. "Oh, thank God.

You're sure?" After a moment, she dashes away a tear and continues. "Okay. I'll wait to hear from you," she says and then snaps the phone shut.

"Everything all right?"

Her smile, though barely there, brings a hint of light to her eyes, and she nods. "Yes. I...shouldn't have panicked back there." She takes one uneven step towards the kitchen, then winces.

"Sit down. Let me check out your ankle and take care of that cut on your knee, okay? After that...I'll go."

Lips pursed like she's not sure she should let me do anything else for her, she holds my gaze for a second, then limps over to the couch. "First aid kit's under the bathroom sink."

By the time I return with a washcloth soaked in warm water and the small metal kit, her eyes are closed, her head resting on the back of the sofa.

"You still with me?"

She lifts her head and then rubs her eyes. "Sorry. This time of night...I get kind of spacey."

The cut isn't bad, just dirty, and once it's bandaged, I ease her shoe and sock off. "You should have kept this wrapped another couple of days," I say as I probe the swollen flesh.

"Stretches my shoe out." Her words are softer now, slower. If she lasts another hour upright, I'll be amazed. Not that I plan on being here that long. "Can't afford new ones."

"Okay. Watch me carefully, then. I'll show you how to wrap it so it won't do that." She meets my gaze, and shit. Flecks of bronze within the brown depths, along with the warmth of her skin, and the trust she's giving me...

*Cut it out. You're going to make sure she's okay, then get the fuck out of here.*

But when I'm done and she gingerly gets to her feet to test

out the wrap, she smiles, and my gut churns. No one's smiled at me like that in...years.

Shuffling into her sparse kitchen, Cara runs water into a teapot. "I...um...need to take my meds. And have a snack. Do you...um...want anything?"

Shoving my hands into the pockets of the jeans that still feel too tight, too new, too restrictive, I hunch my shoulders as I try not to focus on the fact that I'm behind a locked door with the drapes closed, at night.

And then a familiar scent hits me. Cardamom. With cinnamon. Ice fills my veins, and I start to shiver so hard, I can't manage to reply as I stagger for the door.

My hand slips off the deadbolt as my vision darkens, and I sink to my knees, covering my head with my arms as I brace for a blow.

*"You have displeased me, Isaad. As restitution, you will fast for seven days. You will be allowed tea and water only. Damsa!" Faruk calls for the slight woman who cooks meals for the compound's residents.*

*"Yes, Amir Faruk, sir?" She rushes into the room, bows, and stares down at me cowering on the floor.*

*"Isaad will be fasting for the next week. See that he receives plenty of Kahwah tea, but nothing else."*

*"Of course." Sympathy flashes in her eyes for a split second, and then she's gone, and Zaman's vise grip fastens around my arm before he drags me out of the room.*

"Ripper? Shit. Answer me!" Warm hands rest over mine, and I jerk away with a snarl.

"Don't touch me!" My breath wheezes through my clenched teeth as I roll up into a crouch, scanning for ghosts, ready to attack. "Fuck."

"What triggered you? Tell me. Right now." She's kneeling two feet away, her hands raised slightly, and the commanding tone to her voice drags me just far enough out of my panic-induced episode to answer her.

"Cardamom." The single word escapes on a whisper, and she swears under her breath as she rises and limps quickly back to the kitchen. A cabinet door slams, water splashes, and paper rustles.

"What about hibiscus? Peach? Mango? Strawberry?"

"Fruit. Anything fruit is fine." I scrub my hands over my face, equal measures ashamed and curious about this woman who knows exactly what happened and why.

Two seconds later, she's at my side with a paper packet of tea. "Smell this one and tell me if it's okay." She rests her palm against the back of my neck, and I don't pull away as I inhale. Scents of peach and honey reach me, along with whatever she uses in her shampoo, and my heart stops trying to punch through my chest.

"Fine." As I meet her gaze, I find glassy, tear-filled eyes, and the knowledge that I hurt her—even a little—kills me inside. "Fuck, Cara. I'm sorry."

"Don't. You can't control your triggers. I should know." Before I can ask her to explain, her warmth fades, and she's back in the kitchen, peach tea brewing as she rummages around in her fridge. "I have fruit, English muffins, and the lasagna I brought you. Do you want anything?"

"No." After a pause, I shake my head. I can *feel* the hunger, even if I don't recognize it as a desire I'm allowed to have. "I haven't...uh...eaten since breakfast."

"Lasagna then." She slides the box into the microwave, pours the tea into mismatched mugs, and sets them on the small dining room table. "Sit."

This isn't a good idea. I was about to wrestle her to the ground and beat the shit out of her. My nightmares are violent, and more than once I've woken up with a new tear in my sleeping bag or my pocket knife in my hand, ready to kill anyone who approached me.

But I sink down onto one of the chairs and wrap my fingers around the mug of peach tea. It's warm, and I'm still shivering.

*Get your shit together, Richards. Now. You need to hoof it back to your apartment and stay there the whole fucking night. No matter what. Sleep like a normal person. Act like a normal person. And don't ever see Cara again.*

The microwave beeps, and then Cara joins me with plates, silverware, and napkins. Her movements are precise, careful, calculated. As if she's done this a thousand times in exactly this order. Two white pills next to her dish. A paper napkin spread across her lap.

"Cara?"

"Just a minute." The pills disappear one at a time, and she glances at her watch, nods, and then picks up her fork. "Sorry. I...get a little OCD about taking my meds. This late at night, I forget things if I'm not super careful."

"I just had a flashback from the scent of cardamom, of all things, almost threw you across the room, and your response is to make me tea, reheat lasagna, and tell me you're OCD about taking your meds? I thought *I* was a little off my rocker."

"You don't know the half of it. I'm a mess, Ripper. And my meds keep me alive. Dig in. Because while my life might be two steps away from falling apart, there's one thing I know how to do." She digs her fork into the cheesy pasta and meets my gaze. "I'm a great cook."

# CHAPTER EIGHTEEN

**Cara**

Ripper stares at me like I've grown a second head. And when I take a bite of lasagna like it's the most natural thing in the world to eat after the events of the past hour, he braces his hands on the table. "Cara, you don't know anything about me."

"And you don't know anything about me." After another sip of tea, I can feel my meds start to kick in, and the world seems a little less intense as my heart rate normalizes.

Across the table, the former Special Forces soldier grasps his fork like he's never seen one before, then digs into the pasta. Neither of us say a word as we eat, but his shoulders tense a little more every few minutes, and he keeps darting glances at the closed drapes, the door, and me.

"The window in the kitchen opens," I say as I set my fork down.

He lurches to his feet and practically runs for the small window. After a couple of deep breaths, he clears his throat. "I thought...I could do this. Be inside. But...fuck. I was wrong."

His voice cracks, his cheeks tinge red, and he continues to lean close to the window, breathing heavily. I think he'd stick his whole head out there if the sink weren't in the way.

"Ripper, look at me." The haunted look in his eyes confirms I'm right. He's about two seconds away from losing it again. "Go sit on the couch. Open the drapes and the window. Right now."

I'm surprised when he obeys, and I limp over to sit next to him. "I get the idea you don't like people touching you. Am I right?"

After a jerky nod, he clears his throat. "Only been back in the States two months. Before...I was somewhere else. Somewhere...not good."

"Will you try something for me? One word, and we stop."

His brows shoot up, and he angles his head towards my bedroom. "You're not suggesting we—"

"No!" Now it's my turn to blush. He's ridiculously handsome, and as he was holding me earlier, all those defined, sculpted muscles were definitely *not* affecting me. Nope. Not at all.

I rest my elbows on my knees and lean forward, peering up at him through the corners of my eyes. "When I was a teenager, no one knew what was wrong with me. They just knew I'd get overwhelmed and end up in a meltdown. My best friend at the time, Grace, finally figured out how to bring me back when I was in so deep, I couldn't see past the panic."

"How?" His voice is rough, strained, and his hands clench on his thighs.

"By holding me."

Ripper stiffens and starts to inch away. "I can't..."

"Will you let me try?" Slowly, I reach up and cup the back of his neck like I did before, and his entire body goes rigid. "Look at me, Ripper. You're safe. No one's hurting you."

His chest stutters, and I put my other hand over his heart.

"Keep your eyes on me. You're in Seattle. In my apartment. And you can leave at any time."

"Cara." The way he says my name...I want to do whatever I can to keep him safe. I ease myself closer until I have my arms around him and my head resting on his shoulder.

"Sometimes, we all need to be held," I say quietly. "When I was finally diagnosed with ADHD and anxiety a few years ago, my therapist suggested I buy a weighted blanket."

Ripper relaxes by degrees. Each breath a little easier. "A what?" His voice is calmer now too. Deeper. Smoother.

"A weighted blanket. It's supposed to make you feel like you're being hugged." I chuckle a little. "It's not the same thing. Nothing can replace someone else's arms around you. But it does help."

Even though I started this exercise for *him*, to help *him* calm down, it's helping me more than I want to admit. I've been alone for so long. I didn't realize how much I missed...being touched.

When he sighs and we relax against the cushions, I close my eyes, and his voice rumbles against my ear. "I haven't spent this long inside at night since I got back."

"That's good, right?" I stifle my yawn against his shoulder. "What changed? Why did you decide to try to sleep at home tonight?" If I stay upright much longer, I'll start to ramble. And this damaged, handsome, protective man will see me for what I am. A woman who'll put him in danger and probably get him killed. But I get the sense Ripper doesn't open up often. Maybe not at all.

The corners of his lips twitch. "There's this dog..."

---

TEN MINUTES LATER, I'm practically in tears. I still don't know what happened to him before he came back, but since...trying to find his place, wanting to be...better. I understand all of it.

We're still intertwined, and his muscles feel relaxed, loose and warm, but definitely still...strong. "Do you feel safe here?" he asks.

"I don't feel safe anywhere." The words escape before I have a chance to think them through, and I turn my face into his neck, breathing in the light scents of bergamot and sandalwood as my brain scrambles to find something else to say that won't make me sound like an idiot. "I mean...I'll be okay."

He shifts slightly so his cheek rests on the top of my head. "Cara, you don't have any reason to trust me, but I don't like the idea of you being here alone. No one around. The unit next to you is empty."

Whoa. That's...borderline creepy. "It wasn't... But I haven't seen the kid in forever. Are you sure?"

Ripper shrugs. "There's an impressive spiderweb across the top of the door. And the knob's dusty. No one's gone in or out for at least a couple of weeks. Maybe a month."

"That c-could just be...a really industrious spider." I don't want to think about being the only person on this floor. Not that I ever expected the young man living next to me to be my savior—he was all of twenty-two. But maybe he would have called the cops. And now, I'm kicking myself for not realizing he moved out.

"Do you have any friends you could stay with? Or go to a hotel? I don't know what had you so scared tonight—and I'm not asking you to tell me. We all have our secrets. But I know terror when I see it." Shame softens his tone.

"I can't afford a hotel." My own reply is barely a whisper, and I huddle closer to him. His sweatshirt is warm and soft, and I should give it back, but then my thoughts zing back to the question he asked me. "And I can't really go to a friend's. I'll be fine here. I have a baseball bat in the bedroom."

Too bad I don't believe my own words. A baseball bat isn't going to protect me from Jessup and Parr. And while Leland's second call, where he apologized for driving through a tunnel and then said he just wanted to let me know he was going to find a way to send me an additional ten thousand dollars to help me stay afloat for the next few months reassured me, it also reminded me just how precarious my situation is.

Ripper shakes his head. "I still don't like it."

Warning bells go off in my head, so loud, I wonder if he can hear them. But I can't stop myself. The words escape before I can even think them through. "If you're that worried, stay. Here."

"Wh-what?" He jerks out of my embrace. "That's not a good idea."

"No. It's a brilliant idea." I stay as still as I can, not wanting to spook him any further. "Hear me out. You want to sleep inside and you don't think you can. I don't want to be in this apartment alone tonight—and you don't want that either. So... two birds. One couch. You won't be home. So maybe it'll be easier on you. And I won't be alone, either."

I hobble over to the hall closet and withdraw a blanket and a pillow. Is he about to tell me I'm insane? His wary gaze tracks my movements, and when I'm standing in front of him again, he accepts my offerings and clutches them to his chest.

"Can I...keep the drapes and window open?" The shame and desperation in his voice break my heart, and I sink back down next to him.

"Of course." Turning my hand palm up on my thigh, I wait to see if he responds. "Tomorrow, I'll be okay. You can go back to your life, and I'll figure out a way to handle mine."

Ripper covers my fingers with his, and with his free hand,

reaches out and brushes a lock of my hair off my forehead, exposing the long scar down my temple from Jessup's attack almost eighteen months ago. I turn my head, but he stops me by skating the backs of his knuckles along my jaw. "You're a mystery, Cara. Thank you..." he swallows hard, "for taking a chance on me."

# CHAPTER NINETEEN

**Ripper**

THE BEDROOM DOOR shuts softly as Cara disappears inside. I should go. Back to my apartment with the floor-to-ceiling windows, one of which opens out onto the balcony so I can get fresh air. I could sleep out on that balcony. It's small, but it would be...better than this.

Or maybe not. Because I can still smell her. I'm warm from the time she spent holding me. I didn't think I could let anyone hold me ever again. As weak and messed up as I was when Ry pulled me out of that well, I didn't have a choice for a few days. Every time I wanted to move, to change clothes, to bathe, to piss, one of them had to help me. And every time, it sent me into a panic.

Cara calmed me down with just her voice and her touch. And now? I'd give about anything to feel her arms around me again.

There's a soft melody coming from her bedroom, and I

push off the couch and creep silently towards her door. It's some sort of white noise. Peaceful. The door's so thin, I can hear her moving around, talking to herself.

"Shirt, panties, bra, socks. Check. Meds ready to go. Check. Tablet and phone charging. Check. Crap. My box."

The bed creaks, and I rush back to the couch—all of five steps away—sinking down as she opens the bedroom door. Holy shit. She's wearing a dark tank and a pair of loose, flowing pants that highlight her curves. Her nipples tighten as the chill in the living room reaches her, and she hugs herself tightly. "Sorry," she says. "I just needed to get...um..." Darting towards me, she snatches a gray canvas box from the small end table and tucks it under her arm.

"Don't apologize, sunshine. This is *your* place."

Her cheeks pink, and she backs towards her room. "I didn't want to wake you."

"That would require me to sleep. Pretty slim chance of that." The look on her face makes me regret my words almost immediately. "Doesn't matter where I lay my head, Cara. Haven't slept well in six years. Probably won't start tonight. And it doesn't matter. If I can make it until sunrise indoors, that'll be enough."

"I have melatonin," she offers.

"Doesn't do shit for me. I've tried sleeping pills, alcohol, meditation, and pushing my body to its physical limits. There's nothing that can calm me down when it gets dark and I'm alone. I'll be okay. Get some rest." Patting the pillow, I try for a smile. The motion feels strange and unfamiliar, but also good. I don't remember the last time I smiled without forcing it for someone else's benefit.

"Okay. If you need anything..." She takes another step, and I can't decide if I need her to stay or go. I don't want to be alone, but nor do I want to try to face my demons with her in the next room.

At the last second, I ask, "What's the music you have on in there?"

"You can hear that? Crap. I'm sorry. I'll turn it down."

"Don't." Jerking up too quickly, my head spins, and I grab onto the arm of the couch so I don't stumble. Cara's at my side before I can right myself, her warm fingers on my arm. There's no urge to pull away. No need to hide myself, even though her hand is just above my wrist, over the thick scars I'll never be rid of.

"My God," she whispers as she notices the raised, smooth skin. "What—?"

"Not the kind of story you want to hear before bed, sunshine. Or at all. And I'm okay. Just stood up too fast."

"Are...are you sure?" She's only a breath away, and her scent is intoxicating. My jeans, tight before, now feel like they're strangling my dick, and I force myself to nod.

"Yeah. I'm sure." The words scrape over the lump in my throat, and I wish I could hold onto her. I think she'd keep me tethered to reality, and that's all I've wanted for six years.

Her warmth fades as she retreats to her bedroom, but then she turns and peers out a crack in the door. "I can't sleep if it's totally quiet. So I use an app that mixes some low melodies with the sound of waves crashing at the shore. It distracts the part of my brain that wants to over think things...all night long."

In the next beat, she cocks her head. "I could leave the door open. And...turn the music up. If you'd like."

This time, the smile feels less foreign. By the look on Cara's face, it's also probably less "axe murderer" and more "stand-up guy."

"That would be... I'd like that."

———

THE NIGHT SEEMS to last forever. Only the music floating from Cara's bedroom brings me any peace, and even then, it's short lived.

Her couch isn't long enough for me to stretch out on, so I move the blanket and pillow to the floor. Outside, the sounds of cars going by, of young kids chatting as they walk home—or wherever—help, and after a few hours, I start to float. Not exactly asleep, but not awake either.

It's the worst place to be. The place where my nightmares become real.

Images flash through my mind. Bank routing numbers. Stacks of cash. Guns. Missiles. And the worst? Women's faces. Young girls Faruk sold or consigned to his harem.

But when I jerk up to sitting, clutching the blanket to my chest, everything blurs. I can't remember any of it. "Dammit." Slamming the flat of my hand against my forehead, I try to *jar* the memories loose, but that never works.

How the hell can I ever atone for my sins if I can't remember them?

Trudging into the small kitchen, I find a glass and run cold water from the sink. But after three sips, I feel like I'm going to throw up.

From the bedroom, I hear a muffled whimper and almost lose my hold on the glass. Cara. Another cry, this one louder, and I'm moving, at the side of her bed, glass still in my hand, before I even register the carpet under my bare feet.

"Cara?" It's darker in here, but there's still enough light for me to see her curled into a ball, her hands clenching her blanket, a pained expression marring her features. "Shhh. It's okay. You're safe."

Easing my hip onto the bed, I rest my hand on her shoulder, then start to rub gentle circles along her upper arm.

The scream that escapes her lips as she wakes with a violent shudder is full of terror. "No!"

"Cara! It's me. Ripper." I grab her hands as she lunges for me, and she struggles, tears filling her eyes as she gasps for air. "Look at me, sunshine. Say my name. Tell me you recognize me."

"Rip...Ripper." She's shaking, gooseflesh covering her arms. My sweatshirt's folded at the bottom of the bed, and I let her go so I can help her into it. "I didn't think. I should have warned you. But I haven't...not this bad...in forever."

"My shrink would say you shouldn't apologize for the things your subconscious drags up when you least expect it. But he says a lot of things, and I'm pretty sure he's full of shit."

This makes her laugh, and she reaches for a box of tissues on her bedside table, pulls out two of them, and dabs at her eyes. "Did I wake you?"

"No. My nightmare was quieter. This time." My fingers reflexively clench and unclench on my thighs, and I stare down at my feet. One of the few places the scars aren't as evident. Rubber hoses to the soles don't leave marks. Just bone-deep bruises you never forget.

"Where'd you go?" Her fingers are cool on my arm, and as if she can sense how close I am to the edge, she eases herself closer. "Hold onto me."

I shouldn't. Fuck. I should leave and never come back. But when she touches me, the constant stream of self-destructive thoughts running inside my head stops, and I don't feel so broken.

I have my arms around her before I realize I've moved. "Nowhere good. I...I don't know if I can do this, Cara."

If I can't manage a single night—hell, even four hours—I can't take care of Charlie. The idea of abandoning him breaks me, and I squeeze my eyes shut hard enough to give myself a headache. It's either that or start sobbing, and I won't let myself break in front of Cara.

She rests a hand on my thigh, then makes a soft snorting sound. "No wonder. You're wearing jeans. Those can't be comfortable for sleeping. In my bottom dresser drawer, you'll find a pair of loose shorts," she says, her lips close to my ear. "They'll probably fit you. Go put them on, then come lie down with me under the weighted blanket. See if that helps."

"Cara..." I draw back, unsure if she's the most empathetic person on the planet, reckless as fuck, or trying to seduce me. "I can't sleep with you."

"When we were on the couch, you were relaxed. And then... you weren't. Trust me, Ripper. I'm not trying to get into your shorts. Just get you into a pair of mine so you don't have to sleep in your jeans. Then see if we can reclaim some of that calm from earlier."

As ridiculous as I think her idea is—there isn't a damn thing that's going to get me to sleep tonight short of someone knocking me out with a blow to the head—I extricate myself from her arms and go to her dresser.

A few minutes later, once my dick has calmed down and I'm wearing the black basketball shorts over my briefs, my jeans folded under my arm, I emerge from her small bathroom to find she's scooted to the far side of the bed. Making sure there's nothing between me and the door.

When I lie down, she pulls the heavy blanket over us, then fits herself to my side. We're touching shoulder to knee, and damn if it doesn't feel...like I'm at peace for the first time in more than six years.

"I want to ask you for something," she says quietly as I close my eyes. "But if you can't do it..."

"Ask."

"Will you...um...if you're not busy...could you walk me home from the bus stop tomorrow?"

"I'll be there."

# CHAPTER TWENTY

## Cara

MY MUSCLES ARE all loose and warm under the weighted blanket. And then I remember...it's not just the blanket. Ripper's wrapped around me, sleeping on his side, his breath tickling my neck. The thin curtains let in the first of dawn's light. It can't be much later than 5:00 a.m.

Three times in the night, he started shaking, whispering words in a language I've never heard before. But as soon as I drew his arm tighter around me, he settled.

The last time I had a man in my bed, we didn't sleep. Too bad that guy turned out to be a jerk and had sex with my sous chef two days later.

With Ripper, I feel safe. Despite barely knowing him, the valor running through his veins shines so brightly, it's almost blinding. Closing my eyes, I try to eke out a few more minutes of sleep before I have to face the day, but before I drift off, the solid band of muscle wrapped around my waist disappears. By inches, he slides out of bed, and the sound of him shedding the borrowed shorts and donning his jeans leaves me sorely tempted to turn over and pretend I just woke up.

But I don't. I'm shocked he stayed this long, and though my eyes burn a little when he creeps from the room without so much as a whispered goodbye, I understand. Some secrets are too painful to face in the light of day.

---

WITH MORE THAN five hours until I have to leave for my shift at the diner, I start my weekly deep-clean of the apartment only minutes after he walks out the door. I'm about to crush the paper pouch from the peach tea bag when the black scrawl catches my eye. A phone number. And a single word. Ripper.

We're not friends. Not lovers. He's just a man who was in the right place at the right time to make me feel safe. Special Forces. And at one point...a prisoner. The thick scars around his wrists, the way he doesn't like to be touched. His response to the scent of cardamom tea. Something very bad happened to him, and my mind wanders to all sorts of dark places.

I shouldn't care that he left me his number. Yet, I rush to enter it into my phone. Not the burner Leland called me on last night, but Cara Barrett's phone. The one I splurged on when I'd passed the six-month mark in Seattle.

I've been so careful. Lindsey is the only person I'm close to, and she thinks I ran away from a cult when I was in my early twenties.

After I finish the wash—and the repeated trips up and down the stairs to the basement laundry room, I make myself a cup of instant coffee—a sacrilege in Seattle, but it's all I can afford—and then rifle through the industrial size box of assorted teas.

Every single packet of the orange-cardamom blend goes

into a plastic sandwich bag and then into the trash. I don't know if I'll see him tonight—or ever again—but if I do, I won't take the chance that something in my apartment will hurt him again.

Pulling out my precious notebook, I write down every word Leland said to me last night. Every word I remember, at least.

*"Cara, I need you to listen very carefully..."*

And then, a little over an hour later, another call.

*"Cara, I'm sorry. I was driving through a tunnel, dropped the phone, and then my battery died. I'm going to send you some extra cash. I don't want you to have to worry about every penny. Keep this phone on. I'll call you in a day or two and tell you how to access the money."*

Closing my eyes, I try to replay everything that happened. Giving Ripper the lasagna. Sitting down next to him. Seeing his tattoo. My burner phone's ring tone.

Times like this, I hate my broken brain. The meds that help keep my raging ADHD in check wear off by 10:00 p.m., and my thoughts wander. I'm not as observant as I need to be.

I can't remember Leland's voice. What it sounded like. Was he worried? Calm? All I remember is hearing my heart pounding in my ears.

By the time the coffee's gone, I'm on the edge of a panic attack, and the only way I can think to diffuse it is to snuggle into Ripper's sweatshirt with my phone clutched in my trembling hands and send him a text message.

*It's Cara. I wanted you to have my number too. Just in case.*

I don't know what I expect him to say, or how I'll pull myself out of this panic spiral if he doesn't respond. Burrow under my weighted blanket in the bed that smells like him? Probably. At least until I have to leave for the diner.

Before I have to find out, my phone beeps.

*I'll be at the church when you get off the bus.*

It's enough. Knowing that despite how he snuck off this morning, he won't go back on his promise.

As I go through my short routine, making sure I have everything I need for the day, the phone beeps again.

*I ordered a weighted blanket.*

My laugh chases the last of the panic away, and as I head for the bus, I send him an "I told you so" GIF, followed by *"I'll see you tonight."*

I've been safe for a year. Maybe it's time I started to let people in.

---

**Ripper**

When Cara's message comes in, I'm standing on the shore of Green Lake, looking out over the water. Halfway between her place and mine, it's become one of my favorite spots to try to ground myself.

Runners, walkers, cyclists, women pushing baby strollers fill the path around the lake. It teems with activity most of the day. Kids splash in the water, chase the ducks, and laugh with abandon like only little kids can.

I hope Mateen's okay. Ry would know. Or Ford. Scrolling through the phone's contacts, I wonder if I'll ever feel comfortable just texting or calling someone out of the blue. And then Cara's second message comes through.

The corners of my lips twitch, and before I know it, I'm smiling. Actually smiling. It doesn't feel forced. Foreign, maybe. But not forced.

Snapping a photo of the calm lake, sunshine just breaking over the tops of the tall trees to the east, I start another message to her, but stop when I can't figure out what to say.

Who is she to me? A friend? I slept with her, for fuck's sake. Actually slept. In her bed. With my arms around her. And though I woke up with the world's worst hard-on, what we did...it wasn't sexual. Comforting. Calming. Reassuring.

I can't open myself up to more than a friendship. Not after what Faruk's men did to me. Hell, I haven't even rubbed one out since before Hell. I tried. A month ago. Ended up on the shower floor shaking, remembering the agony, the helplessness, and how I'd curled into a ball in the bottom of that fucking well, the God-awful stench clinging to me, knowing I'd never feel anything but broken again.

Shoving the phone back into my pocket, I stalk across the path and head up the hill to the street. *Walk her home tonight. Walk her home every night if you want. But don't get close. It won't end well for either of you.*

I've almost convinced myself I can do this when my phone buzzes. The photo looks out over Puget Sound. There's a green and white ferry on the left and a cruise ship almost out of frame on the right.

And a message.

*Cara: There are days my job sucks ass. But at least it comes with this view. When does your blanket arrive?*

I stop, the sudden desire to *talk* to her, to keep this connection going, almost overwhelming.

*Ripper: Tonight by nine. Of all the shit that didn't exist when I left the States years ago, same-day shipping might be my favorite.*

I attach the picture of Green Lake, and only hesitate a few seconds before I hit send. Maybe I can do this. Make a friend. Talk. A little. It's easier with someone who doesn't know about my past. The guilt creeps in slowly, then rushes over me like a tsunami.

Ryker and Dax are my brothers, our family bond forged through training, combat, and the tortures of Hell. And yet, these text exchanges with a woman I barely know are easier than anything I could possibly say to them.

An hour later, when I code myself into my apartment, I make a beeline for the windows and my balcony. With the sun on my face and the cool breeze carrying the scents of orange and passionfruit to my nose, I feel strong enough to send Dax and Ry a message.

*Ripper: Before Dax heads back to Boston, maybe we could all get together for a beer?*

I know they're giving me space. Trying to let me heal. I'm not sure I ever will, but after last night, I know one thing. I can't do this alone.

---

WALKING into my apartment a little after midnight, I clutch my phone tightly. When Cara got off the bus, I met her with a thermos of hot tea—passion fruit and guava, like her shampoo —and a cupcake from this little place around the corner from my building.

She brought gourmet grilled cheese sandwiches from the food truck, and we spend a couple of hours together, eating, dancing around various subjects until we landed on a discussion about the best coffee shops in Seattle.

Before I left, she gave me the name of the relaxation app she uses on her phone, and I pop my ear buds in before I close and lock my door. "I can do this. This is *my* place. *I* have the lock code. I'm safe here." Still, my heartbeat skyrockets, and I rush for the window. Once I'm out on the balcony, I can breathe again.

And then she texts me.

*Cara: Home yet?*

*Ripper: On my balcony. Going to stay out here a while.*

*Cara: Get the weighted blanket. And check your backpack. I put something in there for you.*

Telling myself I'm only going inside for a minute, I pull the new weighted blanket off the bed. Twenty-five pounds of little glass beads sewn inside a navy blue shell. It's ridiculous to count on something so simple to chase away my panic attacks, but once I have it around my shoulders, I do feel marginally better.

In the front pocket of my backpack, I find a tissue paper-wrapped cylinder that smells like passionfruit. A candle in a glass jar. Once it's lit, I set it on the little table next to the bed in the center in the room, then sit with my back against the door jamb. I'm not inside, but I'm not outside either.

*Ripper: The blanket's helping. And the candle smells like you.*

*Cara: It's my favorite. Good night, Ripper. If you need to, you can text me. I'll keep my phone on.*

The phone goes next to the candle, and I'm suddenly more inside than out. It shouldn't be this hard for me to sleep in a bed or this easy for me to share my problems with a stranger. But nothing else in my life makes sense. Why should this?

Out on the lake, a solitary boat cuts across the water, its lights floating across an inky black expanse. The city lights frame the darkness, and the candle's scent wafts over me. Maybe...I can move a little closer.

With the heavy weight all around me and Cara's scent filling the room, I can take myself back to last night. To the few hours I felt at peace. And soon, I'm lying on the floor next to the bed, my eyelids heavy, a deep sense of calm spreading through my limbs, and I let myself go.

# CHAPTER TWENTY-ONE

**Ripper**

"WHERE ARE YOU RIGHT NOW?" Ryker asks when I pick up the phone.

"Safe Haven Animal Shelter. Woodinville. Why?" Charlie nudges my hand, and I skim my fingers along his good ear. He hasn't stopped wagging his tail since I let him out of his kennel and told him he was coming home with me tonight.

"We'll be there in thirty minutes. Stay out of sight."

"Out of sight? What the fuck is going on, Ry?" Heading for the office, I hold the door open for Charlie, then point at the blanket Melissa has folded under the desk for him.

"Not over the phone." The call disconnects, and my stomach twists into a knot. For three days, I've tried to be a normal guy. It's getting easier to clean the kennels, and at night...I walk Cara from the bus stop to her apartment. We talk about...normal things. Her favorite—and least favorite—customers at the diner, the antics of the kittens at the shelter, even the weather. Nothing serious. Nothing risky. Hell, Ry would probably read me the riot act if he knew I hadn't introduced myself to her as Rick.

Last night, though, things turned serious for a few minutes. When she got off the bus, she was on edge, distracted—almost confused. I had to press. And she admitted that she has a sensory processing disorder. That certain scents and sounds actively hurt her, and yesterday afternoon, her food truck boss came to work wearing one of the scents that turns her stomach. A scent she had to work next to for hours. She was practically in tears by the time we made it to her apartment, and I bundled her into bed and made her a cup of raspberry tea.

Caring for someone felt good. Like maybe I'm not worthless. I almost offered to stay, but she knew I needed to go.

So I walked home. To the apartment Ry pays for, but that I'm slowly making mine. Two days ago, I bought a plant. Last night, I texted Cara a picture of the dog bed I picked up for Charlie.

It feels good. Making a friend. One not tied to my old life. She has her secrets, but in some ways, she's the most honest person I've ever met. Only problem? Every time I'm around her, I want more. And that's something I can't ever have. Not after what Faruk's men did to me.

But I fall asleep at night with her scent all around me. Under the weighted blanket that reminds me of her. And while I don't sleep well—unsure I ever will—I do sleep. For a full two hours last night, I even managed to find peace in the bed before moving to the floor.

Melissa comes in from the stable with bits of hay stuck in her gray hair. "That new filly is a piece of work. She won't eat if she can see another horse." After a pause, she frowns. "Something's wrong. What is it?"

"I don't know. One of my buddies is on the way. Can we... um...finalize Charlie's paperwork? I might need to get out of here in a hurry once he shows up." Fuck. If there *is* something wrong, I can't bring the pup into it. But he raised his head when heard his name and the look in those eyes...

Melissa pulls out an adoption application, then calls for Charlie to get his license number off his tag. When the dog pads back to my side, I bend down and show him the new collar and leash I picked up on the way in today.

"What do you think, Charlie?" He's wriggling like he just won the lottery, and I try to buckle the collar around his neck, but my equilibrium picks that moment to go sideways. I end up on my ass, Charlie licking my face, and then I'm laughing. Actually laughing. It feels so good, tears spring to my eyes, and I remember a little more of who I used to be.

Melissa stands over us, hands on her hips. "Okay, you two. Enough rough housing. Charlie? Sit. Rick? Sign this." She passes me the clipboard once I lumber to my feet, and I stare at all the crossed out fields—including the ones for my address and last name.

Arching a brow, I angle the paperwork towards her. "Breaking the rules is one thing. Ignoring them completely...?"

"Rick Mercury." She snorts. "I've known too many vets to believe that, son. You're a hard worker, and I think I'm a pretty darn good judge of character. But if your name's Rick Mercury, then Charlie there's a pure-bread toy poodle. Now scribble something on the signature line and we'll call it good."

Last time I checked, I was a grown-ass man who's seen the worst of humanity, yet there's no way I'm going to cross Melissa. She hands me a carbon copy of the adoption certificate and a folder with Charlie's tracking chip info, coupons for dog food, vet services, and numbers for some of Seattle's doggie daycare options, then smiles. "There you go. Charlie's officially yours."

I'm not prepared for the overwhelming wave of emotion that hits me, and I drop to my knees in front of the dog—my dog. "No more cages," I whisper to him. "No more bars. No more nights alone. Okay?"

His wet nose presses to my neck, and if I weren't so worried about Ry's phone call, we'd head for the bus right now and go home. Or we'd find out where the food truck is parked and go see Cara.

Instead, we spend twenty agonizing minutes sitting by the windows, Charlie resting his muzzle on my thigh. When tires finally crunch on the gravel, I stand and wipe my hands on my jeans. This is Ry. And I'm safe. But I can't shake the fear that all the progress I've made isn't going to mean shit after today.

Ryker leaves the engine running as he strides toward the office. "We need to go. Now," he says, holding the door open.

"You call me and let me know how Charlie's doing," Melissa says. "And when I can expect you back." She levels a gaze at Ryker. "You, young man, better have a very good reason for leaving *Rick* hanging like you did."

Ryker's brows shoot up. "Yes, ma'am. I do." As I follow him out to his truck with Charlie at my side, he stares down at the dog. "This is new."

"This is Charlie. Charlie, meet Ry. And Dax."

Opening the back door of the truck, I motion for Charlie to get in, and he jumps up, sitting up on the bench seat like he's done this all his life. Dax turns around. "You got a dog?"

"No. He's a pot-bellied pig."

Dax chuckles, though his expression doesn't match the sound. "Found a little of the old you, huh?"

"Maybe. How many fingers am I holding up?" I extend only one, and Dax huffs as he jabs Ryker lightly in the shoulder.

"He's flipping me off, isn't he?"

"Yup." As we turn onto the main road, Ry clears his throat. "We've got a problem. A big one. So I have to ask. Have you told anyone your real name? Like that woman who gave me the stink eye?"

"No. I understand the risks, Ry. I might *deserve* to spend the rest of my life in jail, but I'm sure as hell not going to tell anyone who I am. Not after everything you and Dax have done for me."

"No one? Not one person. It didn't slip out anywhere?" he demands.

Another few seconds of this and I'm going to lose my shit if he doesn't tell me what's going on. "The shrink you set me up with knows. But that was *your* doing." After a beat, I swear under my breath. "Well, there's this woman...I told her my name was Ripper."

"Fucking hell, Rip. Who is she?" Ry asks as he shoots me a glare in the rear view mirror.

"No one who's going to expose me. She works at a diner and a food truck. Thought I was homeless and started bringing me dinner. I walk her from the bus stop to her apartment at night before I go home. What's going on?"

Dax rubs his temples, then shifts in his seat so he's almost facing me. "Someone showed up at Second Sight's offices this morning asking for me. Trev was there and had them pegged as a spook within five seconds. The guy, a Francis Jessup, was asking about J.T. Richards."

"Fuck. What did Trevor tell him?" A cold sweat breaks out over my neck and chest and I drape my arm around Charlie, needing something real to hold on to.

"Said he didn't know a damn thing about J.T. Richards. When Jessup told him the three of us were deployed together, Trev gave him the standard cover story. As far as he knows, Ryker and I were Hell's only survivors, and if Jessup wanted any other information, he'd have to wait until I got back from my trip."

"And then half an hour later, I got a call from a blocked number," Ry says. "Different guy—or different name anyway. Parr. Says he's in Seattle and needs to see me. Today."

I don't respond. I can't. Two months. Is that all I get? Fuck. I tighten my hold on Charlie, and he climbs into my lap. "Ry. If I...if they come for me...if I have to go away, will you take care of Charlie?"

"Stop. Right fucking now," he orders. "There is no question here, Rip. We're not going to let anyone come for you or take you anywhere. Wren and Trevor are digging up everything they can on Jessup and Parr. The apartment isn't in your name or mine. Hell, nothing in this town can be traced to me other than my fucking phone. This truck isn't even registered to Ryker McCabe."

"We need the woman's name and address," Dax says quietly. "Because right now, she's your biggest liability."

"Cara. I...don't know her last name. Just...Cara."

"VoiceAssist: New text message to Wren Kane." Dax passes me his phone. "Type it in. Plus, anything else you know about her."

It feels like an invasion. One I'm going to regret. But I don't have a choice. The name of the diner she works at, the food truck, her address and phone all go into the message body, and I send a silent apology to the universe for what I'm doing to the first new friend I've made in years.

"I know it's asking a lot, Rip," Ryker says as he guides the truck off the highway and heads towards my apartment. "But you need to stay inside. Out of sight. As much as you can until we figure out what the fuck is going on."

Tension locks my muscles, and in my lap, Charlie whines. "I can't. You know that, Ry. Plus, what the hell am I supposed to do with Charlie? Have him shit in the bathtub? I don't think so."

Dax shoots Ry a look that clearly says, "Dumbass." After a

quick shake of his head, he turns to me. "Put on a hat and sunglasses. Make sure your scars and tats are covered. And stay alert. We'll know more in a few hours. Until then, be careful. Keep the security system armed at all times, and above all, answer your phone when we call. Got it?"

I nod, then for his benefit, manage to rasp, "Got it."

Ryker pulls into a parking space in the underground garage, then spends a full five minutes scouting the place before he gives me the all clear. "We'll take care of this, Rip. I promise."

With Charlie's leash in one hand and the other loose at my side, ready to go for my pocket knife at a moment's notice, I head for the stairs and the one thing in my apartment I never wanted to have to use.

My computer.

# CHAPTER TWENTY-TWO

**Ripper**

THE DOOR LOCK beeps as I finish entering my code, and Charlie looks up at me when I hesitate. "Yeah, I know, buddy," I say quietly. "I shouldn't be so scared of my own damn apartment. Come on."

As soon as I lock the door and unclip his leash, he runs around the small space, sniffing every corner, checking out the bathroom, the kitchen, and the balcony. I curl my fingers around the top of the railing, and he stands on his two back legs, his front paws on the metal next to my hands.

"Welcome home. We're probably going to spend a lot of time out here. I hope you like the view." I'm talking to a dog. Like he can understand me. But too many times since I first laid eyes on him, he seemed to know exactly what I was thinking.

His tongue is hanging half out of his mouth, and I jerk my head back towards the main room. "Let's get you some food and water."

I'm stalling. Anything to avoid setting up that damn

computer. But if someone with the government suspects Jackson Richards is still alive, I have to get over my fears. Someone would have had to tell them. And Cara's phone call from Fort Bragg the other night is just too much of a fucking coincidence.

If it's her, though, I might never trust another person again. She's so *real*. Or am I so desperate to feel something close to normalcy that I can't read people anymore?

As Charlie goes to town on his bowl of kibble, I pull out my pocket knife. My hands shake when I slide the blade through the tape on the laptop's box. There's so much of my time in Afghanistan I've blocked out. What's going to happen when I delve into those memories?

An hour later, I can no longer see the sun, but the laptop is finally set up and connected to the internet. Charlie's curled up on his new bed a foot away, yipping happily in his dreams. In a little over an hour, I'm supposed to meet Cara and walk her home, and I have to know who called her from Fort Bragg first.

*"Just ask her,"* my inner voice screams at me. But instead of picking up my phone to text her, I type in the number I memorized the other night. I can't remember half the shit I did working for Faruk, but I can't forget a single number I saw for less than ten seconds.

Damn Ryker and his memory tricks. I wish he'd never taught them to me.

My search doesn't bring up anything concrete, so I open a private browser window and head into the dark web. My stomach twists itself into knots, and more than once, I wish I had a bottle of bourbon or vodka to dull the pain. But that's not a solution. Not one I'm willing to use, anyway.

Eventually, I find a name. Leland Steel. Nothing else. It's like he doesn't exist. With another few hours, I could track him down. Even as rusty as my skills are. But if I don't leave now, I'll miss Cara at the bus stop, and I don't care what Ry says. I don't break promises.

"Come on, Charlie. Time to go for a walk."

---

## Cara

All day, I've felt off. Like someone's following me. Hovering over my shoulder. I even caught a whiff of Jessup's terrible cologne when I left the diner. Or so I thought. Until another man brushed by me and headed into the bakery next door. I wish I could find that cologne manufacturer and shut them down for good.

Twice, I thought I saw Parr—the first time though the front door of the diner and the second time from the window of the bus I took to get to the food truck for my evening shift. But both times, when I looked again, he was gone.

My broken brain is playing tricks on me. One of the dangers of buying prescription medications off the streets? I have no idea if what I'm getting is pure and authentic. The pills *look* normal, but I have no guarantee they are. Maybe this last batch of my ADHD meds was only half strength. Or the anti-anxiety pills could be cut with aspirin or even baking soda.

Ripper's sweatshirt—the one I still haven't returned—gives me a little bit of comfort as I ride a mostly empty bus towards the University District. When I see him, I'm going to have to tell him I'm scared. That I don't want to be alone tonight. Maybe he'll stay with me. Or find some way to reassure me I'm seeing things.

I've played through every level of the day's Solitaire achievements, finished five online crossword puzzles, and now, I'm working my way through a series of six word search challenges, just to keep my brain from hyper-focusing on the worst-case scenario—that Parr and Jessup are in town and I'm going to have to run.

"Last stop, ma'am," the young bus driver announces, and I jerk, too wrapped up in trying to distract myself to realize where we are.

*Stupid, Cara. Just stupid.*

A quick glance out the window, and I smile. Ripper's sitting on the steps of the church, a big German Shepherd at his side. They both watch me as I head for the bus door, and when the trolly pulls away, he stands and waits for me to cross the street.

"Is this Charlie?" I ask as I hold out my hand for the dog to sniff. He immediately licks my fingers, and I laugh as I wipe my hand on my skirt. "You're a friendly one, aren't you?" And then it hits me. Ripper hasn't said a word. His blue eyes look darker than usual, and his shoulders are hiked up around his ears. "What's wrong?"

"Have you told anyone about me?" He doesn't move, and my anxiety shifts into overdrive as I take a step back.

"N-no. I...who would I tell? And what would I tell them? Ripper, you're scaring me."

I'm pretty sure that's the worst thing I could have said to him, because he flinches like I've just slapped him in the face, then his shoulders cave inward and he runs a hand through his hair. "Sorry. I just...no one knows me in this town, Cara. You're the only person I've talked to—besides my shrink and my brothers."

"Did something happen?" My chest tightens, and all I want is for him to hold me and tell me everything's going to be okay, but whatever has him so worried won't let him. "I'd never put you in danger, Ripper. At least not...on purpose."

If I let go for even a second, I'll start crying, and when my voice breaks, it seems to shock him out of this gruff, detached persona. "Fuck. I'm sorry, sunshine. I should have known..." He's down the steps and has his arms around me in a single breath, and the dog presses his big body against our legs with a little whine.

I have to tell him. I can't keep my secret if it's going to hurt him. Or even make him think—for a second—that he can't trust me. "The past few days, you've seen the real me. But... there's another me." My entire body shudders as I realize what I'm about to do. "I have secrets, Ripper. An old life. And all day, I've been worried that old life is going to catch up with me."

He releases me slowly but keeps hold of one of my hands. "Mine has," he says quietly.

Across the street, another bus pulls up to the curb, the hiss of the brakes and the creak of the suspension making both of us stand up a little straighter. A group of laughing college-age kids heads south, while a man dressed in a pair of black pants and a black jacket, a baseball cap pulled down over his eyes, stands across the street, his phone pressed to his ear.

He takes two steps north—in our direction—and now I know I wasn't imagining things all day. As I turn to Ripper, he tightens his grip on my hand. "Cara, we're leaving. Right now."

---

**Ripper**

I first saw the man through the bus window. Standing up front, by the driver, he peered across the street, right at us. I could have ignored it—if it weren't for how he moved. Like me. And Ry and Dax and Trevor. He's been trained. Not a sound from his shoes, a casual air to him, but he's hiding his eyes and heading right for us.

Holding tight to Charlie's leash, I rest my other hand at the small of Cara's back and urge her down the street, taking a left on forty-second, cutting through an alley, and coming back out onto University. Here, the crowds from college starting back up again will help us blend in and disappear.

Cara didn't hesitate. As soon as I told her to move, she did. I can feel the tension radiating off her, and I take her arm and pull her into the overflow crowd from one of the more popular bars. Charlie stays pressed to my side and whines at me like he knows we're in deep shit.

"Stay, Charlie," I order, and he stills. Draping my other arm around Cara's shoulders, I pull her close and pretend to kiss her neck so I can peer behind her. "I don't see him."

"Are you sure?" Cara asks, her voice shaky.

"As sure as I can be with this many people on the street. We need to get out of here." She's shaking, despite the press of people around us, and I draw her closer. "This is the warmest sweatshirt I own, you know."

With her cheek to my chest, her words are muffled, but I think I'd hear them no matter what. "I'm sorry. I...should have given it back."

"Nah. Looks better on you anyway." At my side, Charlie starts to fidget, and then his growl rumbles against my leg. Pressing the leash into Cara's hand, I tip her chin up so she meets my gaze. "We're going through the bar. I doubt they let dogs in here, so we're going fast. As soon as we move, put the hood up, don't let go of Charlie's leash, and stay right behind me. Got it?"

She nods, a little noise escaping her throat, and then ducks her head. We dart forward almost as one, weaving through the crowds, among the tables, and towards the back door. Charlie doesn't lose focus for a second, staying right next to Cara despite the smells and the people and the food all around him.

As we burst out into the alley, Cara shoves Charlie's leash at me. "You don't want to follow me, Ripper. It's too dangerous." Before I can react, she darts away, so fast she's at the corner before I can take two steps.

Charlie whines, and I shake my head as I pick up the pace, breaking into a jog. When I come up next to her and take her hand, she tries to pull away. "Cara, stop. You're only going to draw attention to yourself. We're going to stroll through the University quad, just like two people—and a dog—on a date."

"Ripper, don't. Please. I'm just putting you in danger." Despite her words, she tightens her fingers on mine. The contact shouldn't steady me, but it does, and I lean down so my lips are close to her ear.

"Cara," I nuzzle her neck, savoring the scent of her skin. Fuck. She tastes like salt and rain, and if we weren't being chased, I'd do more than just pretend to kiss her. "You know what I used to be. Special Forces fight for those who can't fight for themselves. I don't know what the hell is going on here, but I'm not leaving you to deal with it on your own. Do you trust me?"

Her free hand cups the back of my neck, and I remember how good it felt the other day, just having her hold onto me. "I trust you."

"Then let's go. Is there anything at your apartment you need tonight?" Before I draw back, I plant a single kiss to the delicate skin behind her ear, and she shudders, goosebumps rising on her skin.

"No. I have my meds with me. Enough for two days, at least."

The stoplight changes, and we amble hand-in-hand across the street, up a well-lit path, and all the way to the center of the quad. I never stop looking around, pausing every fifty feet or so to thread my fingers through her hair under the hood, or cup her cheek, or slide my hand around her waist.

More than once, my attempts to fake a kiss end up with my lips close to hers, and fuck. My jeans are painfully tight. Against me, even though the thick sweatshirt, I can feel her nipples pebble, and for the first time in years, I remember what it's like to have...needs.

But I can't let myself give in. As soon as we get to my apartment, I'll call Ry, and he'll know what to do—how to protect her. And maybe then, I can convince my broken body and soul to walk away.

"I don't see him anywhere," I say after twenty minutes. "But keep the hood up. We're going to my place, and after that, you're going to tell me what's going on."

She nods, tears shining in her eyes. Whatever it is, she's terrified, and I know in my heart, I can't ever walk away from her.

# CHAPTER TWENTY-THREE

**Ripper**

IT TAKES us almost an hour to reach my apartment. I don't trust ride shares—not when there's someone potentially after one or both of us—and though Ry would come get us, he'd also probably tear me a new one for being with Cara, and I'm not in the mood.

"This is like a fortress," she says after the door locks disengage.

"Yeah. You spend six years with no privacy, you lock your shit up tight."

Cara flinches, huddling deeper into my sweatshirt, and I kick myself for not watching my fucking mouth.

Charlie goes right to his bed and lies down with his head on his paws, staring at me expectantly. Great. I'm being judged by my dog now. Mouthing, "I know," to him, I double-check the security system as she stands at the window.

Keeping the overhead lights dim lets me see the city, even at night, and the privacy coating Ryker had a contractor install on the windows ensures no one can see in. "Cara, I'm sorry. It's late, and—"

"You're inside. *Stuck* inside. *Trapped.* Because of me." Turning away from the window, she swipes at her cheeks. "I can't do that to you."

That one word rattles around in my brain. *Trapped. I'm trapped. It's dark, and I'm trapped. Get it together. Relax.*

"I—" my heart rate spikes, and I suck in a wheezing breath, "—brought you here. This isn't your—"

My jacket falls from my hand, and I can feel the scorpion's legs skittering along my shoulder. The dread coiling in the pit of my stomach as I try to hold my breath. The searing agony as the stinger burrows into my muscle. My fingers skim one of the older, deeper scars on my upper arm, long healed, but still too vivid a memory.

"Ripper?" Cara's dark locks tickle my cheek, and I blink hard. I'm on the floor next to my bed with Charlie on one side of me, Cara on the other. "Breathe."

As she presses her hand to my chest, my throat tightens. Faruk's voice echoes in my ears. Then Kahlid starts in. My vision tunnels until all I can see are Cara's brown eyes. My ass throbs where I hit the ground, and I clamp my hand over hers. "Don't. Let. Go," I rasp.

"I won't." Warm fingers curl around the back of my neck, and slowly, she eases herself around me. "Charlie. Come here," she whispers, and the dog wriggles into my lap. "You're safe. Wherever you think you are, you're not. You're in Seattle with me and Charlie. In a fortress of an apartment with a gorgeous view, and a huge bed, and—"

Tangling my hand in her hair, I pull her closer and crush my lips to hers. She tastes like mint, and I'm only vaguely aware of Charlie scrambling off to his bed and Cara wrapping her legs around my waist. "Ripper," she whispers when we come up for air, "it's been so long..."

Her hips grind against me, and more memories threaten. Being held down. Stripped. Laughter. I can't do this. With a choked cry, I lift her off me, then stumble for the balcony door. The cool air hits my cheeks, and even though my dick feels like it's going to explode behind my zipper, I know I'll never have *that*—intimacy, sex, a relationship—again.

After a few minutes, I've calmed down enough to face her, but I don't go inside. "There's a lot you don't know about me, Cara. I shouldn't have kissed you."

She squares her shoulders and marches over to the door, stopping just short of the threshold. "Why not? I like you, Ripper. No, I wasn't looking for a relationship. And God knows I shouldn't let myself have one. Because what you don't know about me could kill you. But that—" she points back to the floor next to the bed, "—wasn't either of us starting a 'relationship.' It was...two people needing one another."

Before I can protest, my phone rings, and I push past her to retrieve my jacket from the floor. "Ry? What's going on?"

"Nothing. Not a goddamned thing. This Parr's a fucking ghost. Wren can't find a single reference to him anywhere, and she's been on the dark web for the past three hours. Trevor's coming up blank on Jessup too."

"Shit." Glancing over at Cara, who's still standing at the balcony doors, her arms wrapped tightly around herself, I know what I have to do. But if I tell Ry about the man following us tonight, he'll be over here in ten minutes, and Cara won't ever forgive me. "Let me..." The words die in my throat, but I take a deep breath and try again. "Let me see what I can find."

Ryker doesn't say anything for a minute, and when he finally does, there's a mix of shock and pride in his voice. "Are you sure you're ready, Rip?"

"No. But it doesn't matter if I am or not. This could burn all of us. And you and Dax...you're my family."

"Hooah," he says quietly. "Brothers. Till the end."

---

**Cara**

I don't want to intrude on Ripper's phone call, especially when his face shutters, all emotion vanishing in a single blink after he asked someone named Ry what was going on. But balconies trigger me. Even standing at the door looking out over Lake Washington, I remember the terror of Jessup standing over me, telling me I never should have eavesdropped on a man like him.

Still, the breeze helps mask his words, as does my pounding heart, which is almost the only thing I can hear.

He's full of contradictions. This place is gorgeous. Top of the line appliances, a view to kill for, and a king-sized bed, perfectly made. It's the most secure building I've ever seen. But the studio is smaller than my place, and I thought my apartment was tiny. How could I think he was homeless? He's far from it.

"Cara?" he says from behind me, "what do you need to take your meds?"

"Oh, God. I forgot. What time is it?" My phone's in my bag, not far from the door, and after traipsing through the UW campus for half an hour, then making our way back here, my usual routines have all gone out the window, and I feel like my entire life has been turned on its head.

"Almost one."

I'm two hours late. For most people, most meds, that wouldn't matter. For me... I rush for my bag, pawing through it with shaking hands. I must look as horrified as I feel, because Ripper kneels next to me and rests his fingers on my arm. "My turn to tell *you* to breathe. What does your pill case look like?"

"It's purple."

He fishes it out in under five seconds and drops it into my hand before pointing at the bed. "Sit."

"I'm not Charlie, you know." The dog raises his head and yips, and I stare into his brown eyes. "Sorry, pup."

"No, you're not. You're *definitely* not." Ripper helps me to my feet and keeps his arm around my waist as he guides me to the bed. "What you are is exhausted. And we're going to need to talk. About a lot of things. So you're going to relax while I make you some tea."

He's right. Now that we're not on the run, my adrenaline's crashing, hard, and I kick off my too-sensible shoes and curl around one of Ripper's pillows. It smells like him, and with that, his sweatshirt zipped up to my neck, and Charlie's soft fur under my fingers as I drape my arm off the side of the bed, I feel safe.

A teapot whistles, and I force my eyes open. I'm so tired, and the world is soft and fuzzy as Ripper moves around the small kitchen. "Charlie?" I say quietly, and the dog sits up and nudges his whole head under my hand. Once I tell Ripper about my past, he's going to hate me for putting him in danger like this, and I'll have to leave. "I'm glad I got to meet you. Take care of him, okay?" He licks my fingers, and I skim them around the shell of his mangled ear. "Whoever did this to you was an asshole. You know that?"

"Grade-A asshole," Ripper confirms as he joins me on the bed and presses a cup of tea into my hand. "Take your meds."

I do, sipping the fruity tea slowly while Ripper strokes Charlie's head. "I didn't understand," I say as Charlie looks up at Ripper with pure, complete adoration in his brown eyes.

"When you said there was something about him you couldn't ignore. I do now. He's yours. Completely."

"Yeah. I think we're a lot alike." Ripper clears his throat, and his voice thickens. "About earlier. That kiss..."

"You don't have to—"

"I do." He pushes to his feet and heads for the open balcony door. When he's half in and half out, he rests his back against the jamb. "I spent six years in Afghanistan. Well, no. Longer than that. We were deployed for a couple of years before it all went to shit."

"We?"

"My team. Ryker and Dax and me—we're the only ones left." Sinking down to the floor, he rests his elbows on his bent knees and drops his head into his hands. "Some wet-behind-the-ears comms operator didn't encrypt his broadcast, and the Taliban knew exactly where we'd be and when. Shot us down, trapped us on a mountainside with no escape." His voice cracks, and he tugs on his hair, as if he needs the pain.

"They took five of us. Ry, Dax, Hab, Gose, and me. Our sixth, Naz...he died in the firefight. Gose died after a few days. He'd been shot twice, and our captors weren't exactly concerned with good medical care."

*Oh, God.*

My stomach twists into a knot, and I set the tea down, suddenly worried another sip will make me vomit. He's going to tell me he was tortured.

"Eventually, we landed in a place called Hell Mountain. They'd dug out a whole system of caves deep underground. There were half a dozen cells. A pit we called 'the hole.' It was a fucking maze, and they kept us blindfolded and tied up most of the time. Separated. Until they picked one of us to torture for the day. At first, they wanted intel. After a while, I think we were just punching bags."

He meets my gaze, and I can see it in his deep blue eyes. He's not in Seattle with me. He's back in Afghanistan. "Come here," I say, holding out my hand. "You don't have to do this alone."

As he stands, I think he's heard me, but then he strips off his shirt, and my gasp makes him flinch. Scars run all along his torso. Some straight, others jagged, and still more are shiny ropes from burns. When he turns his back, tears spring to my eyes.

He's been whipped. Over and over again. The lines criss-cross one another, and when his shoulders hunch, they stand out even more dramatically. "After Hell," he says, his voice rough, "everything got so much worse."

Worse?

I'm off balance as I shuffle towards him, my meds starting to take effect, and I almost crash into him, but right myself at the last minute and wrap my arms around him from behind. He holds on like I'm the only tether he has to sanity, and I rest my cheek against his shoulder blade.

"I can't..." he says finally with a deep, shuddering breath. "I can't do this. Not at night. In the dark. It's too much."

After another minute, he turns, and I drop my arms. Dragging a knuckle along my jaw, he frowns. "You're exhausted."

"Meds kicking in," I say and rest my hand over his heart. A thick scar runs across his chest and peeks out from under my fingers.

"Don't. Not now." Ripper jerks away, stalks over to the closet, and fishes two t-shirts and two pairs of shorts out of a drawer, then passes a set to me. "Use whatever you need of mine in the bathroom. Then, the bed's yours."

"No."

He arches a brow like I've forgotten how to speak English. "What?"

"I'm not sleeping in that bed without you. So if you don't want me sleeping on the floor, you'll get in."

I expect him to argue with me, but he doesn't say a word as I slip into his bathroom and shut the door. When I emerge five minutes later, he's under the weighted blanket, the candle I gave him flickering on the bedside table.

My nipples tighten under the thin cotton t-shirt. He still has the balcony door open, and the crisp night air feels good on my skin.

"I'm going to hold you. Okay?" I ask as I wriggle under the blanket.

He nods, but the tension radiating off his body speaks volumes. It's not okay. Not yet. "We'll take it slow. Just like the other night. Did you get that sleep app I told you about?"

Without a word, he grabs his phone and starts the meditative music. I rest a hand on his shoulder, and he stiffens, then after a deep breath, relaxes a fraction.

I don't know how long it takes him to get used to me next to him. An hour? I'm so tired, my eyes burn, but I don't let myself sleep until he's rolled onto his back, and I'm snuggled up to his side, my hand over his heart.

"Cara?" he says, sleep edging into his tone. "How can you understand when no one else does?"

"I don't. But sometimes...comfort is universal." Lifting my head from his pillow, I make sure his eyes are closed, then press a chaste kiss to his cheek. "Sleep, Ripper. You're safe here."

# CHAPTER TWENTY-FOUR

## Ripper

SOFT HAIR TICKLES MY NECK, and I open my eyes. Out the window, a dull glow over the lake marks the transition from night to day. The candle burned out—hours ago, most likely—but it didn't matter. Cara's dark locks carry the scent of passion fruit and mango, and her deep, rhythmic breathing almost lulls me under again.

Shifting slightly, I tuck my hand behind my head and stare out over the water. I slept. All night. Inside. And while I remember having a nightmare where Faruk's men surrounded me, taunting me and beating me, I only woke for a moment. Long enough for Cara to mumble an exhausted reassurance and snuggle closer.

She understands me. My brokenness. Last night, I wanted more. For one passionate kiss, I thought I could have it, too.

"Ripper?" Cara shifts, and fuck. Her body feels so *right* against mine. "Are you okay?"

Am I? Definitely not. There's a beautiful, caring woman in

my bed, and my hard on is straining against my shorts, but I'm not making a single move. "I owe you an explanation," I manage. "About last night."

"You don't owe me anything." She stretches, and the movement highlights her breasts, the tight nipples pebbling under my t-shirt. "I'm a big girl, Ripper. I can handle rejection."

"No. Fuck, no." I brush a lock of hair behind her ear. "I wasn't rejecting you." Her brown eyes hold such confusion, and I blow out a breath. Once I tell her what happened to me, she'll never look at me the same way again. "Six months after they sent us to Hell Mountain, I managed to get access to a computer. Dislocated my shoulder to get free, and I sent—or tried to send—a message to COMSAT to let them know we were alive. But one of Kahlid's guys found me. Knocked me out, and I woke up somewhere much worse."

"What could be worse than a place they tortured you for six months?" Cara's whisper holds so much emotion, and I guide her against my chest, needing to feel her solid weight, her soft curves, to keep myself grounded.

"Amir Abdul Faruk." Even saying his name sends me careening towards a panic attack, but Cara's hand strokes up and down my arm, and I force myself to breathe. "I woke up at the bottom of a well. I don't know how long I was down there. Days, maybe a week?

"Over the next few months, he took everything from me. Even my name. Called me Isaad. I fought him. For so long. He told me my team was dead. That I'd killed them. Even that didn't break me. Not completely. Not until..."

Cara digs her fingers into my bicep, and I tighten my arm around her, dropping my voice to a whisper. "He told his men to do anything they wanted with me."

I don't want to say the words. But I have to. Charlie jumps up onto the bed and lies down on my other side, and I squeeze my eyes shut. "I could handle the torture. Broken bones. Starvation. The scorpions that would come out at night and sting me. I can still feel them crawling all over me." A half sob escapes, my throat raw, my heartbeat pounding in my ears. "But when they stripped me naked and held me down..."

*Finish it. Just tell her the rest.*

"They used me. And they *laughed* while they did it. Taking my name, my honor, that wasn't enough. They had to take my soul too. Over and over and—"

Cara presses her finger to my lips. "Stop, Ripper. Look at me."

*I can't.* Shaking my head, I bury my face in her hair. "I wanted to die. Prayed for it. Begged. And I did. I couldn't *be* myself anymore. Not after what they did to me. Ripper died, and Isaad? He did so many terrible things. For years. Until Ryker and Dax rescued me two months ago."

Unable to say another word, I wait for her to go. To give up on me. Instead, she shifts, and her lips brush mine. "You did what you had to do." Another kiss, this one at the corner of my mouth. "You lived." The other corner. "You found Ripper again."

Straddling me, Cara cups my cheeks and gently wipes away my tears. I still can't face what I might see in her eyes. "I let him—"

"You didn't *let* him do a damn thing." The harsh edge to her voice demands I listen, and I swallow hard before I meet her gaze. Amber streaks in her irises flare, and her mouth is set in a grim line. "I don't know what you did as Isaad. And I don't care if you tell me." Her cheeks turn bright red. "That came out wrong. I mean...crap. Before my meds, it's like my brain's ten steps ahead of my mouth." With a huff, she rocks back slightly, her hips pressing against my dick, and feelings I have no right to have stir to life.

After she rubs the back of her neck, she returns her hands to my chest and tries again. "You did things. Things you're ashamed of. Things *Ripper* would never do. But answer me this. Did *Ripper* do them?"

"Ripper couldn't stop Faruk's men." I can barely get the words out, but once they escape, it's like a dam breaks, and I'm being swept away. Out to sea without a boat or an anchor or even a life preserver. I'm drowning, gasping for air, and alone.

Cara's kiss brings me back. Her warmth all along my body. Her hands in my hair. And when her tongue traces the seam of my lips, I let her in. She tastes of my tears, and for a second, I want to pull away, but then my arms are around her, and I'm holding on like she's the only thing tethering me to this world.

Rolling her onto her side, I let my hand skim her breast, and when I find her nipple, I pinch lightly, and the noise she makes...it sends my dick rocketing to attention. Deft fingers slide under my t-shirt, her warmth traveling up my back, over my scars. "Off," she demands, and the first rays of the morning sun stream through the window as I strip off my shirt.

Cara lets her gaze rove over my chest, over the scars, the muscles that are just now, with semi-regular meals, starting to look like they used to. Rising up on an elbow, she kisses one of the round welts from the scorpions. "You survived," she whispers.

For the first time since Ryker pulled me out of that well, I think maybe I did. Tugging at the hem of Cara's shirt, I expose her breasts. She's perfect. Soft, yet strong. With real curves, a pink blush spreading from her neck almost down to her waist. Dipping my head, I fasten my lips around one dusky nipple, laving my tongue over the pebbled nub until she's practically panting.

I can smell her arousal, and when I dip my fingers under

her waistband, I find lace, then slick heat, and Cara whimpers, her hips thrusting against my hand.

"Turnabout," I manage as I help her out of her shirt, then drag the shorts down her hips. A flash of embarrassment darkens her eyes, but once I press my lips to her lace-covered mound, she shudders.

"Oh God, Ripper. Please..."

"I want to taste you." Her panties land next to the shorts, and I cup her cheek and meet her hooded gaze. "Tell me you want this? You're not just...this isn't..."

"A pity fuck?" Her huff might be my new favorite sound. "I want *you*, Ripper. I want the man who refused to let me limp home on a sprained ankle. The man who brought me to his apartment and offered me his bed because it was the best way to keep me safe. I want the man who trusted me enough to tell me his secrets." Cara arches a brow as she takes my free hand and presses it to her mound. "I'm naked. And about ready to beg. You going to do something about that?"

*Hell, yes.*

When I spread her thighs, the scent of her shoots straight to my dick. Her brown curls glisten in the morning light, and my first taste...fuck. Tracing patterns with my tongue, I savor each mewl, her little gasps, the way her hips thrust against me when I score my teeth along her clit.

"Ripper..." Cara claws at the sheets, her breath coming in short pants as I slide a finger inside her. "Please. I need to come..."

Adding another finger, I twist and find her G-spot as I suck at her clit. Cara's entire body bucks, and she cries out, flying over the edge with my name on her lips. I drink her in, my salty tears mixing with her taste.

This moment—this perfect, beautiful moment—heals a

part of me I thought was too broken to ever see the light of day again.

As she comes down from her release, our breaths the only sounds in the quiet room, my head starts to swim. My vision tunnels. The sensation of her hands on my skin and the sound of her voice in my ears fades, and I hear that name.

*Isaad.*

I try to hold on. To stay with Cara. With this woman who understands me. But I can't. I slide down, so far that I can't feel the soft sheets or see the freshly minted sun. There's nothing but darkness, sand, and desperation.

Warm hands cup my cheeks, and I brace for whatever they're going to do to me next. For the humiliation. For losing my tenuous hold on reality. For Faruk to take whatever of *me* is left.

"Ripper. Come back to me, handsome."

Cara's face swims into focus, and I expect to find horror—or pity at the very least—because she sees everything. Every memory. Every inch of my shame. Before I can push her away, she coaxes me closer with her soft gaze.

And then she's under me, her palms still molding to my face. Her hips tilt, and my tip grazes slick heat. As if she knows I can't take this last step without help, she presses her mouth to mine.

"It's okay," she whispers against my lips. "You're okay."

"Protection," I manage. "I don't have—"

Another kiss and she cups my jaw, her thumb tracing my cheek. "Are you clean?"

"Y-yes. I made them run every test under the sun when I got back." *And then had to relive every moment of my humiliation in front of the medical staff treating me.*

"I'm on birth control. And it's been years for me. I...I want you, Ripper. Any way I can have you."

My eyes burn, but I won't let myself break down. Not now. Not when I have this amazing, beautiful, perfect woman in my bed, and she's mending my broken soul one piece at a time. "You're sure?"

"I've never been more sure of anything."

My breath catches in my chest as my crown slips between her folds. The memories flare, but just for a second. Then, it's nothing but her. Her hands on my skin. Her kisses. Her soft reassurances. Redemption lives in her eyes, and I lock on, desperate to feel like me again. Like I'm not a failure, not afraid, not...broken.

With each thrust, I heal a little more, and fuck. She feels like heaven. "I won't last," I whisper as my need builds.

"I'm right here, Ripper. With you." Cara cups the back of my neck, and I reach down and find her clit. Her keening cry sends me closer to the edge, and when I feel her inner walls clench around my dick, I shout her name and let go.

# CHAPTER TWENTY-FIVE

**Ripper**

AN HOUR LATER, after taking Charlie out to do his business, I let myself back into the apartment. Cara's sitting at my breakfast bar, meticulously counting out pills. Charlie heads right for his water dish, and the choppy sounds he makes as he slurps make me smile. It's getting easier—smiling.

And then I turn my focus to Cara. She's wearing another one of my shirts, and under the shorts I lent her...well, her underwear's in my hamper, and the ideas floating through my head of what I'd like to do with her? They're getting easier too.

"Hemp milk latte with vanilla?" I say as I slide the cup in front of her. She beams up at me like I just gave her the moon and rests light fingers on my cheek as she leans in to brush her lips to mine.

"What is all this?" I ask as I grab an anti-depressant and a single anxiety pill and wash them down with my own drip. She has six pills arranged in precise order in front of her, along with a little notebook with checkboxes on the page. Taking a seat next to her, I try to figure out how not to offend her. "You don't seem…"

"Sick? Someone who needs all these meds?" She arches a brow, but there's a small smile curving her lips.

"Yeah."

"These," she points to two orange capsules, "are for ADHD. If I forget these, you probably won't notice much change in me until mid-afternoon. Then, I'll be extra tired, but I'll also start forgetting things and I probably won't make eye contact regularly. If I don't take them a second day, you'll swear I have a hearing problem."

"Why? There was a kid with ADHD in grade school with me. He could never sit still. But that's literally all I know about it."

"Women have different symptoms, usually." She takes the two orange pills, then checks off the boxes in her notebook. After another sip of coffee, her shoulders slump a little, and she fiddles with a lock of her hair. "I was okay until I got to culinary school. Or, I thought I was, anyway. Then I started feeling stupid. Like I couldn't learn anything. If I had to carry on a conversation with anyone in a room that wasn't completely silent, I'd miss stuff. I thought my hearing was going. But at the same time, I could hear someone chewing in the next room and it would drive me batty. Still does. Turns out, it wasn't that I couldn't hear the person talking. I'd get distracted halfway through their sentence by something else, and my brain just couldn't keep up."

"When were you diagnosed?" I rub small, slow circles on her lower back. Touching her grounds me, and even though it's daylight, I'm still a little on edge being inside.

"Four years ago. It was like suddenly, my entire life made

sense. And after a couple of days on my meds, I..." Her cheeks flush red and she looks down at the remaining pills. "I called my best friend at the time and asked her if this was what it was like to feel like a person. I'd never felt it before."

"What?" She's so open about her challenges that she makes me want to be better. With her *and* with Dax and Ry.

"Like I could keep up. I remember riding the subway to work the second day and pulling up a news article on my phone. I always scanned the headlines. But that day, I read the whole article. When I got to the comments section, I almost dropped the phone I was so surprised." Her smile widens, and she shakes her head. "Reading that stupid article about landing a satellite on a comet? It made me happier than I'd been in ages."

After another sip of coffee, she points to the other three pills. "The yellow ones are for anxiety. And the last one is a beta blocker. I was born with a genetic condition that produces a really high heart rate. It was manageable before I started treating my ADHD, but now, without the beta blocker, my blood pressure spikes and I'm in legitimate danger of having a heart attack. I need one of these in the morning and one at night."

Checking them all off as she takes them, Cara taps her pen on her notebook, double-checks the list, and then carefully packs everything back up in her purse. "And that's just the start of my crazy, Ripper. We...we need to talk about last night."

Shame crawls up the back of my neck, and I can feel myself shutting down until she cups my cheek. "Not this morning, handsome. Not the sex. Or anything you told me. The guy last night. And why—"

Someone pounds on my door, and Cara yelps and clutches her purse to her chest. But I know that knock. "It's all right, sunshine. It's just a friend of mine. And whatever you have to tell me, you should probably tell him too."

---

## Cara

I don't share Ripper's confidence. The more people who know my secret, the more danger I'm in. But I gave him a part of me I didn't think I'd ever share again, and I trust him.

Until he opens the door and a massive bear of a man ducks his bald head in order to enter the room. He's followed by a second man, shorter, maybe six-foot-four, wearing a pair of tinted glasses and carrying a white cane.

As the taller man focuses on me, his multi-hued eyes narrow. "Fucking hell," he mutters. "Caroline Phillips."

My heart leaps into my throat and I jump up. "How do you know that name?"

Ripper looks back and forth between me and the giant. "Ry, what's going on?"

"Those two spooks trying to get a hold of us? Asking about you? Trevor finally tracked one of them back to Fort Bragg. He can't be sure, but he thinks the guy worked out of JSOC." After pinning me with a hard stare, the big guy continues, "And Caroline Phillips was a chef at JSOC for three years. Until she disappeared twenty-two months ago."

"Cara?" Ripper turns to me, his blue eyes full of confusion. "What's going on?"

"Have you told anyone I'm here in Seattle?" I ask as I take a step closer to the door. Not that I'll be able to go anywhere with these two men blocking my way. "*Anyone?*"

"Not yet. Want to give me a reason I shouldn't?" Ry says.

Drawing up to his full height, Ripper places himself between me and the Neanderthal with more scars than I've ever seen. "Because she doesn't want you to. Now take a step back. We're all going to calm the fuck down and figure this shit out."

I can't decide if I should run or cling to Ripper like my life depends on it. But he doesn't give me much choice when he puts his arm around my waist and leads me back to the stool. "Sit down, sunshine. Ryker and Dax are on our side, and you're safe here with me."

Glancing over my shoulder, I fight for a steady breath. "Not if the two spooks he's talking about are Francis Jessup and Bill Parr. Jessup tried to kill me the night I disappeared from Fort Bragg, and again eighteen months ago in Tulsa."

"What does he want with you?" Ryker crosses his arms over his chest. Crap, the man looks like he could bench press a semi-truck, and even though Dax is obviously blind, his shirt strains over impressive muscles, and he's holding onto that cane like he could easily use it as a weapon.

And then it hits me. These are the other two members of Ripper's Special Forces team. The two who escaped Hell.

"Caro?" Ryker asks again.

"Cara," I say defiantly. "I'm Cara Barrett now."

Dax snorts. "Not the most effective alias."

"Give me a break. I had a broken arm and a concussion at the time. I'm lucky I got out of Tulsa alive." Despite Ripper's warmth at my back and his arm around my waist, I'm terrified.

"Give us a minute," Ripper says. He stalks out to the balcony, my hand held tight in his, but I skid to a stop at the threshold. "Cara?"

"I-I can't." My voice cracks, and I grab the door jamb, swaying slightly.

Ripper slides his hand to the back of my neck. "Tell me. Just me."

I have to. The man who shared the worst of his life with me just hours ago won't hurt me. I can confess my secrets to him.

"It was late when I left work that night. Well after eleven. We had this big retirement party planned the next day for one of the analysts, and I'd stayed to make sure the cake was perfect. I was in the garage when I heard them. Jessup and Parr. Jessup, I knew. He always used to leer at me when he'd come in to the dining hall. But Parr...I had no idea who he was. They were talking about a 'friend' in Afghanistan. How they needed to pressure him to cut them in on some of the bigger deals. They never said his name. But they said the guy had an American working for him, a traitor, and all they had to do was threaten to release the American's name, and..." Horror washes over me, and I think I'm going to be sick.

"And...?"

"And the Special Forces would go in and blow the guy off the map..." Pressing my hand to my stomach, I try to force air into my lungs.

*Oh my God.*

"Cara?" Ripper tries to pull me closer, but I duck out of his hold.

"What's your name? Your *real* name. Ripper...that's your nickname. What's your *name*?" My voice rises half an octave, and my heart races, so fast it feels like I'm running sprints.

"Jackson Richards."

"J.T. Richards. The American, J.T. Richards." I cover my mouth with both hands, trying to stop the sound of my heart and soul shattering into a million pieces. "It was you. They were talking about *you*."

Ripper backs up until he hits the railing, then sinks down

onto the ground. Within two seconds, Charlie's in his lap, licking his cheek, but Ripper doesn't move or react at all.

Tears stream down my cheeks, and Ryker and Dax burst past me out onto the balcony. "What the hell is going on?" Ryker asks. "Rip? Say something! And you—" Ryker points at me, "—what the fuck did you tell him?"

"They knew. Oh God. They knew. For years." Huge, hiccupping sobs escape around the words, and I can't do this. I can't face this man I think I'm falling for, knowing I could have saved him if I'd just been braver. "I didn't know. I tried to go to my security contact, tell him everything I overheard, but then he died, and I...I just ran."

"What?" Ryker grabs my arms, but I can't stop crying and staring at Ripper, who's gone glassy-eyed, his face devoid of all emotion. "Cara! What. Happened?"

I meet Ryker's gaze, and the anger I find there sobers me enough to choke out the truth. "Jessup and Parr knew Ripper was alive. For years. But they didn't care. They used him as leverage against the guy who had him. For money."

Ryker lets loose with a string of obscenities, and his fingers tighten to the point of pain. When I cry out, he releases me with a jerk, as if he forgot I was still there. My legs don't want to support me, and I stagger back, my hands on my knees.

A loud *crack* impacts the glass right above my head, Charlie barks, then growls, and someone shoves me inside. A barrage of bullets hits the windows, and then two large forms barrel towards me. I have to blink hard to understand what I'm seeing. Ryker's dragging Ripper with Charlie at his heels, and Dax is holding on to Ryker's arm.

"Move!" Ryker barks at me. "Out the door. To the right. Down the stairs. We're getting the fuck out of here."

"How'd they find us?" Dax asks.

"My guess? Her." Ryker shoots me a glare over his shoulder

as he carries Ripper into the hall, and I lunge for my bag, hugging it to my chest as I follow them.

But when we reach the garage, Dax and Ryker head for a big, black truck, and I turn on my heel and run as fast as I can in the other direction. I have to get as far away from Ripper as I can. He just got his life back. I won't be the reason Jessup and Parr kill him.

# CHAPTER TWENTY-SIX

## Cara

CHARLIE KEEPS pace at my side. At the far end of the garage, another set of steps lead out into an alley. It's how Ripper brought me here last night. Wedging open the door, I lean down and cup his muzzle. "Go to Ripper."

He whines, and I swear the damn dog shakes his head. "I can't wait, Charlie. I have to go. And you can't come with me."

"Cara? Caroline? Where the fuck are you?" Ryker's booming voice echoes through the garage, and I sling my bag over my shoulder and try to force Charlie back through the door, but he won't go.

"Fine. Keep up." Tears burn my eyes. If anything happens to Charlie, I'll never forgive myself. My heart won't let me run all out, but I manage a fast jog up Latona until my lungs feel like they're going to burst. Down Fiftieth, across the freeway, and over to Roosevelt Way, and I find a bus stop with a bench and collapse, wheezing.

Crap. I can't take Charlie on the bus without a leash.

Unhooking the strap on my bag, I fasten it to his collar, then wrap my arms around his solid body. "I don't know what to do, Charlie," I whisper. "They're going to kill me." The dog nuzzles my chin, and when I look into his eyes, I start to cry. "I know. I left him. I destroyed him and then I left him."

I have to get somewhere with people. Somewhere Jessup and Parr won't want to start a riot by shooting me. Swiping at my cheeks, I stand as a downtown bus pulls up to the stop. Pike Place. I can hide out there. This time of day, it'll be packed, and since I've worked down there for almost a year, I know my way around.

---

BY THE TIME the bus drops me off three blocks from Pike Place Market, my stomach is twisting in on itself. I need food. My meds leave me shaky if I don't eat. Charlie trots at my side, looking up at me every time I slow to figure out which way to go next. One level down, a whole bunch of tables and benches wait for lunch patrons who want a view of the water. Not crowded enough. But up amid the farmers market stalls, it's so loud, I don't know if I can make a call.

Ducking into a corner left vacant for the day by an absent vendor, I dig into my bag for the burner phone, then call Leland.

"Hello?" His voice is scratchy. Cautious.

"I need help. They found me."

He clears his throat, coughs, and swears under his breath. "Where are you?"

"Seattle." I scan the crowds, searching for anyone who looks out of place. For Jessup's dirty blond beard and pale blue eyes, Parr's slight limp and ruddy skin. You spend long enough down here, you get to know the tourists from the locals, but those who don't belong? Who've been trained to blend in? I shudder as I crouch down behind the empty table. The tile floor's dirty, and I tug at my shorts, suddenly very aware I ran out of Ripper's apartment with no panties on. "You have to help me. Tell me where to go."

"I'll send someone for you. Within the hour. Can you get to the Space Needle?"

"The...Space Needle?" My hand shakes, and my shoulder hits the wall as I fall over. "You have someone in Seattle?" This is wrong. Leland didn't know where I was until a few seconds ago, and now he has someone *in* Seattle? Staring at the phone in my hand, I swallow a sob as I end the call.

Leland told me to keep the phone on.

*So they could track me.*

"Come on, Charlie. We can't stay here." Wrapping his makeshift leash around my hand and tucking my bag under my arm, I check all around us, then dart out of the empty stall and weave my way through the crowds. If I can get down to the lower level, I'll reach Alaskan Way. Cruise ships. Cabs everywhere.

The phone lands in the first garbage can I find, and I head for the stairs. A strong hand grabs my arm and pulls me back, hard. Charlie growls, and I stare into Jessup's light blue eyes. His cologne burns my nose, the harsh scent making my head swim. "Let go!" I scream, and Charlie growls and rears up on his hind legs, sinking his teeth into Jessup's forearm.

Metal flashes in my periphery, and I knee Jessup in the balls before he can aim the gun at Charlie. "Run, Charlie. Come on!" We sprint down the stairs, and I take us left, down a ramp, and to another set of stairs. Pounding footsteps echo on the concrete. It's deserted here, the tourists opting for the elevators. Another left should get us to the last set of stairs.

*Please, please, please...*

I can barely breathe, and when we turn, my heart seizes, and I clutch at neck of the t-shirt. Construction has the walkway blocked. An eight-foot-high metal gate is locked in place, and there's no way I can climb it. We're trapped. Charlie's low growl has me whirling around, and my gaze locks onto the gun pointed right at me.

"Ms. Phillips. It's been a long time."

Charlie growls again, and Jessup shifts his aim. "No!" I wrap my body around Charlie, whispering in his good ear. "Find Ripper, buddy. Go now. You have to *go!*" I end the command on a scream and slap his flank, and the dog bolts through a small gap in the chain-link fencing.

Springing up, I launch myself at Jessup, trying to force his hands skyward so he can't shoot at Charlie. But the scent of his cologne is too much, and I retch, stumbling back, and then sinking to my hands and knees to heave up what little is in my stomach.

The world spins around me, and pain sparks across the back of my skull. Bile fills my mouth, something impacts my jaw, and now I taste blood. I can't see anymore. He's killing me. My head hits the ground, and my thoughts fuzz and slow.

*Charlie got away. I know Charlie got away.*

---

**Ripper**

Bits and pieces of conversation float around me. I'm moving, sitting, stuck. I can't breathe and clutch at my shirt until hands fumble for my shoulders.

"Rip. Stop!" Dax. His deep voice registers through my panic, and my body stills, even though I'm close to hyperventilating. "You're safe. We're out of there."

Ry's truck. I'm in the back seat with Dax, and the engine rumbles as Ryker accelerates onto Highway 99 towards downtown. "Where's Cara? And, fuck. Charlie?"

I remember Charlie in my lap, trying to get my attention, then shots, Cara's scream. "Ry? Where are Cara and Charlie?" I slam my fist into the back of his seat, and Dax grabs my arm.

"We don't know, brother. We ran down the stairs. They were both with us. I heard her footsteps, and Charlie was right next to you. But once we got to the garage, she bolted. Charlie took off with her."

"And you didn't go after them?" If Dax weren't blind, I'd probably punch him. My dog and my... I don't even know what Cara is to me. I just know I need her.

*"What's your name? Your real name?"*

*"They knew. The American. J.T. Richards."*

The horror in Cara's eyes. The shame.

I lunge for the window, rolling it down so I can stick half my head out, feel the wind on my cheeks. "They'll. Kill. Her."

Curling against the door, I try to make myself as small as possible. My head goes right to the worst-case scenario. Jessup and Parr torturing her. Violating her. Causing her as much pain as they can before they end her life.

I can feel every blow. Hear every taunt. Zaman's fists, Kahlid's whip. The rubber pipe on my feet, the brass knuckles to my back.

"Rip! Ripper!" Dax shakes me, but I can't respond. I'm locked deep inside my mind, Faruk's men holding me down. Laughing. Kicking. Using bottles. Their rifle barrels. Fists.

"Goddammit, Sergeant. Get yourself back here right fucking now!" Ry roars, but even his orders don't pull me out. I know I need come back. Know it's important. But all I can do it cover my head with my arms and pray that this time, they'll kill me.

MOVING AGAIN. An elevator. Thrown over a shoulder. Ryker. I can smell his soap. Along with a hint of honeysuckle. Dax's cane taps against the baseboards. Forcing my eyes open, I can see it sweep back and forth.

Beeps of an electronic lock.

"Oh, my God. What the flippin' flapjacks happened?" Wren asks as light footsteps rush towards us.

"Put me down, asshole," I grunt as I pound on Ry's back. "I'm not a sack of potatoes."

"Thank fuck." This from Dax, and as my feet touch the ground, I stumble into him. He's a solid wall—not as solid as Ry, but still pretty damn unmovable. "Whoa there, brother."

I don't have time for my messed up head, and grab onto Dax's arm. He stiffens, but then drops his cane and steadies me.

"You're safe, Rip. Ry's place is a fortress. No GPS signals in or out. No wifi, just the hardline. And there's a cyber-net over the whole top floor. It'll mask any GPS trackers."

"I have to find Cara," I wheeze. "Get outside..." Dax turns me towards the windows.

"Best I can do, brother."

I rest my palms on the glass, then my forehead. Sun warms my chilled skin, but there's still only ice flowing through my veins. Fuck. I wish Ry's windows opened. They're almost as large as the ones at my place. The ones someone shot at.

"You put in bulletproof glass at my apartment?" I ask Ry, only sparing him a glance before returning my focus to the city skyline.

He shrugs. "Couldn't afford to do it here when I moved in. But after what happened in Russia, I had them swapped out. Wasn't going to do anything less for you."

"Is anyone going to tell me what's going on here?" Wren

says. She's tiny. Barely reaches Ry's shoulders. Red hair, green eyes, freckles. If it weren't for her attitude, I'd think of her as Strawberry Shortcake. But she's fierce as fuck when she wants to be.

"They came after us," Ry says. "Shot up Ripper's windows."

"And?" Wren huffs as she wedges a hand on her hip and looks from Ry to Dax to me. "What about Cara? And I thought Ripper adopted a dog?"

The rage sparks, then catches flame, spreading out from my core until I whirl around, grab Ry's shoulder, and land a punch to his jaw. He doesn't move, and I rear back for another go until Dax grabs my arms. I growl an oath and shove him away, and he tumbles over the back of the couch, coming up on his feet and banging into the low table with two laptops and the remnants of a long, sleepless night: coffee mugs, protein bar wrappers, and crumpled pieces of paper.

"Calm the fudgesicles down right now before you destroy my equipment," Wren snaps.

I hear her, but Ry's next words fade away as I stare at one of the laptop screens. A man's photo sits next to a wall of text, and his eyes...I know those eyes. Pushing Ry, then Dax out of the way, I grab the laptop.

"Hey, get your hands off—"

"Wait, sweetheart," Ry says.

Sinking down onto the couch with the computer in my hands, I stare at the man—Jessup, according to the name under the photo—and will my broken brain to work.

*"As you can see, my compound is quite secure," Faruk says as he walks through the courtyard with Jessup.*

*"And him?"*

*Faruk chuckles. "Isaad is loyal. He knows what will happen to him if he fails me."*

*I lower my head. Jessup's eyes unnerve me. As if he knows some secret I don't.*

*"Do you have the transfer information?" Faruk asks.*

*"Here. See to it the money's in place within twenty-four hours of receiving the shipment."*

*"Watch your tone, Mr. Jessup. You are in my home, and you will be respectful." Faruk turns to me. "Isaad, when the latest sale is completed, transfer fifteen percent of the proceeds here."*

*"Yes, Amir Faruk, sir. Of course." With the paper clutched in my hand, I rush as quickly as I can back to my little office. Jessup...I don't know who he is, but I know he's a danger to me.*

"Rip?" Dax. He's keeping his voice low, but the familiar southern twang is enough to bring me back. "Rip, what is it?"

"I remember him. And I think I know what he wants." I set Wren's laptop back on the table and run a hand through my hair. *Breathe. You're safe. With your brothers. And you're going to find Cara and Charlie.*

"What?" Ry asks.

"Money. A lot of it. When you killed Faruk, you cut off a huge amount of Jessup's income. And there were," I rub the back of my neck, willing my jumbled memories to untangle themselves, "at least half a dozen transactions in process when he threw me into the well."

A puzzle piece clicks into place, then another, and another. But not enough to see the picture. To know what the hell to do next. I'm only certain of one thing.

"I need to do this alone, Ry." Wobbling to my feet, I face my two best friends—my family. "Where I'm going, I can't have you with me."

"Not a chance." He takes a step towards the door, but I shake my head.

"You don't understand—"

"Then explain it to me."

Rolling my eyes, I stalk over to him so we're only a few inches apart. "That's what I'm *trying* to do, asshole." Before I can, though, my phone rings. I forgot it was in my pocket, and Cara's name flashes across the screen.

"Are you okay, sunshine?" I ask.

"I'm afraid *sunshine* isn't going to be okay ever again unless you do exactly what I say." The thin voice holds a note of a sneer, and I grip the back of Ry's couch hard enough my knuckles turn white.

In my periphery, Ry motions to Wren, who darts over to her laptop and starts furiously typing.

"Jessup, what have you done to her? Where is she? And where's my fucking dog?"

The phone buzzes with an incoming video, and my vision tunnels as I stare at the screen. Cara's sitting on a dirty floor, her ankles tied, her wrists handcuffed around a yellow pipe coming out of the wall at an angle. Dried blood stains her chin, and one of her sleeves is ripped, exposing deep bruises on her arm. Her chest stutters with each breath, and another man—Parr, I'm assuming—holds a pistol to her head.

"What do you want?"

"Our money. All of it. That's four hundred million U.S. dollars. Along with another six hundred million of the late Amir's reserves. After all, it's because of you he's dead and our little *arrangement* is over." Jessup turns the phone and holds up a blurry image that might be Ryker outside of Faruk's compound. "Pretty sure you know this guy, Richards. Ryker McCabe? I wonder what the United States government would say if I sent them evidence McCabe and his team entered Afghanistan illegally, slaughtered at least a dozen men, and then executed one of our best weapons traffickers."

*Shit.*

"That picture's grainy as fuck, Jessup. And Ryker McCabe

would gut you like a pig if you tried to take him down." Wren's motioning for me to keep them talking, but they're too smart to let themselves be traced—unless they're ready for us to come at them with everything we have. "I can get your money. But only if you let Cara go."

He laughs. "We'll consider letting her go once we get our money. You have twelve hours. I'm texting you the account number now. For every million missing after the twelve hour mark, you'll hear Ms. Phillips scream."

The video refocuses on Cara, and Parr flicks open a switchblade, holding it to her exposed inner arm. She chokes behind the gag, her already pale skin turning bone white, and tries to pull away, but he has his other hand clamped down on the back of her neck. A drop of blood wells at the tip of the knife, then trails down her arm.

Every part of me wants to shut down. To let the panic take over. But Cara needs me. The terror and confusion in her eyes shatter my heart into pieces, and the way she's breathing...I don't like it. Cracking my knuckles, I take a slow breath as I focus on her, hoping she can somehow see me on the tiny screen ten feet away. See my eyes and know I'm coming for her.

"Jessup, if you hurt her, I'll cut off each one of your fucking fingers before I feed them to you. Then your dick. Then, for good measure, I'll feed you Parr's dick too."

"I don't think so," he says, the screen still focused on Cara's terrified face. "If we so much as hear a whisper, see you or McCabe or any of his team, we'll expose all the evidence we have against you. I hear Guantanamo is a fucking party these days." Jessup moves the phone again so all I can see is his self-satisfied smirk. "Twelve hours, Richards."

"Wait! I'm not doing a damn thing until I talk to Cara. Put her on. Now."

With a roll of his eyes, Jessup brings the phone over to her, then rips the gag from her mouth.

"Ripper," she rasps, then starts to retch, leaning over as best as she can and vomiting on Jessup's shoes. He gives her a kick to her hip, and her entire body jerks.

"I'll fix this, sunshine. I promise."

She looks so weak and shaky when she finally raises her head, and her brown eyes are bloodshot and swollen. "You can't. Find Charlie. I told him to go home." Her tears turn to full-on sobs, and the words escape between them. "Tell him he's a good dog. Tell him for me."

"Cara! No. Don't think—" The call disconnects, and the black screen mocks me. She's going to die. Even if I do exactly what Jessup wants, they can't keep her alive. As soon as I transfer the money, they'll kill her. She knows their faces. Their secrets.

The time flashes on the screen. Before eleven tonight, Cara's going to die, and I won't be able to live with myself anymore. She was my only hope of finding a shred of valor left in this broken body, and now...that hope is gone.

# CHAPTER TWENTY-SEVEN

## Ripper

I HAVE to get out of here. Outside. Back to my apartment. Find Charlie. Then go somewhere I can be alone. Wren's still at her laptop, muttering to herself like she's about to send that damn computer to the principal's office, and Ryker claps a hand on my shoulder.

"Sit down, Rip. Let Wren work her magic."

I duck out from under his grip and head for the door. "No. Keep working. Find out where she is. I'll call you in a couple of hours. But what I have to do now...I have to do alone."

I'm already out the door and five steps down the hall when Dax calls my name. The strain in his voice—I can't ignore it, despite knowing any delay could mean Cara's life.

"Don't try to stop me, Dax. And I swear to fuck, if Ry picks me up again—"

The corner of Dax's mouth twitches. "He won't." Shoving his hands into his pockets, he leans against the wall, somehow managing to look right at me, even though I know he can't see more than a fuzzy outline. "But you're going to listen for five minutes before you take off on your own."

"Two."

"Fine. Two." Dax mutters something under his breath that might be, "Stubborn bastard," then falls silent for a moment. "I almost didn't call him."

"What?"

A few months ago, Ry walked into my office. Hadn't seen him..." He chuckles. "Well, I hadn't *seen* him since a few days before he escaped Hell. But after he got me out, I remember him talking to me on the medevac. But then he bailed. Never came to see me in the hospital, never returned my calls. We didn't speak for six years. When he showed up in Boston three months ago, I kicked him out of my office. And a couple of hours later, the asshole followed me to my gym where I beat the crap out of him."

"Really?"

Dax pulls his folded cane from his pocket, tosses it in the air, and catches it easily. "Everyone underestimates the blind man. Plus, I'm faster. Always have been." Taking a few steps towards me, he reaches out and clasps my forearm, his palm over the new tattoo. "Point is, after Ry got back from Russia with Wren and they were about to move out here, I told him to call me. Maybe we could salvage something of our friendship. And when he did? I ignored him."

"The two of you always were the stubbornest sons of bitches on the planet." The short, rough laugh isn't much, but it feels good. Almost normal. But the feeling only lasts a few seconds before I blink and see the terror in Cara's eyes.

Dax rubs the back of his neck and shakes his head. "You're giving us a run for our money." After a beat, he continues. "Look, I'm not trying to stop you. But you're not alone now, Rip. You have friends. Family. We can help."

"Dax, I don't remember half of what Faruk made me do. It's blank. Ry's memory tricks? I knew 'em all. Still do. I remember every minute after we landed back in the States. But before? It's this dark hole that's going to pull me down so deep, I might not come out again. I'm pretty damn sure all those secrets are locked in my head because they're so awful, I can't face them."

I blow out a breath. Despite how scared I am, admitting my fears to Dax turns the massive weight on my shoulders into something lighter. Something I can almost carry. "I can't delve into all that shit in the middle of Ry's apartment. I need to find Charlie, and I need to do this next part alone."

With a nod, Dax extends his hand. When I take it, he pulls me in for a quick clap on the back, and I hold on. "Just promise me one thing, Rip."

I know what he's going to say, and I head him off. "I won't go after them alone. The minute I have what I need, I'll be back. I promise."

At the top of the stairs, I hear his reply. "Come back safe, Rip. That's an order."

---

**Cara**

I can't stop shaking. My arms ache, and I have to keep moving my fingers so they don't go numb. It's like a sauna in here, the sun beating against the walls, seeping through painted-over windows—the only light in here other than a bare-bulb lamp plugged into an extension cord.

But the worst part of where I am? The smells. This building feels huge, and it's definitely been abandoned for years. As Jessup dragged me out of the trunk of his car, up some stairs, and into this massive space, I saw a dead bird, at least three live rats, and something big...a raccoon or coyote or something, half-decomposed in the corner of the room.

The floor's coated with dirt, leaves, and God knows what else. The air's so thick, it makes it almost impossible to breathe, and at some point, Jessup took off his necktie, doubled it over, and used it to gag me. That awful cologne he wears? The tie's saturated with it, so much I can *taste* it.

I keep retching, and the only reason I haven't choked to death is that I don't have anything but a small amount of bile in my stomach. So far, I've been able to spit it out around the gag.

The incessant drum beat of my heart is getting faster and faster. I don't know what time it is or how long I've been here, but my meds didn't have time to kick in before I threw up the first time when Jessup grabbed me.

*Think.*

My captors left the room a few minutes ago, and I rest my temple against the angled metal bar. It's slightly cooler than the surrounding air, and it eases the pounding in my head. I can't get out of the handcuffs. This is some kind of material chute that exits the ceiling maybe fifty feet away and then disappears into the wall above my head. No gaps.

As soon as Ripper gives Jessup and Parr what they want, they'll kill me. I have to find some way out of here. Under the stench, there's a hint of seawater, and I think I can hear it lapping against the shore. But I could be five minutes or a couple of hours away from Pike Place. I passed out seconds after I saw Charlie wriggle through the gap in the fence.

A door bangs, and I suck in a sharp breath through my mouth, then immediately regret it. My stomach turns, and I struggle not to retch.

*No. Not Jessup. Not again.*

I can't handle any more of his disgusting cologne. But as I blink rapidly and try to focus, I find a small measure of relief.

Parr. As he approaches, I curl inward, trying to make myself as small as possible, though the way I'm bound leaves me little ability to move.

"Can't have you dying yet," Parr says. He sets a bottle of water next to me, then grabs my hair and turns my head so he can untie the gag. I make it a point to spit more bile on his shoes, and he grumbles something that might be "bitch." But then he twists the top off the bottle and holds it to my lips. "Drink."

Anything to get the taste of Jessup's cologne out of my mouth. I suck down half the bottle before he pulls it away. Panting, taking short, shallow breaths, I peer up at him and whisper, "Please. I need my meds. They're in my bag. My heart..."

His eyes widen for a split second. "We tossed your bag. You're going to have to calm down on your own."

"Doesn't...work like...that, asshole." The dark, disgusting space starts to spin around me, and I can't hold my head up any longer. Even if Parr uncuffed me right now, I couldn't run. I don't think I could even stand.

He crouches so we're almost level, and his voice softens— just a little. "We need you alive until Richards gets our money. I don't have your meds. Tell me what else to do."

My mind races, thoughts flying so fast, I can't pluck a single one from the garbage heap of my brain. And then it hits me. "Music. There's an app...on my phone. *BrainRadioWaves.* Helps..."

"I'm not that stupid, Caroline. Richards could track your phone's GPS. No way. It stays off until the deadline."

My tears lend a shimmer to the dirty, industrial space, and for a moment, it's almost pretty. *Think, Cara!*

All I want to do is feel normal. Stop my racing heart, my frantic thoughts. But I can't. I've failed. Everything I tried to do. Leland's probably dead—they wouldn't tell me. Ripper's going to die. Or go to prison, and that would kill him. And Charlie...

A gentle melody floats over the air, and I blink hard to dash away the tears. Parr holds his own phone up, the *BrainRadioWaves* app on screen. "This the right one?"

I nod, so grateful for this single act of kindness, I don't even protest when he ties the disgusting gag around my head again. Setting the phone a good twenty feet away—too far for me to have any hope of reaching it, he gives me one last glance as he stalks out of the room. "It's almost one, by the way. Ten hours left."

*Ten hours. I only have ten more hours to live.*

---

**Ripper**

I should have asked Ryker for the keys to his truck. Not that I've driven in more than six years. But it's supposed to be like riding a bike. Instead, I take off at a run for my apartment. The three miles pass in agonizing slowness. If we live through this, I'm going to start running again. Hardcore.

We.

The thought isn't lost on me. Cara's mine. Just as much as Charlie—but in a very different way. I need both of them back. Unharmed. Otherwise, I might as well give up.

Taking the stairs to my apartment two at a time, I'm so out of breath, I have to lean against the wall to enter my code. But once I'm inside, Cara's scent lingers. I can't stay here. Not after they shot up the windows. Bulletproof or not, they know where I live, but they also need me alive for the next ten hours.

Grabbing my ruck, I pack up my laptop and power supply, then add a black t-shirt, a pair of black pants, and my shitkickers. I'm getting her back, no matter what, and once it's dark, I need to be able to blend in.

I'm almost out the door when I see the shirt she wore to bed folded on top of the pillow. I strip out of my own shirt and replace it with the one she borrowed. Now her scent is all around me, and I can focus again.

I need privacy. Maybe Cara's apartment? It's not like those two assholes are going to go there looking for her. No. Too risky. A hotel room would do. As I push through the front door of the building, I freeze.

"You didn't *really* think he was going to let you do this alone, did you?" West asks. He leans against the passenger door of a fully restored 1954 F-150 Ford pickup.

"Yeah. I kinda did. I was pretty fucking clear."

West holds up his hands. "I'm not here to get in your way. Think of me as your chauffeur. Your very well-trained chauffeur. Who's armed." He nods towards his hip and I take stock of his outfit.

"Seriously? Never pictured you for a Hawaiian shirt kind of guy."

His eyes hold little humor as he shakes his head. "You know a better way to hide a sidearm when it's hot as fuck in Seattle? Trust me. This was my best option. Even if Cam nearly laughed herself right off her chair when she saw me."

As much as I want to tell him to go home, I don't have a vehicle. And outside of the five mile perimeter around my apartment where I walk every day, I don't know my way around the outskirts of the city. "Fine. The call came ninety minutes after Cara bolted. So, they're probably not right in the downtown core. But Charlie might be. Head towards Green Lake. That's where I walked him yesterday."

I slide into the passenger seat and open the laptop as West turns the engine over. Five minutes later, I've pulled up the data on Charlie's tracking chip. "Shit. Never mind. Pike Place. Now."

West slams on the brakes, executes a quick three-point turn, and ten minutes later, starts down the hill towards the busiest public market in the country. The chip's GPS isn't the most accurate, but we're close. "Let me out, then circle the block a couple of times," I say as I reach for the door handle.

"You're not going to rabbit on me, are you, soldier?" He keeps his tone light, but when I meet his gaze, his icy blue eyes tell me he's not going to take any shit. A car behind us honks, and West sticks his arm out the window to motion them to go around.

"I was wrong." Squeezing my eyes shut for a long second, I see Cara's face and hear the tremble in her voice. "I can't do this alone. But, there's a lot of baggage between me and Ry and Dax. He was right to send you. I'll be back."

West's nod is all I need to hop out and jog down the hill to the market.

*Too many people.*

My heart starts pounding so hard, I can hear it, even over the din of the crowd, and I wipe my damp palms on my jeans.

*Stay focused. Charlie and Cara need you.*

I weave among the stalls, scanning all around me. Back out to the street, down to the corner, and my panic rises even higher until three loud barks have me whirling around.

Charlie bounds towards me, and I crouch down to wrap my arms around him. "Good boy. So good. You tried to help her, didn't you?" He licks my cheek, then yips at me, grabs the hem of my t-shirt in his mouth, and starts to back away slowly.

"Charlie, let go." He does, but keeps backing up, yipping at me the whole way. "Fuck. You want me to follow you? Okay. Go."

The second I give him permission, he takes off, and I have

to run to keep up. Back through the market to a set of stairs, all the way down, to the right, and then he wriggles through an opening in an eight-foot-tall chain-link fence and sits.

"Really?" I'm about ready to tell him to come back to me when I notice what he's sitting in front of. Vomit. And next to him...red smears. Blood. I'm up and over the fence in thirty seconds, and land in a crouch. The strap from Cara's bag lies against the wall, and as soon as I pick it up, Charlie barks again and takes off.

"If you know where she is, you're getting nothing but steak for the rest of your life," I mutter as I follow him. This place is a maze. Up a ramp and then to another set of stairs that lead all the way down to the street—at least three floors. He stops at a garbage can, barks at me, and paws at the metal.

"You want me to stick my hand in *there*?" Still, Charlie hasn't steered me wrong yet, so I grab the rain-proof lid and twist, hard. The metal clatters to the ground, and the first thing I see is Cara's bag. "Steak might be overkill, but you're definitely getting all the hamburger you can eat," I say as I pull out the bag and check the contents.

Wallet, pill case, notebook, pen, battery pack, tissues, and water bottle. All intact.

Charlie whines, grabs the corner of the bag, and pulls gently. "Go on. I'll follow you, buddy." We come to a stop at a parking lot, and he goes right to a dark spot on the pavement. More blood. "They were here, huh? Is this where they took Cara?"

I swear this dog understands English. I wrap my arm around his solid body and bury my face in his neck. "We're going to find her. I promise."

HALF AN HOUR LATER, West pulls up to Hidden Agenda's warehouse. I texted Ry the address of the parking lot, and Inara's guy, Royce, is helping Wren by checking the traffic cameras all around the area.

"What do you need from me?" West asks as I plug in my laptop at the conference table.

"Get Charlie some water? Otherwise..." I stare at the screen, my stomach in knots and a cold sweat breaking out over the back of my neck, "unless you know how to unlock all these memories buried in my fucked up head..."

"No, but I've got my own horrors up here." West taps his temple as he sets a bowl down for Charlie. Ambling over to the coffee pot, he starts spooning grounds into a filter. "Including more than I'd like about how to do...what Faruk did to you. I'm going to touch base with Ry. You need me, I'm here."

West slips outside, and soon the only sounds are Charlie's quiet breathing, the *drip, drip, drip* of the coffee brewing, and my fingers on the keys.

# CHAPTER TWENTY-EIGHT

**Ripper**

FIDDLING WITH THE EARBUD, I tap the keyboard to activate comms. "Wren?"

"Gotcha. What do you need?"

Dropping my head into my hands, I give up all sense of pride, and go for honesty instead. "I don't know where to start."

It's been two hours. And the only thing I have to go on is that fourteen character code I added to every single transaction I ever made. I've traced fifty of them so far, but every trail leads nowhere.

"I only found three accounts when I was looking into Faruk's transactions. One was old account. Someone created it a year or so before you, uh, left Hell." She clears her throat, and I think I hear her murmur something off comms. "That's what we used to set you up with everything in Seattle. The account had been earning interest for so long, it had almost two million in it. The second one—that one was created the day after Joey arrived at the compound, and had a balance of sixty thousand dollars. And your code attached to the transfer. When I asked her about her personal finances, she said she had that much at a brokerage account. That ring any bells?"

"Shit. Yeah. I was going to find a way to get it to her family. Eventually."

"I'll send you everything I have on that transfer. It came from half a dozen different sources. Maybe one of them will lead you somewhere."

"Thanks." I want to ask her if she's found anything about Cara's location, but she'd have led with that.

"Ripper?" Her voice softens. "We'll find her. Royce identified twenty-five cars traveling on Alaskan Way during the time we *think* Cara was taken. We've eliminated four of them so far. We won't give up on this. I promise."

*I promise.*

Ryker told me what those words mean to her. Through the lump in my throat, I thank her again and close comms. Thirty seconds later, Wren's info flashes up on my screen. I stare at the lines of code, the account numbers, the dates and times, and pull up a calendar.

"Please," Joey whispers. "You can't just make me disappear."

But I did. Closing my eyes, I let my fingers rest lightly on the keys.

*Think. It's all muscle memory.*

I moved money for Faruk every few days. Invested it. Watched the markets. Codes and passwords start to come back to me. "Paper. I need paper."

West is on the climbing wall. I'm not sure the man ever sits still unless he's on a mission. With no idea where the fuck anything is in this place, I open up Cara's bag and pull out her notebook. "Sorry, sunshine," I say quietly as I undo the elastic cord and flip through the pages.

*Afghanistan. Their "friend." Has contacts everywhere. Runs guns, missiles, drugs, and people.*

*J.T. Richards. American. Works for the guy in Afghanistan.*

*Jessup and Parr want a bigger cut. They're going to threaten to tell their superiors about Richards. If they do, the Special Forces will blow the guy off the map.*

Cara's notes. Everything she overheard the night that changed her life. Turning the pages, I read every line until I come to what happened in Tulsa.

*Jessup found me through the pharmacy. Ordering all three of my prescriptions together was too easy to trace. He grabbed me when I was asleep, dragged me to the balcony, and tried to throw me over. He said he was sorry. Sorry? Really? I don't even know who this Richards is. Or how to find out. I was so lucky. I should have died, not just broken my arm and ended up with a concussion. Leland*

A few pages later, I find a detailed accounting of every penny she's spent.

*New identity - Cara Barrett: $1500*
*Backup identity - Carrie Barstow: $1500*
*Doctor (Leland's friend): $2000*
*Bus ticket to Seattle: $212*

All of it. Her meds. The deposit on her apartment. Rent. Clothing from Goodwill. The occasional bottle of wine. Drinks with someone named Lindsey.

"Wren?" As I wait for her to respond, I page to the end of Cara's notebook and start writing down all the various banks I can remember.

"Go," she says.

"There's a name in Cara's notebook that might be something. She got a call from a Leland Steel a couple of days ago. It spooked her. I started looking into the guy, but then everything went sideways." After I rattle off this Leland's number, I disconnect without signing off and keep writing.

I have to remember. Everything. If I don't, Cara's dead. And I can't let that happen.

---

WEST BRINGS back burgers and fries at 5:00 p.m. Cara's been gone for six hours now, and every minute that passes, my anxiety climbs higher.

I remember now. Most of it, anyway. All the women I made disappear. All the shipments of guns, heroin, opium, and cocaine Faruk financed.

Three hundred million and change. That's all I've been able to account for, but every few minutes, I find another cache. I can do this.

"You managing, Rip?" West asks as he sits across from me and unwraps a double cheeseburger.

"Haven't offed myself yet."

"Say anything like that again, I'm calling Ry." With the burger halfway to his mouth, West pins me with a stare that could melt glass.

SEALs are the scariest fucks in the world. There's something that happens to you in BUD/S. Had a few friends who were SEALs before Hell. I don't know if they're even still alive, but they all got that same look in their eyes.

"Calm down, frogman. It's a joke. You remember those, right?"

West raises a brow at his shirt. "If I didn't, do you think I'd be wearing this monstrosity?"

"Good point." Reaching for my own burger, I pause. Are they feeding Cara? Why would they? I give serious thought to tossing the whole thing in the trash, but she needs me to be at my best.

"So?" He's not going to let this go. I can hear it in his voice.

"You want the truth? If I had a time machine, could go back six years, and find a way to kill myself before Faruk started in on me, I would. But since no one bothered to invent something like that while I was being drugged and brainwashed and beaten, the only thing I can do is try to make up for all the bad shit he had me do. And get Cara back so I can tell her how fucking sorry I am that I ever got her into this."

The burger tastes a lot like dust, but it's fuel. And once Cara's back with me—and feels up to it—I'm taking her out to the best fucking restaurant in Seattle.

West stares off over my shoulder as he chews and swallows, then meets my gaze again. "I watched that fucker die."

"Faruk?" I don't even want to say his name, but if I don't, it gives him more power in death than he should have ever had in life.

"Yeah. Graham and I were on Alpha Team. Infiled with Ry. He headed for a barn. Some dog trapped inside."

At my feet, Charlie's dreaming, and I reach down and give his chest a rub.

After a swig of water, West continues. "We killed twelve of his men. I took down ten. Graham got the other two. Kid never saw much combat. I try to protect him when I can."

"He's the one who looked like he was eighteen?" I don't remember a lot from the first couple of days after they rescued me. Faces. Panic. Pain.

West grins. "Yeah. He's twenty-six. But you'd never know it."

"Holy shit, really?" I'm starting to feel every one of my forty-two years.

"Really." The light leaves West's eyes—not that there was much there to begin with. "When we found Faruk's office, he was holding a kid hostage. Maybe eighteen? Twenty? Had a knife to his throat. Told us he'd kill the boy if we took another step." West shakes his head. "And for a second...maybe two...we hesitated. The kid looked terrified. But as Graham lowered his sidearm, the kid pulled one of his own."

West runs a hand through his hair. "I put a bullet through his heart. And Faruk didn't even flinch. He was one sick-ass son of a bitch. Whatever he made you do, Rip, it wasn't your fault. The sooner you accept that, the sooner you'll get your life back."

---

## Cara

It's been hours. At least with the music playing, my brain isn't totally useless. My heart races, I can't breathe easily, and everything hurts, but a few of the thoughts playing tag in my head slow and solidify from time to time.

I fell asleep for a few minutes, and when I woke up, I was half-bent over, my fingers totally useless. But my lapis pendant was dangling from my neck, and it was all I could see. The blue stone and the wire wrapped around it.

*"You need to be able to protect yourself, Caro,"* Leland says as he *pours rubbing alcohol over the bullet wound to my thigh.*

I took his advice to heart. Learned how to shoot, how to find the prescriptions I need on the streets, and how to pick locks.

It takes me forever to rock up to my knees so my neck and hands are close to the same level. My legs are numb, as are my fingers. But if I do nothing, I'll die here. Seconds after I manage to grab the pendant and pull hard enough to break the clasp, the door across the room bangs open.

*Shit. No.*

I scramble to hide the pendant and chain in my fist.

Jessup stalks over to me, Parr on his heels. "Lover boy hasn't given us more than a quarter of what we asked for," he says with a sneer. "Time for a little motivation."

*Oh God.*

Clenching my hands as hard as I can, I brace for whatever they're going to do to me. Jessup flicks open his pocketknife, while Parr holds my phone. I swear, regret swims in his hazel eyes. Just a hint of it. But maybe I'm so desperate to believe my death will be quick that I'm searching for any shred of decency.

"Smile for the camera, Caroline," Jessup says as the light on the back of my phone turns on. "Richards, you're running out of time. Your girl here only has four hours left, and she's not going to be happy about how she'll spend them if you don't get a move on."

Wrapping his fingers around my upper arm, Jessup deepens the earlier cut, and I whimper through the gag as the blood soaks into my shirt. And then he grabs my hair and slams my head into the pipe.

My vision swims, and it takes everything I have to keep my fingers curled tightly around my pendant. My moan doesn't travel far, the gag muffling the sound, but when Jessup wraps his hand around my neck, panic takes over and I gasp for air, thrashing to try to get away.

"Enough," Parr says as he taps the phone and the light turns off. "Can't kill her yet. He's going to want proof of life before he sends the last bit."

"Fine. You're too fucking soft, Parr." Jessup stalks back out of the room and slams the door behind him.

"More water?" Parr asks as he loosens the gag.

"Y-yes," I croak. It's so hot in this place, I've sweat through my t-shirt, and my heart still feels like it's going to explode out of my chest, even with the music playing.

I suck down the other half of the bottle as Parr holds it to my lips, and when he pulls it away, he stares down at me. "You know we're out in the middle of nowhere, right?"

"Figured." My hands ache from being clenched so tightly, and I just want him to leave me alone so I can try to get out of here. But that regret I thought I saw earlier? It's stronger now.

"I won't gag you again. Don't scream. If you do, Jessup will cut out your tongue."

"No screaming." I nod, which is a terrible mistake, as the whole room starts to spin. Parr steadies me with a hand on my shoulder, and I flinch, but then lean into him.

*Work him. You can use his pity.*

"Can you change the music?" I rasp. "There's one for...meditation." Letting a few tears escape down my cheeks, I peer up at my captor, letting him hear the desperation in my voice. "I need to find some peace before the end."

Parr sighs. "So you know."

"That he won't let me live? I've always known." I don't have to pretend to cry now. If I can't get out of these cuffs, I'm dead. And I'll never see Ripper again. Never get to hold him. Never get to tell him how very much I care about him.

Parr's whole face softens, and he trudges over to his phone and picks it up. "You want to say anything to Richards before the end? I can record a message for you. Nothing about us. If you try, I'll have to hurt you. But if you want to say anything personal?"

"Please...?" Keeping my gaze locked on the phone, I watch as he enters his passcode.

*Eight-seven-two-one-three-seven-nine.*
*Eight-seven-two-one-three-seven-nine.*
*Eight-seven-two-one-three-seven-nine.*

I say the numbers over and over to myself as many times as I can before Parr launches the video app and nods at me.

"Rip? I should have told you from the beginning. Who I

was. You made me feel so safe. Normal. And I ruined it all. I think I could have loved you. I wanted the chance to try. You're not broken. You're perfect. I'm so sorry."

My sobs make any other words I might want to say impossible, and Parr stops the video, then shifts the music to the meditation track I asked for. After he returns the phone to the table, he stares down at his feet. "It'll be quick. I'll do it myself. That's all I can give you."

The door slams a moment later, and I'm alone.

*Eight-seven-two-one-three-seven-nine.*

I did it. I remembered. Relaxing my fingers, I look up at the pendant clutched in my hands. "Please," I whisper as I start trying to unwind the metal wrapped around the stone. "Please let me live."

---

BY THE TIME I have the wire broken into two distinct pieces, my entire body's shaking and the sun's mostly down. The single bare bulb in the room doesn't help chase away the shadows from the pipe that falls over the handcuff locks, and I have to contort my entire body to be able to see what I'm doing. Not to mention manipulate the two pieces of wire with my wrists bound.

More than once, I give in to despair. This was a stupid idea, and if they catch me, my death won't be the quick, painless one Parr promised me. But then I think about Ripper. How he looked when he admitted what had happened to him. When we made love. When he left to take Charlie for a walk.

Relieved. Accepted. Happy.

I want to see him again. See all those emotions and more. And now that he's learned who I am, I want him to know the real me.

Wedging the first piece of wire into the lock, I hold my breath. Moment of truth. The second piece slides in next to it, and I whimper through a painful hand cramp, but manage to keep the makeshift lockpicks in place until it passes. Slowly, I maneuver them back and forth, hoping the constant tingling running up and down my fingers doesn't hamper my ability to feel the tiny tumblers move.

Ten seconds. Twenty. Thirty. And then...there's a click, and my right hand is free.

The pain of my arms falling to my sides after so long stretched over my head almost makes me cry out, but I bite my lip hard enough to draw blood. After I shove the two pieces of wire into the cup of my bra, I go to work on the rope around my ankles. I don't know how much longer I have before one of them comes to check on me, hurt me, or kill me. It's dark outside, so it has to be after nine.

Crawling over to Parr's phone, not confident my legs will support me yet, I enter his unlock code. Now what? I can't call the police. Who are they going to believe? A fugitive? Or two government agents? And I don't know Ripper's number. It's in my phone.

Parr's texting app is the only thing I recognize besides the app he downloaded for me, and I launch it.

There are dozens of messages. Mostly to Jessup. Oh, crap.

*Parr: I'm tracking her phone. She's at an apartment off of Latona.*

*Jessup: Send me the address. I have a sniper on standby.*

Then, half an hour later.

*Jessup: Got her. Some fucking dog almost took my arm off. She's still alive. Headed to the rendezvous point. She means something to Richards. We can use her to get our money, then kill her.*

I take a bunch of screenshots, find Parr's email app, and send them all to myself. If I don't get out of here alive, though, they won't help me.

*Think, Cara!*

It's too hard. My head aches, the throbbing getting worse every time I try to move. My heartbeat, so high for so long, starts skipping. *Shit, shit, shit.*

Using the wall for support, I stagger to my feet. There has to be a way out of this huge room besides the door Jessup and Parr keep using. Heading in the opposite direction, I stumble more than once, almost losing my grip on the phone.

My eyes don't want to focus for more than a second or two. The world around me pulses and shifts every time my heart goes into arrhythmia. The only other time this happened, I passed out and woke up in the hospital four hours later. If I lose consciousness here, I'm dead.

There! Up high on the wall, there's a vent I think I can fit into. The cover's gone, and cobwebs stretch across the space. Another angled pipe runs from the ceiling to a few feet below the vent, and if I can get up there, I might be able to pull myself into the ductwork.

Sliding the phone into my pocket, I put one foot on the pipe. My stomach lurches, but I force myself to take a slow, deep breath, and step up.

Another breath, and I reach up, sliding both arms, my head, and shoulders into the duct. It stinks like a dead animal—even more than the room below, but I can stand it if it leads me to safety.

Using the last remaining strength in my legs, I jump and wriggle forward. I want to cry when I feel my feet slip over the edge, and I start to slide on my stomach, only a couple of inches at a time, until I come to a bend.

This is harder. Contorting my body around the ninety degree angle leaves me panting, and I have to stop for a minute or I'll pass out. As I lie there panting, one thought pings in my head. *Parr called Ryker. How many Seattle numbers would there be in his call log?*

I can't reach the phone in this tight space, but if I can get out of the ducts, maybe I can find out.

Ten, maybe fifteen minutes later, I find another room, this one smaller than the one they kept me in, with a broken window that looks out over water. Lights from the city provide the only illumination, but it's enough to tell me I can get out. I just don't know how high up I am.

Carefully, I lower myself down, but fall the last few feet. I'm not far enough away. Jessup and Parr could have heard me. This might be my last chance. Running for the window, I climb over the sill and fall onto a corrugated metal roof five feet below.

A door bangs several rooms away, and I pull out the phone. *Eight-seven-two-one-three-seven-nine.*

Thank God my broken brain remembers something. There's only one Seattle number. "Please..." I whisper as I tap it and start to creep along the roof, hoping to find somewhere I can hide where they won't find me.

"McCabe."

"Help me," I whisper, but before I can say anything else, I hear Jessup. Too close.

"Find her! What the fuck were you thinking leaving your phone where she could get a hold of it?"

"Caroline? Cara?" Ryker asks. "Where are you?"

"There's evidence. In my email," I gasp as I stumble along the roof. I rattle off my email address and my password, but then my foot lands wrong on the uneven metal, and I go down, hard. The phone slips from my grasp and tumbles off the edge and onto a grassy slope that leads down to the water.

"No. God, no." I can't go after it. I'm more than twenty feet up. Instead, I crawl, as quickly as I can, until I see a long, sloped greenish pipe that looks like it angles *almost* down to the ground. It's at least ten feet across, fifty feet long, with huge, curved ventilation shafts at the end that look out over the water. The only problem? It's a ten foot drop to the pipe.

"Find her!"

The voice is too close, too angry, and if I don't move now, I might not get another chance. Saying a quick prayer, I squeeze my eyes shut and call up Ripper's face in my mind.

"Find me, soldier. Please."

And then I jump.

# CHAPTER TWENTY-NINE

**Ripper**

"GRAB your tech and let's go," West says as he hefts two large bags, one for each shoulder. His Hawaiian shirt is gone, replaced with a full complement of tactical gear.

I shoot him a look of disbelief. There's less than two hours left until Jessup and Parr are going to kill Cara, and I'm still more than twenty million dollars short. Each transaction is taking me twice as long as it should because I won't let them keep a cent of the money in the end. Not if Ry can find them and get to Cara. "I'm not going anywhere."

"Suit yourself." He cracks a half-smile. "Just thought you might want to be there when we take down those fuckers and save your girl."

I'm out of my seat, the laptop tucked under my arm, in half a second and racing after him as he heads for the back of the warehouse. "What the hell are you talking about?"

"Apparently, she got a hold of Parr's phone and found Ry's number. They're on Harbor Island. Ten minutes away." West bursts through the rear door of the warehouse and out into a parking lot, where he heads for a black van. "Get in the back and gear up. If the dog's coming, he better damn sure stay quiet."

I didn't even notice Charlie at my side, but the German Shephard is in the van before I am. "I don't have any gear."

As the engine rumbles to life, West turns from the driver's seat with an amused grin. "What the fuck do you think I've been doing for the past five hours? Everything you need is in that go bag."

Shit. He's right. Black fatigues, a black t-shirt, boots, a tactical vest, and enough weapons to take down a small army. Charlie lies down under one of the bench seats while I change, and West taps on the in-dash display. "We're on our way. Where are you?"

"Five minutes ahead of you," Ry says.

I pull a chest harness from the go bag and strap it on. "You have Cara on the phone?"

"No." A sigh carries over the connection. "I don't know what happened, Rip. She said, 'help me,' rattled off an email address and password—which, by the way, contained screenshots of a whole lot of Parr's incriminating text messages—and then I think she dropped the phone. They didn't take it from her. That's all I can tell you. The connection stayed open long enough for Wren to trace it. Hell, it's still open now. But all Wren can hear is the wind."

*Help me.*

Glancing at my phone, I blow out a breath when there aren't any new messages. I didn't tell Ry about the last video. The one where Jessup cut up her arm and slammed her head into a pipe. I transferred another ten million within seconds of seeing that and didn't bother with a tracer code.

"What's the plan?" I ask.

"Ask the guy driving," Ryker replies. "In the field, I don't do shit until he tells me. Pulling up to Terminal 18 now and going dark."

"So?"

West shoots me a look. "I found out where we were going exactly two minutes before you did. I've never been here before, and I don't know what the fuck we're dealing with. At this point, the plan is to take down Jessup and Parr without getting ourselves killed, find Cara, and get the hell out."

As soon as West stops the van next to Ry's truck, I'm out the door. "Charlie, stay here." He whines once, and I wrap my arms around him. "You can't come, buddy. It's too dangerous. But I'll be back with Cara. Soon."

Charlie sits, and I grab the go bag, close the door, and join West and Ry as they gather around a map spread out on the truck hood. "Wren pulled up photos of the inside of this place," Ry says. "The room they had Cara in is here, and the phone is here."

West narrows his eyes at the poorly lit map. "There's only one door out of that room. Unless she managed to subdue Jessup and Parr, she didn't use it. But see this?" He points to a line that starts in the third floor processing room and bends at a ninety-degree angle after twenty feet. "I think it's a ventilation shaft. If it was big enough for her to squeeze through, she'd come out in this smaller room here and could get onto the roof."

The NVGs West hands me are so much lighter than any night vision we had the last time I geared up, and I slide them on, adjust the magnification, and examine the corrugated metal roof on the side of the facility. "She's not there now."

Ry kneels, opens a black case resting on the ground, flips a couple of switches, and taps his ear. "Wren? Take her up."

"What the...?"

A drone rises from the case, wobbles slightly in front of our eyes, and then speeds off towards the facility. "New toy," West says. "Courtesy of Cam and Royce. Thermal imaging drone. Get out your laptop, Rip. Wren'll send the images directly to your screen."

It's an agonizing five minutes before the screen flashes with an incoming transmission. "Two heat signatures in the north-west corner," Wren says. "That's it. I took the drone around the whole building. Up and down all three floors. Cara's...not there."

No. She has to be. Or...she is and her body's no longer warm. I stumble back, my heart pounding. They killed her. I think...I think I might have loved her. Or at least, I was close to loving her.

"Ripper. Focus," Ry snaps. "Jessup and Parr are going to pay for this. All of it. What happened to you, what may or *may not* have happened to Cara. If she's dead, so are they."

I meet his gaze, then look to West. The SEAL pulls a knife from a sheath at his hip, turns it over in his gloved hand, and then slams it back into place. "They hurt one of us, they hurt all of us. My conscience is clear."

My phone vibrates with an incoming photo, and I tap the screen. Cara's tear-stained face comes into focus. Jessup holds the blade to her neck.

Another message follows almost immediately. Only two words.

*Time's up.*

West snorts. "They don't have her."

"What?" I whirl around to face him, not quite sure how he ended up behind me.

"Open the picture again."

When I do, he nods. "What's that in the corner there, geek?"

All I can see is Cara, but I squeeze my eyes shut for a second and then focus on the room behind her. "Sunlight."

"Yep. This was taken at least three hours ago. If they still had her, they'd show you a video. Reply. Stall."

*That last forty I owe you? Tucked away in an account only I have access to until Cara's free. But I just found another five accounts in Antwerp. Give me one more hour and you'll have all of your money and then some. I want her returned to the apartment you shot up this morning in sixty minutes, or no deal.*

I only have to wait a minute for another message to come in.

*You fuck with us, she'll die screaming. One hour.*

I shove the phone into one of my pockets, reach into the bag West packed for me, and pull out my knife. The one Ry used to kill Faruk. "We end this. Now."

"Hooah," Ry says as he holds out his fist.

West mirrors the motion. "Hooyah."

I haven't uttered the army battle cry in more than six years, but it rolls off my tongue like it's the most natural thing in the world. And maybe...it is. "Hooah."

---

THE DRONE TAKES another pass around the abandoned facility. "They're on the move," Wren says over comms. "Fast. Frantic."

West chuckles. "They're scrambling because they don't have a fucking clue where she is. This is going to be like shooting fish in a barrel."

Until he slams his hand against my chest seconds before I'm about to slip through a side door. I'm about to say something less than polite when he nods towards the floor and the small red laser light on one side of the jamb.

Ry and West snap on their NVGs and twist a little knob on

the side. After I put mine on, Ry reaches over and flicks that same knob, and...holy shit. Infrared. "I've got a lot of catching up to do," I mutter as I follow them through the door, stepping over the motion sensor and sweeping my gaze around the room.

"They're separating," Wren says. "Based on body mass, Jessup's heading for the roof and Parr's coming down. Straight for you."

Taking up flanking positions on either side of the stairwell, we wait. As Parr flies into the room, West crouches, grabs the man's legs, and flips him upside down and onto his back.

Parr stares up at the three of us. Ryker has his Beretta pointed at Parr's head, and I crouch down and press my knife to his throat. "Where is she?"

"I don't know. She got away. Jessup's tracking my phone—she took it—and we know she was on the roof at one point. We lost her after that."

"Give me a reason why I shouldn't slit your throat right now, asswipe. You hurt her. Repeatedly. And you left me in Afghanistan for years, let that sick fuck destroy everything I was."

The split-second realization that I care more about him hurting Cara than all the pain I endured at Faruk's hand hits me hard, but I shake it off and press the knife harder against his windpipe.

"Jessup called in backup. They'll be here in five minutes. Please. I don't want to do this anymore. I never wanted to kill Caroline in the first place. I *tried* to help her. Or at least, make her more comfortable. Jessup...he threatened my family."

"Your call, brother," Ry says.

"Um, guys?" Wren's voice isn't steady as she breaks in over comms. "There's an SUV approaching your location at high speed. Four heat signatures inside."

I slam my knife back into its sheath, grab Parr by the upper arms, and haul him up. "You get to live—for now. But only because we might need you before the end. If she dies, so do you."

Ryker pulls a pair of flex cuffs from one of his pockets and binds Parr's wrists behind his back. "Up the stairs, asshole. I know just the place to stash you."

West makes a sharp clicking sound, then gestures out the door, two fingers in the air. *We've got company.* Ry goes up, and I follow West until we reach the corner of the main building.

*Go left,* he signals, and I nod, the weight of my knife in my hand so familiar, and yet so foreign at the same time. Keeping low, I use a rotting fence as cover, moving almost soundlessly through the tall grasses. No one's used this place in a dozen years, if I had to guess. Peeling paint, crumbling walls...

Cement explodes just above my head, and I tuck and roll, then slither on my belly until I can take cover behind a large vent shaft maybe four feet high and easily that wide.

Tapping my comms, I whisper, "Base, got a visual?"

"One hundred yards at two-fifteen," Wren says.

I hope I remember how to shoot straight. The H&K submachine gun with its internal suppressor should be quiet enough, but I was always more of a close quarters guy. Dax, Gose, and Ry all beat my ass in sniper training.

"Eighty yards," Wren says quietly. "Approaching at a fixed angle."

*You're gonna regret that move, idiot.*

I can feel my heartbeat in my neck, the anxiety crawling up from my stomach to settle in my chest, but I can do this. For Cara. For myself. For Ry and West and this whole family of men and women who want me with them.

Drawing down on the shadow creeping towards me, I blow out a breath and squeeze the trigger. The shots land center mass, and the guy's down. Probably not dead if he's wearing body armor. Holstering the weapon, I leap over the decrepit fence and sprint for him, knife at the ready.

When I reach his prone form, he's clawing at his chest, the wind knocked completely out of him, but when he sees me, he tries to raise his gun.

My knife slides across his throat, severing his windpipe and his carotid artery like they're made of butter, and I've just killed a man. "Target down."

Falling back on my ass, I want to be sick, but a quiet series of pops behind me pulls me out of my panic. I race back to the main building, weaving back and forth to make myself a more difficult target.

"Pinned down on the top floor," Ry says in my ear. More pops echo from inside the building, too many to be from only one gun, and definitely not the sound of our H&Ks.

"How many?" I trade speed for stealth as I reach the rusty metal stairs, creeping slowly, testing each step.

"Three."

"Second target neutralized. And I disabled their vehicle." This, from West, whose voice is rougher than normal. "Headed to you now."

The gunfire doesn't let up as I climb, and at the top, a long, dark hallway looms ahead of me. Cobwebs hang from the ceiling, leaves cover the floor, and the stench of dead animals fills the air.

But floating on top of all that? Sweat. A lingering hint of harsh cologne, and gunpowder. Five doors in this hall, all yawning open, and I have to clear each room before I can get to Ry.

The first is nothing but broken down pallets. The second, an odd closet through which half a dozen pipes crisscross, some with shut-off valves on them. As I head for the third, a solid weight slams into me, taking me down to my knees. The knife tumbles from my hand, and the barrage of punches to my back leave me gasping for breath.

"Where's. My. Money?" Jessup hisses in my ear as he grabs my hair, yanks my head up, and then slams it back down. I see stars, and then he straddles me.

The flash of terror fades when a pistol presses to the back of my neck. He won't kill me. He needs me. "Where's Cara?"

Ry and whoever he's fighting continue to exchange gunfire, and then an explosion rocks the far side of the facility.

"She got away. You want the chance to find her, give me my goddamned money or I'll put a bullet in your brain."

I don't know what it is in his voice that makes me believe him, but I do. He doesn't know where she is, which means it's possible she's still alive.

"You have ten seconds, Richards. Or make peace with your God.

*Not a chance, asshole. I survived six years of hell, and I'm getting my fucking happy ever after.*

"You want your blood money? Fine," I spit out. "I just need my phone, shithead. Reaching for it now." The barrel presses harder against my skull, and I dig into one of the pockets of my tactical vest. "Got to see to initiate the transfer. Or are you just *that* stupid?"

The pressure lets up as he rises, and he mutters, "I should kill you anyway. Get the fuck up."

Slowly, I get to my knees, then stand, keeping my back to him. "Sixty million coming at you in three, two—" Whirling around, I punch Cara's kitty cat brass knuckles into Jessup's forearm, sending the gun flying across the hall. My next punch pierces his cheek, the cat ears digging into the soft flesh just above his jaw.

He howls in pain, and I sweep his legs out from under him,

aim a swift kick to his mid-section, and pick up my knife. "You're the worst of humanity, Jessup. Profiting off the suffering of others. You *knew* what Faruk was doing to me. You fucking *saw* me there and did nothing. Didn't tell my brothers. Or JSOC. You know what he did to me?"

When he doesn't answer, I kick him again, and he curls on his side in the fetal position. "Do. You. Know?"

"Fuck you, Richards. I don't care." Jessup pulls a small pistol from an ankle holster, and as he fires, his aim so far off it's almost comical, I drive the knife through his heart.

"No. Fuck you."

# CHAPTER THIRTY

**Cara**

THE GUNFIRE STOPPED a few minutes ago. I should try to climb out of my hiding place, but I can't move. Sliding down the pipe was easy. Stopping? Not so much. Everything hurts. In order to wedge myself into this broken-down industrial fan hood, I had to wade out into the murky, frigid water of the Duwamish. I fell over when my foot caught in a soft patch of mud, I lost both shoes, and I'm still soaked to the skin.

"Cara!"

*Ripper.* The voice is so faint, I wonder if I'm imagining things.

But then I hear it again. Along with barking. Charlie. He found Charlie.

"Here," I try to call, but my teeth are chattering so badly, I barely make a sound. "Ripper!" My heart pounds and I feel like my head's about to explode, but I use the metal walls to try to push myself up. I almost make it. But my legs cramp from crouching in this position for so long, and I collapse, one hand clawing at the edge of the fan housing.

I try again. "Ripper...here..."

Flashlights sweep over the area, and Charlie's barking gets louder until it's right below me. But my hands are wet, and I lose my grip and fall onto my ass with a tiny yelp.

"Help me up," Ripper says, and three seconds later, his face appears above me. "Thank God. Cara? Sunshine, can you take my hand?"

"Uh-huh." I'm so cold, but he'll keep me warm. All I want is his arms around me. I'll be fine if I can just get to him.

"Hold my legs," he calls behind him, and then wriggles forward until half his torso's inside the fan housing. "Push up, Cara. Just a foot or two. I'll take it from there."

I can barely see his eyes in the darkness, but he's so confident, I don't hesitate. My thighs tremble, and a sharp pain snakes across my chest, stealing my breath, but I grit my teeth and inch upwards until Ripper can grab me under the arms.

"Pull," he calls. I don't know who's out there, but he wouldn't be so calm if Jessup and Parr were with them. Wrapping my arms around his neck, I hold on for all I'm worth as we slide up the shaft and onto the edge of the housing. And then he's trying to loosen my grip on him, and I whimper. *No. Don't let go.*

"Cara, sunshine, look at me." As his warm hand cups my cheek, I meet his gaze. "I'm standing on Ry's back. I need you to swing your legs around so you're sitting on the housing. Once I'm back on the ground, I promise, I'll hold you as long as you want. As long as you let me."

I'm still shivering so violently, I can't answer him, but I nod, and he snakes an arm around my back, then helps me spin around.

Ryker's bent over, his hands braced on his thighs, knee deep in the water. Another man, one I don't recognize, stands a few feet away out of the water with Charlie pacing around him.

Jumping off the platform Ry made for him, Ripper lands with a splash, then straightens and holds his arms out to me. "Just let yourself drop. I'll catch you."

He does just that, crushing me against him, and I start to cry, even though I didn't think I had any tears left. "You're freezing," he says, and after he's back on dry ground, crouches down with me cradled to his chest. "Charlie, get over here."

The dog presses himself against me, and I'm sandwiched between two warm bodies, safe. "Can't breathe," I gasp. "Heart."

"Ry?" Ripper says. "In the back pocket of my vest, there's a purple case. Get me one of the white pills."

*He has my meds.*

When he holds a metal flask to my lips, I manage a healthy sip of water to wash down the pill that will calm my racing heart.

Charlie licks my cheek, and then the other man, the one I don't know, clears his throat. "I don't want to interrupt this touching reunion, but we set off a grenade six minutes ago, there are five dead bodies in that mill, and we have an army intelligence officer tied up in the van. Can we get out of here now?"

"Let's go, sunshine," he whispers to me, and I nod, then rest my cheek on his shoulder.

As he carries me to a four-door pickup truck, no one says a word. The other man climbs into a black van, while Charlie jumps up into the backseat of the pickup.

"Is it o-over?" I stammer as Ryker pulls a black bag out of the truck bed and throws it on the passenger seat.

Ripper accepts the blanket Ryker hands him and tucks it around me. "It's over. It's finally over."

I ONLY REMEMBER pieces of the ride back to Ripper's apartment and how I ended up in his bed. The tension radiating off of him as he carried me into the elevator. The warm water in the tub. His naked body against mine as he washed away the dirt and blood and that terrible cologne Jessup wore that clung to me the whole time. Bandages to my upper arm. A soft t-shirt, thick socks. A man—a doctor—who came to examine me, assuring me a dozen times there would be no record of his visit. A pill to help me sleep, another for the pain, and an order to call him if I had any nausea.

Now, we're snuggling together under the weighted blanket with Charlie pressed up against my side.

I'm so tired, but I need to know what happened. Ripper's quiet. Almost like he's retreated into his own head.

"Talk to me," I say softly.

"You should sleep." He brushes a lock of my still-damp hair away from my swollen cheek. "After the meds the doc gave you, I'm amazed you haven't passed out already."

"Worried about you." He's not wrong. My words feel like they weigh a hundred pounds, and I have to concentrate on every syllable.

"You're safe. The rest...we can talk about the rest tomorrow." Ripper brushes a gentle kiss to my lips. Maybe it's the drugs or even wishful thinking, but there's the promise of so much more in that kiss. Maybe even forever.

I don't want to let him off the hook. He needs something. Forgiveness? Reassurance? Acceptance? If I weren't so banged up, exhausted, and still lightheaded from my heart going haywire for half the day, I'd give him all three—and more.

Instead, I wriggle a little closer and whisper, "You're safe, too."

## Ripper

My phone rings a little before 7:00 a.m. With Cara in my arms, I slept almost six hours straight. In my own bed. She was so chilled, I didn't even open the balcony doors. Reaching back to the bedside table, I check the screen. Ry.

"Hang on a minute," I say quietly. Easing myself out of bed, I freeze when Cara makes a small noise and Charlie raises his head, but I motion for the dog to stay with her, and he does. He's getting a steak today. Jessup's backup found our van and let him out, but must have bolted, because there isn't a scratch on him.

By the time we got outside with Parr, he was barking like crazy close to where we found Cara. If he wasn't a police dog in his last life, he should have been.

I'm only wearing a pair of loose shorts, and when I slip outside onto the balcony, it almost feels like fall. A cool breeze raises goosebumps all along my arms. "What is it?" I ask.

"Trevor's landing in two hours. He wants to meet with you and Cara at eleven. Along with Commander Austin Pritchard from JSOC."

Tension stiffens my shoulders, and I stare out at the lake. "You trust this guy? I mean, fuck. He helped get me out. But according to JSOC..."

"Jackson Richards died six years ago," Ryker finishes for me. After a long pause, he sighs. "Dax vouched for the guy. And we'll both be there. No one's taking you into custody. Not without going through us."

"That's suicide, Ry." Running a hand through my hair, I wish I'd opened up to him a long time ago. Shared even a fraction of what happened to me. "If that's what Pritchard's here to do, you let him do it. Understand?"

"Rip—"

"No. You've been protecting me since we landed back in the States. Don't think for a minute I don't appreciate every fucking thing you've done. Talked to the church staff? Set me up in this apartment? Gave me enough of that bastard's blood money so I didn't have to work until I was ready? Hell, even the shrink, the doctor last night who treated Cara. But you will *not* throw your life away for me."

"We're brothers, Rip. You know that." Ryker's voice takes on a strain I haven't often heard since I got back. "Dax and I...we'd die for you."

My eyes burn, and I sink down onto the single chair in the corner of the balcony. "I know. And I'd do the same for either of you. But you and Dax—you deserve that double wedding. Think of Wren. And Evianna. Whatever happens today, don't interfere. Promise me."

"You know I can't—"

"Promise me. Or I'm hanging up right now and I'll disappear. Forever."

"Fucker," he mutters. "I promise. Dax and I will stand down."

"Then I'll be there. Cara's still asleep. If she doesn't want to go, will you...?"

"Cara who?"

I try three times before I can force a response over the lump lodged in my throat. "You're... I... Fuck it. Ry, you and Dax? You're family. I...uh..."

"Say it. I can't. Only to Wren."

"Love you, brother."

"Same here, Rip."

WHEN I SLIP BACK INSIDE, Charlie's pressed up against Cara like he's going to guard her from the whole world. I ease a hip onto the bed and stroke a hand over his side. "You're pretty amazing, buddy."

"Ripper?" Cara starts to stretch, then winces. "Shit."

"What hurts?"

After a groan, her eyelids flutter open. "Everything."

I lean over Charlie to cup her cheek. "The doc left one more Vicodin. You want it?"

"No." She covers my hand with hers, and the look in her eyes, fuck. I want to see that look every day for the rest of my life. But there are so many secrets between us, and all her pain...it's my fault. "I don't like how they make me feel. And I'll sleep all day if I take it."

"What can I do?" Anything she asks, I'll give her. Even if she begs me to take her home and never see her again.

"Talk to me."

Charlie hops off the bed and pads to the door. That dog is a mind-reader, and as soon as I can get to a grocery store, he's getting anything he wants. For the rest of his life. "I have to take him out. But I'll bring you back a latte. Then, I'll tell you anything you want to know."

TWENTY MINUTES LATER, I code myself back into the apartment to find Cara sitting up in my bed, a half-empty bottle of water and her pill case on the side table. She's staring at her little notebook, her eyes wide.

"Hemp milk latte with vanilla?" I say as I hold out the cup along with a white paper bag. "And an apricot scone."

"You did all this?" she asks. Tipping the notebook, she shows me the page she's reading.

Transaction after transaction, account numbers, amounts, locations, and my recollections of what Faruk was buying or selling for every single line. Evidence of all the terrible acts I committed for the man who nearly destroyed me.

I can't manage another sip of my own cold brew, so I set it on the breakfast bar and head for the windows. I need to see the sun. "Yes. All of it. And more. Over six years, I probably moved three billion total. And every single transaction added more blood to my hands."

"Ripper." Cara hisses out a breath and I turn to find her standing. Her steps are uneven, and I start to tell her to get back into bed, but she levels me with a single arched brow. "That's not what I was asking. Or why." When she reaches me, she winds her arms around my waist, and I stiffen until she rests her head against my chest. "You did all of that, dug up all of those memories, to keep me alive."

"I would have done anything to keep you alive."

"What happens now?" she asks.

"Now...we have a decision to make."

# CHAPTER THIRTY-ONE

### Cara

RIPPER HAS to help me with almost everything. Washing my hair. Fastening my bra. And he never leaves my side, not even when tell him I can put my socks on by myself.

I know why. He's terrified after we meet with Trevor and the JSOC commander, he'll never see me again. So am I. But he's going, and I'm not letting him do this alone.

Ryker and Dax are sitting in my living room waiting for us because I wasn't going anywhere without my own clothes—and underwear.

None of my injuries are serious. In a day or two, I'll be back to normal. But I'm bruised from head to toe, and my heartbeat is still a little out of sorts. Standing up is risky. When we got out of Ryker's truck, my blood pressure took a nose dive and so did I. Right into Ripper's arms.

My brain? That's another matter. Being without my ADHD meds for a full day while trapped in the world's worst anxiety attack? It's like I'm operating at half-speed.

"Cara?" Ripper's hand rests on my calf, and he peers up at me from where he's kneeling on the floor next to my bed. "What shoes, sunshine?"

"Crap. You've asked me that twice already. The red ones."

He returns to my side, and I ease the Keds from his hands. "I can put on my own shoes, Ripper. But, I need to ask you again. Are you sure about this?"

"No. But I have to go. Otherwise, Dax and Ry? They'll never be safe. JSOC knows they got me out. If they don't know Ry killed Faruk, they'll figure it out soon enough. That was so fucking illegal, there's no coming back from it."

"You're going to trade your life for theirs." I can hardly form the words as the anxiety and panic sit like a hard ball on my chest. Throwing my arms around him, I hold on for all I'm worth, and he doesn't flinch, just gathers me close and buries his face in my hair. "Don't do this. I don't want to lose you."

"I'm falling in love with you, Cara," he whispers in my ear. I try to pull back, but he tightens his hold. "Shhh. Let me get this out. I didn't think anyone could accept me again. Not after everything that happened. But you—you treated me like I was normal. Homeless, but normal. All the darkness in me...it's like you didn't even see it. Only the good."

I slide my fingers through his hair, then ease myself back so I can see his eyes. His right cheek is swollen and bruised, and I keep my touch feather light as I trace his jaw.

"I saw the darkness, Ripper. All of it." Taking his hand, I rest my fingers over the thick scars at his wrist. "You'll always carry it with you. It's a part of you. But not the *only* part of you. Your darkness doesn't make you unlovable."

His eyes shine, and his lips twitch like he's trying to find the right words. There's so much emotion churning in his gaze, it's almost overwhelming.

"I've never believed in asking someone to change for

me," I rush to continue. "You're perfect the way you are, Ripper. Jackson. Rick Mercury. I don't care what your name is. Or how much darkness you're carrying around inside." Resting my palm over his heart, I lean in and press my lips to his. "This man right here was willing to do anything to save me. This is the man I'm falling in love with. Darkness and all."

THE RIDE to Ryker's warehouse in South Seattle seems to take forever, even though it's probably less than twenty minutes. Dax sits in the front seat, staring straight ahead. Ripper, Charlie, and I take up the back, and the dog rests his head on Ripper's thigh, as if he knows whatever's about to happen is big —and dangerous.

I lost it a little when Ripper asked me to take care of Charlie if he had to go away. But I agreed. And then had to go fix my make-up again.

Ryker stops us before we enter the warehouse, Dax at his side. "Rip? Whatever happens in there..."

Clearing his throat, Dax holds out his arm. The sleeve of his dress shirt is rolled up halfway, and he has the same tattoo Ripper does. Ryker mirrors his movement, exposing an identical piece of ink.

Ripper leans in and kisses my cheek before letting go of me. "Brothers. Till the end," he says, the emotion in his voice making me cry all over again. And when he wraps his arms around these two big, damaged soldiers and they return the gesture, I watch in shock as the three strongest men I've ever seen all tear up in one another's arms.

The moment passes quickly, and they all swipe at their eyes before backing up. "Let's do this thing," Ripper says, then takes my hand and strides into the warehouse, Charlie at his side and Dax and Ry following behind us.

---

### Ripper

I zero in on a man standing in front of the conference table who can only be Commander Austin Pritchard. He's in full dress uniform, stars decorating his shoulders, a full complement of ribbons over his heart. But then I look around.

*Holy shit.*

Ten other men and women stand around the table. Trevor is off to one side slightly, his face completely blank. West holds the hand of a woman with dark hair and almond-shaped eyes. His wife. Cam. Inara is next to an older man with gray at his temples. Royce, I think, with Graham next to her. Wren and Evianna wait for their men to join them, then link arms next to Ford and Joey.

Cara presses closer to me, and I slip my arm around her waist. "It's okay, sunshine. They're all...family."

"Sergeant Richards," Pritchard says as he holds out his hand. "Commander Austin Pritchard."

"I know who you are, sir." I shake his hand, then salute him. "This is—"

"Caroline Phillips," he says.

Her voice trembles a little. "Cara. I'm...Cara now."

"Cara, then. I asked around a little, Cara. And your cooking is sorely missed at JSOC. The words 'genius' and 'gourmet' were tossed about frequently."

She blushes. "Thank you, sir."

"Shall we sit?"

I'd rather stand, but I'm not about to anger the man with

the power to make me disappear forever behind a treason charge, so I nod. Trevor, Dax, and Ryker join us, the rest of the group moving to stand behind me and Cara. A solid wall of family I don't deserve, never wanted, but wouldn't trade for anything.

"Parr was only too happy to confess everything in exchange for being sent to Leavenworth rather than Guantanamo," Pritchard says. He turns to Cara. "Your quick thinking sending all those screenshots to your email, then making sure McCabe could access them? I know seasoned special ops guys who wouldn't have thought that quickly on their feet. What happened to you at JSOC was deplorable. The procedures we put into place should have protected you."

"Hiram Adams tried," she says. "I went to him first." She glances over at me, notes my raised brow, and offers me a small smile. "He was head of internal investigations. I told him every-thing, and he set me up in a safehouse for a week while he investigated. But then..."

Pritchard shakes his head. "We found him dead in his office a few days after you reported Parr and Jessup. The autopsy didn't show anything amiss, but Parr confirmed they'd given him a fatal dose of insulin."

"And Leland Steel?" Cara asks. "He told them I was here, didn't he?"

"He's dead. Jessup's men tortured him. Held him for over a week, forced him to call you and get you to keep that damn phone on."

Cara tightens her grip on my hand and makes a small sound that's almost a sob. I scoot my chair closer to her and wrap my arm around her shoulders. "Bottom line this for me, Commander. Am I going home tonight? Or to Leavenworth?"

He sweeps a gaze over the cadre of men and women standing behind us, Dax, Ry, and Trevor, then gives a small shake of his head. "Pretty obvious which option everyone's expecting."

"Pritchard," Ry says as he flattens his palms on the table. I know that gesture. He's mad as hell, and he's doing his best to keep it in check. "Sergeant Richards went through horrors none of us can even imagine, and men under *your* command could have stopped it. If you even think of sending him to Leavenworth—"

The JSOC commander pushes to his feet. He's six inches shorter than Ry, but he has the presence that only comes with years of leadership. "I'd stop right there, McCabe. I'm a reasonable man. But I don't take to being threatened."

"I don't either," Ry says with a hint of a smile that doesn't reach his eyes.

"For fuck's sake." Trevor looks between the two men. "Both of you need to stand down."

The entire room is stunned into silence. Who the hell does Trevor think he is talking to the commander of JSOC that way? Yet, the man sinks back down, and Ryker takes his hands off the table.

Pritchard pulls a folder from the bag at his feet and removes two pieces of paper. "Sergeant Richards, this sheet on the left is a list of all your war crimes. All the evidence you sent us while you were trying to rescue Ms. Phillips yesterday. The one on the right contains the commendations you're owed for being injured in the line of duty, for bravery in combat, and for valor."

Both sheets are full of typed words that blur in front of me. I'm going to jail. I'll never see Cara again, never be free.

Rustling paper draws my attention, and Pritchard flicks a lighter, the flame brighter than the sun as he sets the sheet of my crimes ablaze. Once the paper catches, he heads for the sink in the small kitchen, holding on until the fire is nearly at his fingers.

Ash and bits of burnt parchment land in the sink, and the Air Force Commander, one of the most powerful military officers in the country—if not the world—turns on the water and washes every one of my crimes down the drain.

When he's returned to the table, he pulls a box from his pocket, frowns, and meets my gaze. "Please stand up for this, Sergeant."

I do, though I keep my hand on Cara's shoulder to help center me.

"Sergeant Jackson T. Richards, I hereby award you the Distinguished Service Cross for extraordinary heroism in the face of great danger from an enemy of the United States. Your actions at Hell Mountain gave us proof of life, which in turn, led to the joint Special Operations Forces, including Lieutenant Commander West Sampson, Sergeant Inara Ruzgani, and Commander Ryker McCabe, destroying the facility and putting an end to one of the most sadistic of the Taliban's interrogators."

He passes me the box and I raise the lid. A golden cross on a blue and red ribbon rests on black velvet. An eagle spreads its wings over the words "For Valor."

"Your subsequent torture and behavior while a prisoner of Abdul Faruk further justify this award. Despite grave danger, you ensured every action you took under duress was traceable, and with the information you provided us in the past twenty-four hours, JSOC will be able to right many wrongs committed over the last six years. Your actions showed true selflessness and embody the very ideals of the Special Forces, and no one—especially not you—should ever question your valor again."

I need to say something. Thank you. I don't deserve this. Anything. But the words won't come. Pritchard's still talking, but I can't make out what he's saying. I trace the contours of the eagle, the rest of the world fading into the background as those two words ring over and over again in my head.

*For Valor.*

"Ripper?" Cara whispers in my ear, now standing next to me. "Come back."

"Sorry," I say with a shake of my head. "What did you say, Commander?"

The expression on his face—amusement—fades. "That isn't the award I wanted you to have, Sergeant. If I could, I'd trade that out for the Congressional Medal of Honor. But after talking to Mr. Moana," he gestures to Trevor, "and doing a little investigation into Commander McCabe and Sergeant Holloway, I thought you might prefer a little less publicity. That is, if you're going to continue the work you're so obviously suited for with them and their teams."

He's giving me my life back. All of it. But more than that, he's allowing me to choose the life I want. I swallow hard and salute.

"Thank you, Commander."

He returns the gesture. "I have to get Parr back to Fort Bragg so he can be processed and sentenced. Ms. Phillips? Should you ever want your job back at JSOC, you only have to ask." Pritchard passes her a business card, and Cara tucks it in her pocket. "But regardless, I promise you, by the end of today, all records of Caroline Phillips ever working at JSOC will be scrubbed from our databases. Permanently."

The commander spins on his heel and heads for the door, his footsteps quick and efficient, almost silent. At the last second, he turns, sweeps his gaze over all of us, and nods. "The United States Armed Forces thank all of you for your service and bravery. Good day." With a final salute, he closes the door.

I'm free.

# CHAPTER THIRTY-TWO

**Cara**

I TURN TO RIPPER. "Is that it? It's over?"

He wraps his arms around me—carefully—and shakes as he presses his lips to my neck. Behind us, the man from last night, West, nods. "It's over. Rip can be Jackson Richards again if he wants to."

"Wait." I pull back to stare at him. "What name *were* you using?"

Dax, sitting next to Ryker, snorts and shakes his head. "Rick Mercury."

"Like...Freddy Mercury?"

Ripper refuses to meet my gaze, his ruddy cheeks turning a duskier shade. "I liked *Queen*."

"I love it." Cupping his cheek, I force him to look at me and lower my voice. "I don't care what your name is. I just want a chance to see where this goes."

"Oh, it's going somewhere," Ryker says as he lumbers to his

feet and heads for the coffee pot in the kitchen. "Like Snoqualmie. At New Year's."

Ripper stares daggers at him, and I look from Ryker to Dax and back to the man in front of me again. "What? Someone better explain—"

And then his lips are on mine, and I don't care because there's so much promise in his kiss, I can feel it down to my toes. I'm vaguely aware of the rest of the group shuffling and moving around us, but until Ripper comes up for air, I can't be sure of anything.

"For now," he whispers against my cheek, "just trust me."

"I do. But I feel like there's some inside joke I'm missing here."

He links our fingers and scans the room. "I don't even know all of you people. So what the fuck are you doing here risking your freedom to stand up for me?"

Despite his words, there's genuine affection and wonder in his voice. A tall, older man with graying temples and his arm around a woman with blond hair steps forward. "Trevor showed up at our apartment at midnight last night. Said he had a plane waiting and you might need backup. We came."

The woman holds out her hand to me. "I'm Joey. That's Ford. Ripper...when he was—"

"Isaad," Ripper says quietly.

"He helped us. Without him, we never would have escaped Faruk's compound."

"I work with Dax," Ford says. "We own Second Sight."

West speaks up next, angling his head to the woman at his side. She leans on a cane, a cup of coffee in her free hand. "This is Cam. My wife. Former army ordinance specialist and owner of Emerald City Security."

"Royce Nadiri," the other older gentleman says. "Army. And

my fiancée, Inara Ruzgani. Former Army Ranger sniper now on Ry's team."

"That's Graham." Ry gestures to the young man currently leaning against the counter alone. "Coast Guard. Reservist now. You know Dax, but Evianna's his fiancé. You've heard of Alfie, the home automation bot that came out a couple of months ago?"

I nod.

"Hers."

My head spins with all the names and faces, everyone here to make sure Ripper wasn't alone.

"Still doesn't explain what you're doing here," he says, his voice thick with emotion. "Pritchard could have arrested all of you."

Ryker and Dax look at one another, then at Ripper. "We're family," Ry says simply. "That's what we do."

---

HOURS LATER, we're all sitting in a backyard not far from Ripper's apartment. West and Cam's house, apparently. A couple of the guys stand around a grill, the scents of meat and corn on the cob filling the air.

I still can't keep everyone straight, and the single beer I've been nursing for half an hour has already gone to my head. At my side, Ripper looks vaguely uncomfortable, but at the same time, happier than I've ever seen him.

"Are you okay, handsome?" I ask, and almost topple over as the whole world tilts on me. Giggling when he pulls me into his lap, I barely notice the pain from my various bruises. Not when he's so very willing to touch me, to hold me, to rain kisses along my neck and up to my ear.

"Gonna take me a while to wrap my head around this

family thing," he says. "But, yeah. I'm okay. Should probably get *you* home soon, though."

Home. To my apartment. My empty, solitary apartment. I don't know why, but I just assumed I'd be staying with Ripper. But, we've only known each other a little over a week. No logical person would ever be ready for the "move-in-together" stage that quickly.

Except me.

Charlie comes running up to us, his tongue hanging out of his mouth. He's been playing with this little white fluffball of a dog ever since we got here, the two of them chasing one another around the yard, both retrieving toys whenever one of the guys tosses one, and generally having a blast.

He rests his head on my thigh, and I lean down to scratch behind his good ear. "Gonna miss you sleeping next to me tonight," I whisper. "Take care of Ripper for me, okay?"

"Cara?" The look on Ripper's face...it's like someone slapped him. "You want to...? I didn't mean—fuck."

I don't know what's wrong, and neither does Charlie. The dog whines and butts his head against the hand Ripper has clenched at his side.

"What is it? What's wrong? Talk to me."

"I thought you might want to stay with me. And Charlie. To move in." Shaking his head, he stares down at the grass under his feet. "It was a stupid idea. My place is so small. And you could go back to your life in Fort Bragg now."

"All of my belongings fit in a small suitcase. Never was one for stuff." Glancing around the yard at the small family, half of whom stood up for Ripper without even knowing him, I blink back a tear.

"Rip, what the hell are you doing. This is a celebration. Cara looks like she's about to face a firing squad," West says as he sets two plates with burgers and ears of corn on the table next to us. "If he's being a jerk, Cara, just tell me—or Cam or Inara. They'll put him in his place."

"I...it's okay," I stammer. "I don't need—"

"You're part of this family now." West grins. "We take care of our own. Even if that means the newest member of Hidden Agenda gets his ass kicked. Hey, Graham!"

The young guy talking with Inara looks over. "What happened to probie?"

"You moved up in the ranks, kid." Pushing to his feet, he claps Ripper on the shoulder. "*This* is the new probie. Feel free to lord it over him for at least a few weeks, you hear?"

"Sir! Yes, sir!" Graham salutes West, then offers Ripper a sheepish grin and a shrug. "Sorry, probie. No one crosses the SEAL."

"We'll see about that," Ripper mutters. But the corners of his mouth twitch into a smile, and for once, the gesture seems to fit him.

I cup his cheeks and turn his gaze to mine. "I'm not going anywhere. Except with you. Probie."

# EPILOGUE

## Ripper

A WEEK LATER, this new life of mine starts to seem real. Cara's clothes hang in my—our—closet. Her tea has its own shelf in the kitchen, and when I come in from a long walk with Charlie, the smells wafting through the small space make my mouth water.

She stands at the stove, earbuds in, humming to Queen's *Radio Ga Ga* as she stirs a bunch of chopped vegetables in some sort of sauce. The dark bruise on her cheek is fading, and the dizzy spells that plagued her for days every time she stood up seem to have passed.

A soft yelp escapes her lips when she notices me watching her, and her cheeks redden. "Sorry. I didn't expect you back until dark."

Charlie pads over to her and sits, waiting expectantly, and she laughs. "All right. Only because you're the best dog *ever.*" The little jar on the counter labeled "Spoiled Rotten Dog Treats" was one of her contributions to the apartment, and she lifts the lid, holds up a biscuit, and waits until Charlie starts wagging his tail. "Good boy."

He retreats to his bed while I wrap my arms around Cara from behind and peer over her shoulder. "This smells amazing. What is it?"

She adds tomatoes, milk, and crumbled bread to the sauce pan, gives it all a stir, and then turns down the heat. "It *will* be my famous Bolognese. In about three hours."

"How much of that time do you need to be at this stove, sunshine?" My lips find her ear, and I score my teeth over the shell.

"Maybe once an hour...for five minutes," she says on a shudder. "God. I've missed you, Ripper."

I haven't touched her like this since before she was taken. Once I got her back, she was so bruised and beaten up, I was terrified I'd hurt her. And now, my own fears return. What if I can't? What if the other day was just a fluke? Desperation born from more than six years of loneliness and pain?

As if she can read my thoughts, she wriggles out of my hold. "Bed. Now, soldier."

I don't hesitate, even though my heart is pounding so hard, I can feel it in my ears. After she angles a lid over the top of the pot, she unties her apron and drapes it over one of the stools at the breakfast bar.

"Talk to me," she says, fitting her body to mine. "I can always tell when you're getting stuck in your own head, you know."

"I know. It's kind of creepy."

She jabs me lightly in the shoulder, then sobers. "You get this look in your eyes, Rip. Like you're bracing for a blow."

"I'm sorry—"

"Don't." Her finger touches my lips. "Don't ever apologize for the darkness inside you. I don't expect you to banish it. Or hide it. Or for it to suddenly disappear. The *only* thing I need is for you to share it with me. When you can."

I want to say the words. The three words we've both been dancing around, but can't force ourselves to say. Instead, I thread my fingers through her hair and guide her on top of me. "I don't know why you want to be with someone so...damaged," I whisper. She smells like passion fruit and mango, and there are times I look at her and I can't believe she's real.

"We're all damaged in different ways." Her brown eyes fill with pain, and she skims the backs of her knuckles along my jaw. "What they did to you was vile, and I hope West and Graham killed every single one of the men who hurt you."

"Pretty sure they did."

Cara sits up and snags the hem of my t-shirt. When it lands next to the bed, she kisses a deep scar along the right side of my chest. "How many of these do you remember?"

"Every single one."

With a sharp gasp, she stops, her palms flat on my skin. "God. Ripper."

Wrapping my arms around her, I flip our positions. "Everything I went through, sunshine, led me to you. I'd love to be able to forget. The scorpions, the whips, all the times they held me down. But if I could, this—you—we never would have met."

Sliding down her body, I loosen the button on her jeans. "I've wanted to taste you for days."

"Well, then get to it."

The soft skin of her stomach quivers as I kiss just above the waistband of her panties, and when I can smell her arousal, I yank the jeans down her hips, followed by the scrap of black lace between her thighs.

"You taste," I say between little licks and one brief nibble to her tight nub, "like the sweetest fruit. Like sunshine and rain and...and love."

She whimpers, and I dig my fingers into the soft, pillowy flesh of her thighs. "More. I need more."

I'll give her anything she wants. For the rest of her life if she lets me. She writhes on the bed, digging her heels, trying to find purchase, but I pin her down with my arm across her belly. "I want to watch you come, sunshine. I want to see you fly apart in my arms."

When she does, soaring higher and higher until her back arches and she's gasping for air, I suck on her clit, and she screams my name.

I drink her release in, her sweetness coating my tongue and healing something broken inside me.

As her trembles subside, I reach behind her and unhook her bra. With her breasts bared, I can lavish attention on each nipple, and Cara moans. "You're going to make me come again."

"That's the whole point, sunshine."

"Nuh-uh." Wriggling away, she strips me of my khakis, then my briefs, and wraps gentle fingers around my dick. "My turn."

The brief moment of panic fades quickly when she whispers my name, and I stare into her half-lidded eyes, seeing nothing but love reflected back at me.

As she slides her hand up and down my shaft, I tense, but then Cara whispers in my ear, "You're safe, Ripper. Let yourself feel."

I am safe. With Cara, I'm always safe.

Her lips wrap around my crown, and all I find is pleasure. I love this woman, and for the first time, the idea of us heading where Ry thinks we're going...to Snoqualmie over New Year's with my two brothers fills me with nothing but peace.

As she runs her tongue up and down the underside of my dick, I groan. "I need to be inside you. Please. I won't last."

Her lips slide over me, and I flip her onto her back, spread her legs with my knees, and position myself at her entrance.

"Cara..." Pushing home one inch at a time, I wait for her to focus those deep brown orbs on me. "I love you, sunshine. I didn't think I could let anyone in again. But you...with you I don't feel broken."

"You're not broken." Her legs wrap around my waist, and she cups the back of my neck, just like the first night we spent together. "You're Jackson Richards. You're a hero. You're *my* hero. And I love you."

Her use of my real name lets something break free, something I hadn't been able to touch since they took everything from me, and the last vestiges of my secret shame fade away. I don't have to pretend with her. Don't have to be anything other than what I am. Who I am.

Ripper.

---

DEAR READER,

Thank you for reading Ripper and Cara's story. This one gutted me. I can't tell you how many times I cried.

If you have a few moments, I hope you'll consider leaving a review on your purchase site of choice. I know it might seem silly, but your review really **can** make a difference.

Up next, you can find Trevor's story. Pre-order *Call Sign: Redemption* today!

Oh, and if you made it this far and were one of the first few people to buy *Fighting For Valor*, then you should be rewarded. Download a whole SET of bonus scenes for the entire Away From Keyboard series now!

---

THE END

# ABOUT THE AUTHOR

I've always made up stories. Sometimes I even acted them out. I probably shouldn't admit that my childhood best friend and I used to run around the backyard pretending to fly in our Invisible Jet and rescue Steve Trevor. Oops.

Now that I'm too old to spin around in circles with felt magic bracelets on my wrists, I put "pen to paper" instead. Figuratively, at least. Fingers to keyboard is more accurate.

Outside of my writing, I'm a professional editor, a software geek, a singer (in the shower only), and a runner. I love red wine, scotch (neat, please), and cider. Seattle is my home, and I share an old house with my husband and cats.

I'm on my fourth—fifth?—rewatching of the modern *Doctor Who*, and I think one particular quote from that show sums up my entire life.

"We're all stories, in the end. Make it a good one, eh?" — *The Eleventh Doctor, Doctor Who*

I hope your story is brilliant.

*You can reach me all over the web...*
patriciadeddy.com
patricia@patriciadeddy.com

facebook.com/patriciadeddyauthor

twitter.com/patriciadeddy

instagram.com/patriciadeddy

bookbub.com/profile/patricia-d-eddy

# ALSO BY PATRICIA D. EDDY

## Away From Keyboard

Dive into a steamy mix of geekery and military might with the men and women of Emerald City Security and North-West Protective Services.

Breaking His Code

In Her Sights

On His Six

Second Sight

By Lethal Force

Fighting For Valor

Call Sign: Redemption

---

## Midnight Coven

These novellas will take you into the darker side of the paranormal with vampires, witches, and more.

Forever Kept

Immortal Hunter

## Elemental Shifter

Hot werewolves and strong, powerful elementals. What's not to love?

A Shift in the Water

A Shift in the Air

---

## By the Fates

Check out the By the Fates series if you love dark and steamy tales of witches, devils, and an epic battle between good and evil.

By the Fates, Freed

Destined: A By the Fates Story

By the Fates, Fought

By the Fates, Fulfilled

---

## In Blood

If you love hot Italian vampires and and a human who can hold her own against beings far stronger, then the In Blood series is for you.

Secrets in Blood

Revelations in Blood

---

## Holidays and Heroes

Beauty isn't only skin deep and not all scars heal. Come swoon over sexy vets and the men and women who love them.

Mistletoe and Mochas

Love and Libations

---

## Restrained

Do you like to be tied up? Or read about characters who do? Enjoy a fresh BDSM series that will leave you begging for more.

In His Silks

Christmas Silks

All Tied Up For New Year's

In His Collar

Made in the USA
Coppell, TX
17 January 2023

11265769R00164